The Fetishist

Michel Tournier was born in 1924, trained as a philosopher, became an expert on Germany and the German language, and spent some years working in French radio, television and book publishing before devoting himself full time to writing. Tournier was described by the *Observer* as 'the most gifted and original novelist to emerge in France since the war'. His first novel, *Friday or the Other Island*, won the Grand Prix du Roman of the Académie Française in 1967; his second, *The Erl King*, won the Prix Goncourt in 1970. All his five novels have been translated into English, including his most recent, *The Midnight Love Feast*, and he has also published an autobiographical volume, *The Wind Spirit*.

Also by Michel Tournier
and available in Minerva

Gilles and Jeanne
Gemini
The Four Wise men
The Midnight Love Feast

THE FETISHIST
AND OTHER STORIES

Michel Tournier

Translated from the French by
Barbara Wright

Minerva

A Minerva Paperback
THE FETISHIST

First published in Great Britain 1983
by William Collins Sons & Co. Ltd
This Minerva edition published 1992
by Mandarin Paperbacks
Michelin House, 81 Fulham Road, London SW3 6RB

Minerva is an imprint of the Octopus Publishing Group,
a division of Reed International Books Ltd

First published as *Le Coq de Bruyère*
by Editions Gallimard 1978

A CIP catalogue record for this title
is available from the British Library
ISBN 0 7493 9941 4

Printed and bound in Great Britain
by Cox & Wyman Ltd, Reading, Berks

CONTENTS

The Adam Family

In the beginning the earth had neither grass nor trees. A vast desert of dust and stones stretched over all the land.

Jehovah sculptured the statue of the first man out of the dust of the ground. Then he breathed into his nostrils the breath of life. And the statue of dust became a living soul and stood up.

What was the first man like? He was like Jehovah, who had created him in his own image. Now Jehovah is neither man nor woman. He is both at the same time. So the first man was also a woman.

He had a woman's breasts.

And at the bottom of his belly, a boy's sex organ.

And between his legs, a girl's little hole.

This was actually quite handy: when he walked, he tucked his boy's tail into his girl's little hole, the way you tuck a knife into its sheath.

So Adam didn't need anyone else in order to be fruitful and multiply. He could be fruitful and multiply all by himself.

Jehovah would have been very pleased with his son Adam if Adam had had a son by himself, and so on.

Unfortunately, Adam didn't agree.

He didn't agree with Jehovah, who wanted grandchildren.

He didn't agree with himself. For on the one hand he felt like lying down, fertilizing himself and having children. But the ground around him was still only a desert. And a desert is no place to sit down, and even less to lie down. A desert is an arena to fight in, a stadium to play games in, a cinder-track to run races on. But how can you fight, play games, or run races, with a child in your belly, a child on your hands, that you also have to give the breast to and make baby food for?

Adam said to Jehovah: 'The ground you've put me on isn't

suitable for family life. It's more appropriate for a long-distance runner.'

So Jehovah decided to create the kind of land where Adam would feel like staying put.

And this was the Earthly Paradise, or the Garden of Eden.

Great trees heavy with flowers and fruit hung over lakes filled with warm, limpid water.

'Now,' Jehovah said to Adam, 'you can have children. Lie down and dream under the trees. It'll happen of its own accord.'

Adam lay down. But he couldn't sleep, much less procreate.

When Jehovah came back he found him walking nervously up and down in the shade of a mangrove tree.

'The thing is,' Adam told him, 'there are two beings in me. One would like to relax underneath the flowers. Then all the work would be done inside his belly, where children grow. But the other can't keep still. He's on pins and needles. He needs to walk, and walk, and walk. In the stony desert, the first was unhappy. The second was happy. Here, in the Garden of Eden, it's just the opposite.'

'That,' said Jehovah, 'is because your nature is both sedentary and nomadic. Two words you must add to your vocabulary.'

'Sedentary and nomadic,' Adam repeated obediently. 'And now what?'

'Now,' said Jehovah, 'I'm going to cut you in two. Go to sleep!'

'Cut me in two!' exclaimed Adam.

But his laughter was soon stilled, and a deep sleep fell upon him.

Then Jehovah took everything that was female out of his body: his breasts, his little hole, his womb.

And he put these pieces into another man that he formed nearby out of the moist, luxurious earth of Eden.

And he called this other man: woman.

When Adam awoke, he sprang to his feet and nearly took wing, he felt so light. He had lost everything that had been weighing him down. He had no more breasts. His chest was hard and dry, like a buckler. His belly had become as flat as a paving stone. All he had between his thighs was a boy's sex organ which didn't get in his way too much, even though he no longer had a little hole to tuck it away in.

He couldn't stop himself running like a hare along the wall of the Garden of Eden.

But when he reached Jehovah, the latter pulled aside a curtain of greenery and said: 'Look!'

And Adam saw Eve, asleep.

'What's that?' he asked.

'That's your other half,' replied Jehovah.

'Aren't I handsome!' exclaimed Adam.

'Isn't she beautiful,' Jehovah corrected him. 'From now on, when you want to make love you must go to Eve. And when you want to go running, you can leave her to relax.'

And he withdrew discreetly.

We have to know that this is the way things began, in order to understand the sequel.

Adam and Eve, as we know, were driven out of Eden by Jehovah. Then they started on a long march through the desert of dust and stone of the dawn of History.

Naturally, this fall from Paradise wasn't at all the same thing for Adam and for Eve. Adam found himself back on familiar ground. It was in this desert that he had been born. It was out of this dust that he had been sculptured. What was more, Jehovah had relieved him of all his feminine appurtenances so he could move around as nimbly as an antelope, as indefatigably as a camel, on his feet which were as hard as horny hoofs.

But Eve! Poor mother Eve! She who had been formed out of the moist, luxurious earth of Eden, and who liked nothing so much as to sleep happily beneath the changing shadows of the palm trees, how sad she was! Her fair skin scorched by the sun, her tender feet lacerated by the stones, she dragged herself along, groaning, behind Adam the fleet-footed.

She thought of nothing but Eden, her native land, but she couldn't even mention it to Adam, who seemed to have completely forgotten it.

They had two sons.

The first, Cain, was the very spit and image of his mother: blond, chubby, and very fond of sleeping.

But whether he was asleep or awake, Eve never stopped murmuring a beautiful story in his ear. And this story was always about mosses studded with anemones, forming cool cushions at the foot of the magnolia trees, about hummingbirds amid the golden clusters of the laburnums, and flights of cranes swooping down on the tall branches of the black cedars.

You might say that Cain drank in nostalgia for the Earthly Paradise with his mother's milk. For these whispered evocations built magic islands in the head of this poor child who knew nothing but the arid steppes and the sterility of the infinite, undulating sand dunes. So he very soon manifested a vocation as an agriculturist, a horticulturist, and even an architect.

His first toy was a little hoe, his second a sweet little trowel, his third a box of compasses with which he made hundreds of scale drawings that brilliantly revealed his gifts as a future landscape gardener and town planner.

How different was his younger brother, Abel! *He* was the very spit and image of his swift-footed father. He couldn't keep still. All he ever dreamed of was departures, marches, journeys.

Every sort of work that called for perseverance and immobility repelled him and filled him with scorn. On the other hand, nothing amused him so much as to trample the flower beds or kick over the sand castles of patient, laborious Cain.

But older children must be indulgent towards younger ones and Cain, duly lectured on the subject, choked back his tears of wrath and tirelessly rebuilt everything in the wake of his brother.

They grew up.

Abel became a keeper of sheep and chased after his flocks over the steppes, the deserts, and the mountains. He was thin, dark, cynical, and smelled like his own goats.

He was proud of the fact that his children had never eaten vegetables and could neither read nor write, for there is no school for nomads.

Cain, on the other hand, lived with his family in the midst of cultivated fields, gardens, and beautiful houses which he loved and tended passionately, and kept a jealous watch on.

Now Jehovah was wroth with Cain. He had sent Adam and Eve forth from Eden, and placed at the east end of the garden Cherubims, and a flaming sword which turned every way. And here was his grandson, possessed by his mother's spirit and memories, reconstituting, through his work and intelligence, what Adam had lost through his stupidity! Jehovah saw insolence and rebellion in this Eden II that Cain had brought forth out of the barren and dry land of the desert.

Jehovah, on the other hand, had respect unto Abel, who chased indefatigably after his flocks through the rocks and sand.

Therefore, when Cain brought as an offering to Jehovah the flowers and fruits of his gardens, Jehovah rejected these gifts.

On the other hand, he accepted with tender emotion the firstlings of his flock that Abel offered him as a sacrifice.

One day, the tragedy that had been brewing came to a head.

Abel's flocks overran and devastated Cain's orchards and ripened corn.

The two brothers had a discussion. Cain was gentle and conciliatory, while Abel laughed viciously in his face.

Then the memory of everything he had put up with from his young brother overwhelmed Cain, and with one blow of his spade he smashed Abel's skull.

Jehovah's wrath was terrible. He drove Cain out from his presence, and condemned him to be a fugitive and a vagabond in the earth with his family.

But Cain, with his inveterate sedentary nature, didn't go far. He headed quite naturally for the Paradise his mother had told him so much about. And he dwelt there, in the land of Nod, on the east of the walls of the famous garden.

There this architect of genius builded a city. The first city in History, and he called its name after the name of his first son, Enoch.

Enoch was a dream city, shaded by eucalyptus trees. It consisted entirely of a great clump of flowers in which fountains and turtledoves cooed with the same voice.

In its centre stood Cain's masterpiece: a sumptuous temple, all pink porphyry and mottled marble.

This temple was empty, and not yet in use. But when Cain was questioned about it, he smiled mysteriously into his beard.

Finally, one evening, an old man appeared at the city gate. Cain seemed to be expecting him, for he immediately made him welcome.

It was Jehovah, wearied, fatigued, exhausted by the nomadic life he had been living for so many years with Abel's sons, being humped around on a man's back in a worm-eaten Ark of the Covenant which stank of ram's suint.

The grandson pressed the grandfather to his heart. Then he knelt, to be pardoned and blessed. After which Jehovah – still grumbling a little as a matter of form – was solemnly enthroned in the temple of Enoch, where he remained for evermore.

The End of Robinson Crusoe

'It was there! There, look – off Trinidad, at nine degrees twenty-two north. There's not the slightest doubt about it!'

The drunkard kept jabbing his dirty finger down on a bit of a tattered, grease-stained map, and each of his passionate assertions raised a laugh from the fishermen and dockers round our table.

We knew him well. He was a character – part of the local folklore. We had invited him to have a drink with us in order to hear him tell some of his tales in his rasping voice. As for his adventure, it was both exemplary and heartrending, as is often the case.

Forty years previously he had been lost at sea, like so many others before him. His name had been inscribed in the church with those of his shipmates. And then he had been forgotten.

Not so completely, however, that he wasn't recognized when he reappeared after twenty-two years, hirsute and vehement, accompanied by a Negro. The tale he spewed out at every possible opportunity was stupefying. As the sole survivor of the wreck of his ship, he was quite alone on an island inhabited by goats and parrots until the arrival of this Negro whom he claimed to have saved from a horde of cannibals. Finally an English schooner had rescued them and he had come home, but not before he had had time to make a small fortune out of the sort of deals which were quite simple in the Caribbean islands at that time.

Everyone had fêted him. He had married a young thing who could have been his daughter, and everyday life had apparently closed the yawning, incomprehensible gap, full of luxuriant vegetation and birdsong, that a freak of destiny had opened for him in his past.

Apparently, yes, for in actual fact, as the years went by, an inner ferment seemed to be at work, eating away at Robinson Crusoe's family life. Friday, the black servant, had been the first to succumb. After months of irreproachable behaviour he had taken to drink – discreetly at first, and then more and more rowdily. Then there was the business of the two unmarried mothers, harboured by the Hospice of the Holy Spirit, who almost simultaneously gave birth to half-caste babies greatly resembling one another. Wasn't it obvious who was the author of this double crime?

But Robinson Crusoe had defended Friday with strange obstinacy. Why didn't he dismiss him? What – possibly shameful – secret linked him to this Negro?

Finally, large sums of money had been stolen from their neighbour, and even before anyone had come under suspicion, Friday had disappeared.

'The idiot!' Robinson Crusoe had remarked. 'If he wanted some money to be able to go away, he only had to ask me for it!'

And he had added, rashly:

'In any case, I know where he's gone!'

The victim of the theft had seized on these words and demanded that Robinson Crusoe should either pay him back the money or produce the thief. After a show of resistance, Robinson Crusoe had paid.

But ever since that day he had been seen hanging about on the quays and in the port taverns looking more and more gloomy and saying, every so often:

'He's gone back there, yes, I'm sure he has, that's where he is now, the rascal!'

For it was true that an ineffable secret united him to Friday, and that this secret was a certain little green spot which, the moment he returned, he had got the port cartographer to add to the blue Caribbean ocean. This island, after all, represented his youth, his marvellous adventure, his splendid, solitary garden! What was he waiting for under this rainy sky, in this glutinous town, among these merchants and pensioners?

His young wife, who possessed the instinctive intelligence of the warm-hearted, was the first to guess his strange, mortal chagrin.

'You're bored, I can see you are. Come on, admit that you're pining!'

'Me? You're mad! Pining for whom, for what?'

'For your desert island, of course! And I know what's stopping you leaving tomorrow, I know, of course I do! Me!'

He protested volubly, but the more loudly he protested the more sure she became that she was right.

She loved him dearly, and had never refused him anything. She died. He immediately sold his house and his field and chartered a sailing boat for the Caribbean.

More years passed. People started to forget him once again. But when he came back the next time, he seemed even more changed than after his first voyage.

He had made the crossing as a galley hand aboard an old cargo boat. An aged, broken man, half-drowned in alcohol.

What he said aroused general hilarity. Nowhere-to-be-found! Despite months of unremitting search, his island was nowhere to be found. He had exhausted himself in this futile exploration, desperate with rage, and expending his strength and money trying to rediscover that land of joy and freedom which seemed to have been engulfed for ever.

'And yet it *was* there,' he repeated once again that evening, jabbing his finger down on the map.

Then an old helmsman stepped out of the crowd and came and touched him on the shoulder.

'You want me to tell you something, Crusoe? Of course your desert island is still there. And what's more, I can assure you that you really did find it again!'

'I did find it?' exclaimed Crusoe, almost suffocating. 'But I tell you . . .'

'You did find it! You probably passed it ten times. But you didn't recognize it.'

'Didn't recognize it?'

'No, because your island has done what you've done: it's aged! Don't you understand? – flowers turn into fruits, and fruits turn into wood, and green wood turns into dead wood. Everything happens very quickly in the tropics. And what about you? Look at yourself in the mirror, you idiot! And tell me whether your island recognized *you*, when you passed it?'

Robinson Crusoe didn't look at himself in the mirror, the advice was superfluous. He cast such a sad, haggard glance over all the men that the rising wave of their laughter suddenly stopped short, and a great silence fell over the tavern.

Mother Christmas

A Christmas Story

Was the village of Pouldreuzic about to experience a period of peace? For years and years it had been split by the antagonism between the clerics and the radicals, between the Catholic school run by the Brothers and the secular State school, between the parish priest and the schoolmaster. The hostilities, which changed their colours with the changing seasons, reached their chromatic peak with the legendary festivities of the end of the year. For practical reasons, Midnight Mass was held on 24 December at six in the evening. At the same hour, the schoolmaster, dressed up as Father Christmas, used to distribute toys to the State school children. Through his efforts, therefore, Father Christmas became a pagan, radical and anticlerical hero, and the parish priest set up in opposition the Little Lord Jesus of his living crèche – which was famous throughout the canton – as one might splash holy water in the Devil's face.

Well, yes – was Pouldreuzic actually going to enjoy a truce? The thing was, the schoolmaster had retired, and he had been replaced by a schoolmistress who was a stranger to the district, and everyone was watching her to see what stuff she was made of. Madame Oiselin, the mother of two children – one of which was a three-month-old baby – was a divorcée, which seemed to be a guarantee of laic fidelity. But the clerical party claimed a victory from the very first Sunday, when the new schoolmistress appeared in church, a fact which did not go unnoticed.

The die seemed to be cast. There would no longer be a sacrilegious Christmas tree coinciding with 'Midnight' Mass, and the parish priest would have the field to himself. Great was the surprise, then, when Madame Oiselin announced to her pupils that there would be no change in the tradition, and that Father

Christmas would distribute his presents at the usual hour. What sort of game was she playing? And who was going to be Father Christmas? Everyone's thoughts turned to the postman and the rural policeman, on account of their socialist opinions, but both swore they knew nothing about it. The general astonishment reached its peak when it was learned that Madame Oiselin was lending her baby to the priest to play the part of the Little Lord Jesus in his living crèche.

Everything went well at first. The Oiselin baby was sleeping like a log as the faithful filed past the crèche, their eyes agog with curiosity. The ox and the ass – a real ox and a real ass – seemed to be tenderly watching over the laic baby so miraculously metamorphosed into the Saviour.

Unfortunately, just when they'd got to the Gospel, he began to stir, and the moment the priest ascended the pulpit he started yelling his head off. No one had ever heard a baby yell so loudly. In vain, the little girl taking the part of the Virgin Mary cradled him against her meagre breast. The brat, scarlet with rage, flailing around with his arms and legs, made the vaults reverberate with his furious vociferations, and the priest couldn't get a word in edgeways.

Finally he called one of the choirboys and whispered an order into his ear. Not waiting to take off his surplice, the boy left the church and the sound of his galoshes could be heard outside, gradually growing fainter.

A few minutes later, the clerical half of the village, the whole of which was gathered together in the nave, saw an unprecedented vision which was henceforth inscribed for all time in the golden legends of the Pont l'Abbé region of Brittany. They saw Father Christmas in person come bustling into the church. He strode up to the crèche. Then he pushed his big, white cotton wool beard to one side, he unbuttoned his red robe, and offered an ample breast to the Little Lord Jesus, who was immediately appeased.

Amandine, or The Two Gardens

An Initiatory Story for Olivia Clergue

Sunday I have blue eyes, cherry-red lips, plump pink cheeks, and wavy blond hair. My name is Amandine. When I look at myself in the mirror, I think I look like a little girl of ten. Which isn't surprising. I *am* a little girl, and I *am* ten.

I have a papa, a mama, a doll called Amanda, and also a cat. I think it's a she-cat. She's called Claude, that's why we aren't very sure. For two weeks she had an enormous stomach, and then one day I found four kittens in the basket with her, no bigger than mice, and they were paddling around with their little paws and sucking her stomach.

Talking of stomachs, hers had become quite flat, so anyone might think the four little kittens had been shut up in it and just got out! Yes, Claude really must be a she-cat.

The kittens are called Bernard, Philippe, Ernest, and Kamikat. That's how I know that the first three are boys. But with Kamikat, obviously, there's some doubt.

Mama told me that we couldn't keep five cats. I really don't know why not. But I asked my schoolfriends whether they would like a kitten.

Wednesday Annie, Sylvie, and Lydie came to my house. Claude rubbed herself up against their legs, purring. They picked up the kittens, their eyes are open now and they're starting to totter around. As they wanted to be sure to get a he-cat they didn't take Kamikat. Annie took Bernard, Sylvie took Philippe, and Lydie took Ernest. The only one I have left is Kamikat, and naturally I love it all the more, now the others are gone.

Sunday Kamikat is a ginger cat, the same colour as a fox, with a white patch over its left eye, as if it had been . . . been what, actually? The opposite of punched. Been kissed. Like those white cakes they call 'kisses'. Kamikat has a white eye.

Wednesday I like Mama's house and Papa's garden. In the house, it's always the same temperature, summer and winter alike. And no matter what the season, the lawns are always green and well-kept. You might think that Mama in her house, and Papa in his garden, are having a competition to see who can be the neatest and tidiest. In the house, you have to wear felt slippers so as not to dirty the parquet floors. In the garden, Papa has put ashtrays down here and there, for walker-smokers. I think they're right. Things are more reassuring like that. But sometimes they're also a little bit boring.

Sunday I'm so pleased to see my little cat getting bigger, and learning everything by playing with its mama.

This morning I went to look at their basket in the sheep pen. It was empty! No one there! When Claude went for a walk, she used to leave Kamikat and its brothers on their own. But today she's taken it with her. Or rather, she must have carried it, because I'm sure the kitten couldn't have followed her. It can barely walk. Where has she gone?

Wednesday Claude hadn't been seen since last Sunday, but she has just suddenly reappeared. I was eating strawberries in the garden when all of a sudden I felt something furry rubbing against my legs. I didn't even have to look, I knew it was Claude. I ran to the sheep pen to see whether the kitten had come back too. The basket was still empty. Claude came up. She looked in the basket and raised her head to me, closing her golden eyes. 'What have you done with Kamikat?' I asked her. She turned her head away and didn't answer.

Sunday Claude doesn't live the way she did before. In the past, she was always with us. But now, very often she isn't there. Where does she go? I'd really like to know that. I've tried to follow her. Impossible. When I'm watching her, she doesn't budge. She always seems to be asking me: 'Why are you watching me? You can see very well I'm not going anywhere.'

But I only have to let my attention wander for a single moment, and pfft! – Claude has disappeared. And a lot of good it does me to look for her! She's nowhere to be found. But the next day I come across her by the fire and she looks at me with an innocent air, as if I'd been seeing visions.

Wednesday I've just seen something strange. I wasn't a bit hungry, so when no one was looking I gave Claude my bit of meat. Now dogs – when you throw them a bit of meat or a lump of sugar, they catch it in the air and gobble it up in all confidence. But not cats. They're suspicious. They drop it. Then they examine it. Claude examined it. But, instead of eating it, she took the bit of meat in her mouth and carried it into the garden, which would have let me in for a scolding if my parents had seen her.

Then she went and hid in a bush – probably hoping we'd forget her. But I was watching her. All of a sudden she leaped over towards the wall, she ran at it as if it were flat on the ground, but it was well and truly vertical and in three bounds the cat was on top of it, still with the bit of meat in her mouth. She looked back at us as if to make sure we weren't following her, and then disappeared over on the other side.

I've had my own idea about it for some time. I had a suspicion that Claude was so disgusted at having three of her four kittens taken away from her that she wanted to put Kamikat in a safe place. She's hidden him on the other side of the wall, and she's there with him whenever she isn't here.

Sunday I was right. I've just seen Kamikat again, after three months. But how he's changed! This morning I got up earlier than usual. Looking out of the window I saw Claude slowly walking down one of the garden paths. She had a dead field mouse in her mouth. But what was extraordinary was the sort of very soft growling sound she was making, like fat mother hens when they're walking up and down surrounded by their chicks. In this case, though, the chick soon appeared, only it was a big chick with four legs, covered with ginger hair. I recognized him at once, with the white patch over his eye, his white eye. But how strong he's grown! He started dancing around Claude, trying to smack the field mouse with his paws, but Claude kept her head so high up that Kamikat couldn't get hold of it. In the end she dropped it, but then, instead of eating the field mouse on the spot, Kamikat picked it up very quickly and disappeared into the bushes with it. I'm afraid this little cat has become quite wild. Naturally, because he's grown up on the other side of the wall and never seen anyone, apart from his mother.

Wednesday I get up before the others every day now. It's not difficult, it's so lovely, then! And I can do whatever I like in the house for at least an hour. When Papa and Mama are asleep, I feel as if I'm alone in the world.

It frightens me a little, but at the same time I feel full of joy. It's odd. When I hear my parents stirring in their bedroom I'm sad, the party's over. And then, I see a whole lot of things in the garden that are new to me. Papa's garden is so well-kept and well cared for that you'd think nothing could ever happen in it.

And yet, what things you see when Papa is asleep! Just before the sun rises there's a tremendous commotion in the garden. This is the time when the night animals are going to bed and the day animals are getting up. But there's just one moment when they're all there. They pass each other, and sometimes even bump into one another, because it's both night and day at the same time.

The owl is in a hurry to go home before the sun comes up and dazzles her, and she brushes up against the blackbird that's just coming out of the lilac tree. The hedgehog rolls itself up in a ball in the depths of the heather just at the moment when the squirrel pokes its head out of the hole in the old oak tree to see what sort of a day it is.

Sunday There's no longer any doubt about it. Kamikat is completely wild. When I saw them this morning on the lawn, Claude and him, I went out and walked up to them. Claude gave me a warm welcome. She came and rubbed herself up against my legs, purring. But with one single leap Kamikat had already disappeared into the gooseberry bushes. It really is strange! He can see perfectly well that his mama isn't afraid of me. Then why does he run away? And his mama, why doesn't she do anything to stop him? She could explain to him that I'm a friend. But no. It's as if she has completely forgotten Kamikat the moment I come on the scene. She really does have two completely separate lives, her life on the other side of the wall, and her life with us in Papa's garden and Mama's house.

Wednesday I tried to tame Kamikat. I put a saucer of milk down in the middle of the path and went back into the house and watched through the window to see what would happen.

Claude arrived first, naturally. She stopped in front of the saucer, her front paws prudently pressed together, and started lapping. After a minute I saw Kamikat's white eye appear between two tufts of grass. He watched his mother, looking as if he was wondering what on earth she could be doing. Then he started to move, but with his stomach flat on the ground, and very very slowly wriggled over to Claude. Hurry up, little Kamikat, or when you get there the saucer will be empty! Ah, he's made it. But no, not yet! He starts circling around the saucer, still flat on his stomach. How fierce he is! A real wild cat. He stretches his neck out towards the saucer, a long, long neck, a real giraffe's neck, all this so as to stay as far away from the saucer as possible. He stretches his neck out, he lowers his nose, and then all of a sudden, he sneezes. He has just touched the milk with his nose. He wasn't expecting it. Because he's never eaten out of a saucer, the little savage. He's sent drops of milk flying all around. He retreats and licks his chops, looking disgusted. Claude has got splashed too, but she doesn't care. She goes on lapping as quickly and regularly as a machine.

Kamikat has finished mopping himself up. Actually, the few drops of milk he's licked remind him of something. It's a very early memory. He flattens himself. He starts crawling again. But this time it's his mother he's crawling towards. He slides his head underneath her stomach. He sucks.

So there you are: the big fat she-cat laps, and the little he-cat sucks. It must be the same milk, the milk in the saucer, that goes into the she-cat's mouth, comes out through her tum-tum and goes into the little cat's mouth. The difference is that it gets warmed up on the way through. The little cat doesn't like cold milk. He uses his mother to make it warm.

The saucer's empty. Claude has licked it so hard that it's

shining in the sun. Claude looks around. She discovers Kamikat still busy sucking. 'Well well, what's he doing there?' Claude's paw snaps like a spring. Oh, not spitefully. With all her claws in. But her paw hit Kamikat's head hard enough to send him rolling over and over like a ball. That'll remind him that he's a big kitten, now. The very idea – still sucking at the breast at his age!

Sunday I've decided to go on an expedition over the wall to try to win Kamikat over. And out of curiosity too, just a little. I believe there's something else on the other side of the wall, another garden, another house, perhaps, Kamikat's garden and house. I believe that if I became acquainted with his little paradise I'd know better how to make friends with him.

Wednesday This afternoon I walked all the way round the next door garden. It isn't very big. It only takes ten minutes to walk right round it, without hurrying, and to come back to your starting point. It's simple: it's a garden that's exactly the same size as Papa's garden. But the extraordinary thing is: there's no door, no gate, nothing! A wall without a single opening. Unless its openings have been blocked up. The only way to get in is to do what Kamikat did, jump over the wall. But I'm not a cat. So what shall I do?

Sunday At first I thought of using Papa's gardener's ladder, but I don't know whether I'd have been strong enough to carry it as far as the wall. And then, everyone would notice it. They'd soon spot me. I don't quite know why, but I believe that if Papa and Mama suspected what I am planning they'd do everything they could to stop me. What I'm about to write is very naughty, and I'm ashamed, but what can I do? I think it's necessary and delightful for me to go into Kamikat's garden, but I mustn't say anything about it to anyone, and especially not to my parents. I'm very unhappy. And very happy at the same time.

Wednesday At the far end of the garden there's an old gnarled pear tree with one branch reaching out towards the wall. If I can manage to walk along to the end of that branch I shall probably be able to get on to the top of the wall.

Sunday I made it! My idea about the old pear tree worked, but wasn't I scared! At one moment, there was I with my legs spread-eagled, with one foot on the pear tree branch and the other on the top of the wall. I was still holding the bough with one hand and I didn't dare let go of it. I almost called for help. Finally I took the plunge. I very nearly fell over on to the other side of the wall but I managed to get my balance, and then right away I was in a position to look down into Kamikat's garden.

All I could see at first was a tangled mass of greenery, a real jungle, a hotchpotch of thorn bushes and trees lying flat along the ground, of brambles and tall brackens, and also of heaps of plants I don't know. The exact opposite of Papa's garden, which is so neat and tidy. I thought I'd never dare go down into that virgin forest which must be swarming with toads and snakes.

Then I started to walk along the wall. It wasn't easy, because often a tree had rested its leafy branches on it and I didn't know what I was stepping on. And then some of its stones were loose and wobbly, and others were slippery with moss. But the next thing I discovered was a total surprise: propped up against the wall, as if it had been waiting there for me forever, was a sort of very steep wooden stairway with a handrail, a bit like the long ladders that lead up into attics. The wood was all green and worm-eaten, the handrail was slimy with slugs. But even so it was very useful, and I don't know how I'd have got down without it.

Right. Here I am in Kamikat's garden. There are some tall grasses that come up to my nose. I have to walk along an old path that must have been hacked out through the forest, but it's fast disappearing. Big, strange flowers stroke my face. They smell of pepper and flour, a very soft scent, but it also hurts a little when I breathe it in. I can't say whether it's a good or a bad scent. It seems to be both at the same time.

I'm a little scared, but spurred on by curiosity. Everything here seems to have been abandoned for a very, very long time. It's both sad and beautiful, like a sunset . . . I turn a corner, go along yet another green corridor, and I come to a sort of round clearing with a paving stone in the middle. And sitting on the paving stone, guess who? Kamikat in person, calmly watching me approach. It's funny, he strikes me as being bigger and stronger than when he's in Papa's garden. But it's him, I've no doubt about that, no other cat has a white eye. In any case he's very calm, almost majestic. He doesn't run away like a mad thing, nor does he come up to me to be stroked, no, he stands up and walks off serenely, his tail as straight as a church candle, towards the other end of the clearing. Before he disappears beneath the trees he stops and looks back, as if to see whether I'm following him. Yes, Kamikat, I'm coming, I'm coming! He closes his eyes for a long time with a contented expression, and then starts off again just as calmly. I really don't recognize him. What it is to be in the other garden! A real prince in his own realm.

In this fashion we go twisting and turning along a trail which is sometimes completely hidden under the grass and weeds. And then I realize that we've arrived. Kamikat stops once again, turns his head round towards me, and slowly closes his golden eyes.

We've reached the edge of a little wood and before us a colonnaded pavilion stands in the centre of a vast, round lawn. It's surrounded by a pathway lined with crumbling marble benches covered in moss. Under the dome of the pavilion is a statue on a plinth: a naked boy with wings. His curly head is inclined, with a sad smile that brings dimples to his cheeks, and he's holding a finger up to his lips. He has dropped a little bow, a quiver, and some arrows, which are suspended down the side of the plinth.

Kamikat is sitting under the dome. He lifts his head up to me. He is as silent as the stone boy. Like him, he has a mysterious smile. It looks as if they share the same secret, a rather sad and very sweet secret, and as if they would like to teach it to me. It's odd. Everything here is melancholy, the ruined pavilion, the crumbling benches, the untamed lawn covered in wild flowers, and yet I feel full of joy. I want to cry, and yet I'm happy. How far away I am from Papa's well-kept garden and Mama's well-polished house! Shall I ever be able to go back to them?

Suddenly I turn my back on the secret garden, on Kamikat, on the pavilion, and dart over to the wall. I run like mad with the branches and flowers whipping my face. I reach the wall, but of course the miller's worm-eaten ladder is further along. Ah, here it is at last! I walk along the top of the wall as quickly as I can. The old pear tree. I jump. I'm in the garden of my childhood. How bright and orderly everything is, here!

I go upstairs to my little room. I cry for a long time, very hard, for no reason, just cry. And then I sleep for a while. When I wake up I look at myself in the mirror. My clothes aren't dirty. There's nothing wrong with me. Oh yes there is, though, there's a little blood. A trickle of blood along my leg. That's odd, I don't have any scratches anywhere. Why, then? Never mind. I go over to the mirror and examine my face really close up.

I have blue eyes, cherry-red lips, plump pink cheeks, and wavy blond hair. What do I look like? I hold my finger up to my cherry-red lips. I incline my curly head. I smile mysteriously. I decide that I look like the stone boy. . . .

Then I see the tears welling up under my eyelids.

Wednesday Kamikat has become very friendly since my visit to his garden. He spends hours lying on his side in the sun, showing his stomach.

Talking of his stomach, it looks very plump to me. Plumper every day.

It must be a she-cat.

Kami-she-kat.

Tom Thumb Runs Away

A Christmas Story

That evening, Captain Thumb seemed to have made up his mind to put an end to the air of mystery he had been affecting for the last few weeks, and to show his hand.

'The fact is,' said he, after a meditative silence, when they had got to the dessert, 'we're going to move. Bièvres, and our crooked little villa, the bit of garden with our ten lettuces and three rabbits – they're all a thing of the past!'

Whereupon he fell silent, the better to observe the effect of this tremendous revelation on his wife and son. Then he pushed aside the plates and cutlery, and with the edge of his hand swept away the crumbs strewn over the oilcloth.

'Let's say that this is the bedroom. That – that's the bathroom, here's the living room, here's the kitchen, and there are two more bedrooms, if you please. Sixty square metres, with built-in cupboards, wall-to-wall carpets, neon lighting and all mod cons. A chance in a million. Twenty-third floor in the Mercury Tower. Can you imagine?'

Could they really imagine? Mrs Thumb cast a scared glance at her terrible husband and then, with a reaction that she had been having more and more frequently of late, she looked round at little Tom, as if she were counting on him to challenge the authority of the chief of the Paris woodcutters.

'Twenty-third floor! Well! We mustn't forget our matches!' he remarked courageously.

'Idiot!' retorted Thumb, 'there are four ultra-rapid lifts. In these modern high-rise buildings they've practically done away with staircases.'

'And when it's windy, watch out for draughts!'

'No question of draughts! The windows are all sealed up. They don't open.'

'Then how do I shake my mats?' Mrs Thumb ventured to ask.

'Your mats, your mats! You'll have to forget your peasant habits. You'll have your vacuum cleaner. And the same with your washing. You don't really want to go on hanging it outside to dry, do you!'

'But then,' Tom objected, 'if the windows are sealed up, how do we breathe?'

'No need for fresh air. Everything's air-conditioned. There's a fan that expels the stale air, day and night, and replaces it with air extracted from the roof, heated to the required temperature. And in any case, the windows have to be sealed because the tower block is sound-proofed.'

'Sound-proofed, at that height? But whatever for?'

'Well, my goodness, because of the planes! Don't you realize that we'll be within a thousand metres of the new runway at Toussus-le-Noble? Every forty-five seconds a jet passes within a hair's breadth of the roof. Just as well we're sealed off! Like in a submarine . . . There you are, then, we're all set. We'll be able to move in before the twenty-fifth. That'll be your Christmas present. A bit of luck, eh?'

But while the captain was pouring himself out the remains of the red wine to wash down his cheese, little Tom was gloomily smearing his cream caramel all over his plate; suddenly, he didn't seem to want it any more.

'That's modern life for you, my children,' Thumb insisted. 'We have to adapt to it! You don't really want us to stagnate in this mouldy countryside for ever, do you? And anyway, as the President of the Republic himself said: *Paris must adapt to the motor car, even at the expense of a certain aestheticism.*'

'A certain aestheticism – what's that?' asked Tom.

Thumb ran his short fingers through his black, close-cropped hair. These kids – always asking stupid questions!

'Aestheticism, aestheticism . . . er um . . . well, it's trees!' he finally came out with, to his relief. '*Even at the expense of*, that means that they have to be cut down. You see, son, the President was referring there to my men and me. A fine tribute to the woodcutters of Paris. And a well-deserved tribute! Because without us, eh, there'd be no question of motorways and car parks, with all those trees. It may not be obvious, but Paris is full of trees. It's a real forest! Or rather, it *was* . . . Because we count for something, we woodcutters. An élite, that's what we are. Because when it comes to the finishing touches we're like goldsmiths, we are. Do you think it's an easy job to cut down a twenty-five metre plane tree in the middle of the city without damaging anything around?'

He was off. Nothing would stop him now. Mrs Thumb got up and went to wash the dishes, while Tom stared at his father with a frozen look that feigned passionate interest.

'The big poplar trees on the Ile Saint-Louis, and the ones in the Place Dauphine, we had to slice them up like salami and lower the logs one by one with ropes. And all that without breaking a single pane of glass, without denting a single car. We even got ourselves congratulated by the City Council. Which was only right and proper. Because the day Paris has become a network of motorways and flyovers that thousands of cars will be able to cross at one hundred kilometres an hour in all directions, who will people owe it to first and foremost, eh? To the woodcutters who cleared the ground!'

'But what about my boots?'

'What boots?'

'The ones you promised me for Christmas.'

'Boots? Me? Ah yes, of course. Boots, well, they're all very fine for messing about in the garden here. But you can't wear them in a flat! What would the downstairs neighbours say? Here, I'll make you an offer. Instead of boots, I'll buy you a colour television. That's really something, huh? Right? – let's shake on it, then.'

And he took his hand, with the warm, frank, virile smile of the captain of the Paris woodcutters.

I don't want any kneeon lighting or air contingents. I'd rather have trees and boots. Goodbye for ever. Your only son, Tom.

'They'll say my writing's still babyish,' thought Tom in some mortification, reading over his farewell note. What about the spelling? There's nothing like one really big, stupid mistake to rob even a pathetic message of all its dignity. Boots. Should it be *u*, like in *brutes*? Or does it really have two *o*s? Yes, it must have, because there are two boots.

He folded the note and stood it up conspicuously on the kitchen table. His parents would find it when they came home after spending the evening with friends. He would be far away. All alone? Not quite. He crossed the little garden and, with a hamper tucked under his arm, went to the hutch in which he kept his three rabbits. Rabbits don't like twenty-three-storey tower blocks either.

So there he was, walking along the RN 306, the main road leading to the forest of Rambouillet. Because that was where he wanted to go. Just a vague idea, obviously. During their last holiday he had noticed a group of caravans round a pond in the village of Vieille-Église. Maybe there were still some caravans there, maybe someone would take him in . . .

The premature December night had fallen. He was walking along the right-hand side of the road, against all the advice he had always been given, but hitch-hiking has its own requirements. Unfortunately the cars seemed to be in a great hurry on this day before Christmas Eve. They hurtled past without even dipping their headlights. Tom walked for a very long time. He wasn't tired yet, but he had to keep shifting the hamper from his right arm to his left and back again. Finally he came to a small island of bright lights, colours, noises. It was a garage with a shop full of gadgets. A big articulated lorry was drawn up by a diesel pump. Tom went up to the driver.

'I'm going to Rambouillet. Will you give me a lift?'

The driver gave him a suspicious look.

'You haven't run away, I hope?'

Here, the rabbits had a brilliant idea. One after the other they poked their heads out of the hamper. Do you take live rabbits in a hamper with you if you're running away? The driver was reassured.

'Come on, then. Jump in.'

This was the first time Tom Thumb had travelled in a lorry. You're perched so high up! It's almost like being on the back of an elephant. Bits of houses suddenly loomed up in the headlights, and phantom trees, and fleeting silhouettes of pedestrians and cyclists. After Christ-de-Saclay the road becomes narrower and more winding. You're really in the country. Saint-Rémy, Chevreuse, Cernay. Right, they'd come to the forest.

'I get off a kilometre farther on,' Tom announced at random.

In actual fact he was scared to death, and he had the feeling that once he had left the lorry he would be completely lost. A few minutes later the driver pulled up at the side of the road.

'I can't stop here for long,' he told Tom. 'Come on, then! All change!'

But even so he thrust his hand down under his seat and pulled out a thermos.

'Here – have a swig of mulled wine before you go. My old woman always puts some in for me. Personally, I prefer dry white.'

The syrupy liquid burned his throat and smelled of cinnamon, but it was still wine, and Tom was a little tipsy when the lorry pulled away, puffing and blowing, spitting and bellowing. 'Yes, a real elephant,' thought Tom as he watched it disappear into the darkness. 'But with all those skyrockets and red lights, it's an elephant that's like a Christmas tree as well.'

The Christmas tree disappeared round a corner and the darkness closed in on Tom. But it wasn't totally dark. A vague phosphorescence was emanating from the cloudy sky. Tom walked. He had a feeling that he ought to turn down a path on the right to get to the pond. He came to a path, but it was on the left. Oh, so what! He wasn't sure of anything. He decided to settle for the left. It must have been the mulled wine. He shouldn't have drunk it. He was dropping with sleep. And that confounded hamper digging into his hip. What if he rested a minute under a tree? For instance, under that big fir tree with its carpet of almost-dry needles all around it? Ah, he'd let the rabbits out. Live rabbits keep you warm. They're as good as a blanket. They're a live blanket. They nuzzled up to Tom, poking their little noses into his clothes. 'I'm their burrow,' he thought, with a smile. 'A live burrow.'

Stars were dancing around him, with exclamations and silvery laughs. Stars? No, lanterns. Held by gnomes. Gnomes? No, little girls. They crowded round Tom.

'A little boy! Lost! Abandoned! Asleep! He's waking up. Good morning! Good evening! Hee hee hee! What's your name?

Mine's Nadine, and mine's Christine, Carine, Aline, Sabine, Ermeline, Delphine . . .'

They were bubbling over with laughter and jostling one another, and the lanterns were dancing faster than ever. Tom felt the ground around him with a tentative hand. The hamper was still there but the rabbits had disappeared. He stood up. The seven little girls surrounded him, tugging at him, and he found it impossible to resist them.

'Our name is Ogur. We're the Ogur sisters.'

Another paroxysm of giggles shook the seven lanterns.

'We live here. Look, you see that light through the trees? What about you? Where have you come from? What's your name?'

That was the second time they'd asked him his name. He said, very clearly: 'Tom'. With one voice they all exclaimed: 'He can talk! He talks! He's called Tom! Come on, we'll introduce you to papa Ogur.'

The house was entirely made of wood, apart from its stone foundation. It was a complicated, wobbly old construction which looked as if it had once been several buildings, now rather awkwardly joined together. But Tom had already been pushed into the big living room. All he could see at first was a monumental fireplace in which tree trunks were blazing. The left side of the hearth was obscured by a big wicker armchair, a veritable throne, but a light, airy throne decorated with loops, and whorls, and crosses, and rosettes, and corollas, through which the flames glowed.

'This is where we eat, and sing, and dance, and tell stories,' seven little voices observed at the same time. 'Over there, in the next room, that's where we sleep. That bed is for all us children. Just look how big it is.'

In fact, Tom had never seen such a big bed, a precise square, with an eiderdown swollen like a big red balloon. Above the bed, as if to inspire sleep, there was an embroidered motto in a frame: *Make love, not war.* But the seven little imps led Tom into another room, a huge workshop which smelled of wool and wax polish and in which all the space was taken up by a loom made of light-coloured wood.

'This is where Mama weaves her fabrics. She's gone to the provinces to sell them. We're waiting for her with Papa.'

'Funny sort of family!' thought Tom. 'The mother works, and the father looks after the house!'

They went back to the living room. The armchair stirred. Then the aerial throne must be inhabited. There was someone in between its arms, which were curved like swans' necks.

'Papa, this is Tom!'

Mr Ogur stood up and looked at Tom. He was so tall! A real forest giant! But a slim, supple giant. Everything about him was gentle: his long blond hair held back by a sort of ribbon across his forehead; his honey-coloured leather clothes covered with engraved silver jewels, chains, necklets, and three belts with buckles one on top of the other; but above all, oh! above all, his boots, his tall, flexible, beige suede boots which came up to his knees and were also covered with chains, rings and medals.

Tom was overwhelmed with admiration. He didn't know what to say, he didn't know what he was saying. He said: 'You're as beautiful as . . .' Mr Ogur smiled. He smiled with all his white teeth, but also with all his necklets, with his embroidered waistcoat, his huntsman's breeches, his silk shirt, but above all, oh! above all, with his tall boots.

'As beautiful as what?' he insisted.

In a panic, Tom tried to find the right word, the word that would best express his surprise, his astonishment.

'You're as beautiful as a woman!' he finally brought out, in a whisper.

The little girls' laughter rang out, and then Mr Ogur's laughter, and finally Tom's laughter, he was so happy at the way he was becoming part of this family.

'Let's go and eat,' said Mr Ogur.

What a lot of pushing and shoving there was around the table, with all the little girls wanting to sit next to Tom!

'It's Sabine's and Carine's turn to serve today,' Mr Ogur reminded them gently.

Apart from the grated carrots, Tom didn't recognize any of the dishes the two sisters put on the table, from which they all immediately started to help themselves liberally. They named them: purée of garlic, whole rice, horseradish, grape sugar, pickled plankton, grilled soya beans, boiled swedes, and other marvels that he ate with closed eyes, washing them down with fresh milk and maple syrup. With implicit trust, he found everything delicious.

Next, the eight children sat in a semicircle round the fire and Mr Ogur took a guitar from the canopy over the fireplace and at first played just a few sad, melodious chords. But when the song began, Tom started with surprise, and looked round at the faces of the seven sisters. No, the girls were all listening, silent and attentive. That thin voice, that light soprano which effortlessly reached the highest-pitched trills – it really did come from the dark silhouette of Mr Ogur.

Would there ever be an end to his surprises? It began to look as if there wouldn't, because the girls started passing cigarettes round, and the one next to him – was it Nadine or Ermeline? – lit one and casually slid it between his lips. Cigarettes that had a funny sort of smell, slightly bitter but at the same time slightly sweet, and whose smoke made you feel as light as could be, as light as it was itself, floating in blue layers in the dark space.

Mr Ogur propped his guitar up against his armchair and observed a long, meditative silence. Finally he started to speak in a quiet but deep voice.

'Listen to me,' he said. 'Tonight is the longest night of the year. So I'm going to talk to you about the most important thing in the world. I'm going to talk to you about trees.'

He remained silent for quite a time, and then he went on:

'Listen to me. Paradise – what was Paradise? It was a forest. Or rather, a wood. A wood, because its trees were neatly planted, with plenty of space in between, and there were no brambly copses or prickly undergrowths. It wasn't like it is now. Here, for example, we have whole hectares of fir trees, and then hundreds of silver birches. What sort of species am I talking about? Why – forgotten, unknown, extraordinary, miraculous species, species which can no longer be found on earth, and I'll tell you why. In fact, each of these trees produced its own fruit, and each kind of fruit possessed its own particular magic power. One of them conferred the knowledge of good and evil. This was the number one tree in the Garden of Eden. Number two conferred everlasting life. That wasn't bad, either. But there were all the others, the one that gave strength, the one that granted creative power, the ones that endowed people with wisdom, ubiquity, beauty, courage, love – all the qualities and powers that are the privilege of Jehovah. And this privilege was something that Jehovah was determined to reserve for himself alone. Which is why he said to Adam: "If you eat the fruit of tree number one, you'll die".

'Was Jehovah telling the truth or was he lying? The serpent claimed that he was lying. All Adam had to do was try it. He'd soon see whether he was going to die or whether, on the contrary, he was going to know good and evil. Like Jehovah himself.

'Encouraged by Eve, Adam makes up his mind. He bites into the fruit. And he doesn't die. On the contrary, his eyes open, and he knows good and evil. So Jehovah had lied. It was the serpent that had told the truth.

'Jehovah panics. Now that he's no longer afraid, man is going to eat all the forbidden fruit and, one thing leading to another, he will become a second Jehovah. And so – first things first – he places a Cherubim, complete with a flaming sword that turns in every direction, in front of tree number two, the one that confers everlasting life. Next, he drives Adam and Eve out of the Magic Wood, and exiles them into a land without trees.

'This, then, was the curse laid upon men: they left the vegetable kingdom. They descended into the animal kingdom. And what is the animal kingdom? It's hunting, violence, murder, fear. The vegetable kingdom, on the other hand, is the peaceful growth that results from a union between the earth and the sun. This is why all wisdom can only be founded on a meditation on trees, undertaken in a forest by men who are vegetarians . . .'

He stood up and threw more logs on the fire. Then he went back to his place and, after a long silence:

'Listen to me,' he said. 'What is a tree? In the first place, a tree consists in a certain balance between aerial foliage and underground roots. This purely mechanical balance contains a whole philosophy in itself. For it is clear that it is impossible for the foliage to spread, to expand, to embrace an ever-increasing portion of the sky, if the roots do not at the same time plunge deeper, and divide into ever-increasing numbers of radicles and radicels to anchor the edifice more firmly. People who know about trees are aware that certain varieties – cedars in particular – are rash enough to develop their foliage beyond what their roots can support. In that case, everything depends on where the tree is growing. If it is in an exposed position, if the ground is light and shifting, just an ordinary storm is enough to topple the giant. So you see, the higher you want to rise, the more you must have your feet on the ground. Every tree tells you so.

'And that's not all. A tree is a living being, but its life is completely different from that of an animal. When we breathe in, our muscles expand our chests and they fill with air. Then we breathe out. The decision is one we take by ourselves, solitarily, arbitrarily, without bothering about what sort of a day it is, whether it's windy, or sunny, or whatever. We live cut off from the rest of the world, the enemies of the rest of the world. But look how different it is with trees. Their lungs are their leaves. They don't change their air unless the air itself feels like moving. A tree's respiration is the wind. A gust of wind is the tree's movement, the movement of its leaves, its tigella, stalks, boughs, twigs, branches, and finally the movement of its trunk. But it is also aspiration, expiration, transpiration. And the sun is necessary, too, otherwise the tree cannot live. The tree is indivisible from the wind and the sun. It sucks its life directly from these two breasts of the cosmos – wind and sun. It is nothing but this anticipation. It is nothing but an immense network of leaves outstretched in anticipation of the wind and the sun. A tree is a wind-trap, a sun-trap. When it stirs and rustles, sending arrows of light darting in all directions, it is because these two big fish, the wind and the sun, have allowed themselves to get trapped in its net of chlorophyll . . .'

Was Mr Ogur really speaking, or were his thoughts being silently transmitted on the blue wings of the strange cigarettes they were all still smoking? Tom couldn't say. He was simply floating in the air like a great tree – a chestnut tree, yes, why precisely a chestnut tree he had no idea but it certainly was that tree – and Mr Ogur's words had come to inhabit his branches with a luminous rustling.

What happened next? He could still see, as if in a dream, the big, square bed, and lots of clothes flying all over the room – little girls' clothes as well as those of one little boy – and a boisterous scramble accompanied by whoops of joy. And then the cosy night under the enormous eiderdown, and the swarm of adorable little bodies around him, those fourteen little hands caressing him so

mischievously that he nearly choked with laughter . . .
A dirty light came filtering in through the windows. Suddenly they heard piercing whistles. There were heavy knocks on the door. The little girls dispersed like a flock of sparrows, leaving Tom all alone in the big, eviscerated bed. The knocking redoubled – it sounded like the blows of an axe attacking the trunk of a condemned tree.

'Police! Open up!'

Tom got up and dressed in a hurry.

'Good morning, Tom.'

He looked round, recognizing the soft, lilting voice that had lulled him all night long. Mr Ogur was there in front of him. He was no longer wearing his leather clothes, or his jewels, or the ribbon round his forehead. He was barefoot in a long tunic of unbleached linen and his hair, parted in the middle, fell loosely over his shoulders.

'Jehovah's soldiers have come to arrest me,' he said gravely. 'But tomorrow is Christmas. Before the house is ransacked, come and choose, in remembrance of me, an object to take with you into the desert.'

Tom followed him into the big room where, under the mantelpiece, there was nothing but a heap of cold ashes. With a vague gesture, Mr Ogur pointed to all the strange, poetic objects scattered round on the table, on the chairs, hanging on the wall, lying on the floor, a whole pure, primitive treasure trove. But Tom didn't even glance at the engraved dagger, or at the belt buckles, or the fox-fur waistcoat, or the diadems, necklets or rings. No – all he saw was the pair of boots standing almost under the table, whose tall stems were flopping awkwardly over their sides, like elephants' ears.

'They're much too big for you,' said Mr Ogur, 'but it doesn't matter. Hide them under your coat. And when you find things too boring back home, lock yourself into your bedroom, put them on, and let them carry you off to the country of trees.'

At this point the door was broken down and three men came crashing into the room. They were wearing policemen's uniforms, and Tom wasn't surprised to see the captain of the Paris woodcutters rushing in behind them.

'So using and pushing drugs isn't enough for you any more,'

one of the policemen barked in Mr Ogur's face. 'You have to corrupt minors as well!'

Mr Ogur merely held out his wrists. The handcuffs snapped. In the meantime, Captain Thumb caught sight of his son.

'Ah, so there you are! I knew it! Go and wait for me in the car! Get a move on!'

Then he set out on an infuriated and disgusted inspection of the surroundings.

'Trees – they are where mushrooms and vice proliferate! The Bois de Boulogne, for instance – you know what that is? An open-air brothel! Here, look what I've just found!'

The police inspector studied the embroidered motto: *Make love, not war.*

'That,' he agreed, 'is evidence: incitement of a minor to immoral behaviour, and attempted demoralization of the army! What filth!'

On the twenty-third floor of the Mercury Tower, Thumb and his wife were looking at their colour television set on which they saw pictures of men and women wearing clowns' hats throwing confetti and streamers in each other's faces. It was Christmas Eve.

Tom was alone in his bedroom. He turned the key in the lock and then pulled out from under his bed two big boots made of soft, golden suede. It wasn't difficult to pull them on, they were so much too big for him! It would be very awkward to walk in them, but that wasn't what he wanted. These were dream boots.

He lay down on his bed and closed his eyes. And then he was far, far away. He became an enormous chestnut tree whose flowers were as erect as creamy little candelabra. He was suspended in the immobility of the blue sky. But suddenly, a slight breeze passed by. Tom made a gentle soughing sound. His thousands of green wings beat in the air. His branches moved gently up and down, dispensing blessings. The sun opened out like a fan, which then closed again in the grey-green shade of his foliage. He was immensely happy. A big tree . . .

Prickly

❧

'You're all prickly!'

The little boy squirmed in the arms of his father, who was trying to kiss him. It wasn't just his stubbly cheeks, it was his grey skin, his smell of tobacco and shaving soap, his dust-coloured suit, his stiff collar that was not enhanced by a too sensible necktie . . . No, really, there was nothing about this man that charmed or caressed, and his efforts to demonstrate affection seemed like punishments. What was more, he had only made matters worse by countering his son's rebuffs with irony, calling him 'Prickly' or, 'my little hedgehog'.

'Come here Prickly!' he commanded. 'Come and kiss Papa!'

When he heard this nickname for the first time, the child had bristled. Yes, he felt precisely that he was becoming a hedgehog, a miniature pig covered with bristles swarming with vermin. Ugh! He screamed with anger and disgust. Luckily Mama was there. He took refuge in her arms.

'I don't want to, I don't want to be Prickly!'

She enveloped him in her perfume. She pressed her creamy, rouged cheek to her child's burning face. Then her deep, calming voice, as if by a miracle, sprang the trap and placed a soothing picture, like a cool hand, over his inflamed imagination.

'But you know, baby hedgehogs don't have prickles – just very soft, very clean down. It's only later. Later, when they grow up. When they become men . . .'

To become a man. Like Papa. No prospect could be less attractive to Prickly. He sometimes watched his father shaving. The folding razor, one of those old-fashioned razors with a mother-of-pearl handle that are sometimes called cut-throats, held in a bizarre way between the thumb and forefinger, scraped at his skin and removed the lather contaminated by the cut whiskers. And that grimy snow disappeared in grey flakes under the water from the tap, while Papa was still scratching away at his neck and jowls, making ridiculous grimaces. He ended with his upper lip, pinching the tip of his nose between his fingers and pulling it back. At this point Prickly ran away, to stop Papa taking him in his arms when he'd finished. But had he *really* finished? What about all those black hairs on his chest?

On the other hand, Prickly had never seen his mother at her dressing table. After her lemon tea, which she took alone in her bedroom, she shut herself up in the bathroom for an hour and a half. And when she came out, still dressed in a chiffon negligée, she was already a goddess, the goddess of the morning, as fresh as a rose, anointed with lanolin, very different, it's true, from the great black goddess of the evening, the one who leaned over Prickly's bed, her face half hidden behind a little veil, and told him: 'Don't kiss me, you'll ruin my hair.' 'At least leave me your gloves,' he begged her one day. And she agreed, dropping these bits of black kidskin into his bed. They were as supple and warm as fresh, living skins, and the child swathed his body in their empty hands, Mama's hands, and fell asleep under their caress.

The beautiful apartment that Prickly and his family lived in in the rue des Sablons provided little nourishment for the child's imagination apart from a huge old painting in the Pre-Raphaelite style which had been hung, to get it out of the way, in the narrow corridor leading from the salon to the bedrooms at the back. Nobody noticed it any more, except Prickly who felt its terrible images weighing heavily on him every time he went along that sombre passageway. This painting depicted *The Last Judgement*. In the centre of an apocalyptic landscape consisting of mountains collapsing one on top of the other, a supreme being made of light was sitting on a throne and presiding over the inexorable division established between the damned and the chosen. The damned were sinking down into an underground passage made of granite, while the chosen, singing and carrying palms, were ascending to heaven up a great staircase made of pink clouds. Now what the child found particularly striking was the anatomy of each category. For whereas the damned had brown skin and black hair, and their nudity revealed formidable muscles, the chosen were pale and slim, and their white tunics concealed frail, delicate limbs.

On fine days Prickly and his nursemaid went out in the afternoon to the gardens in Desbordes-Valmore Square. Old Marie always sat on the same bench, where she held court with the other governesses of the district who also came there to give the progeniture of the bourgeoisie the benefit of some fresh air. They talked about the weather, about family affairs, about the provinces they came from, and above all about their employers. As the gardens were enclosed and therefore safe, they allowed the children to wander off, keeping only a vague eye on them.

Prickly liked these times when there was nothing much to do except explore and discover. They made such a contrast with the dreary mornings he spent at his lessons in the company of a handful of other well-to-do children in a private school in the rue de la Faisanderie. Everything he learned at school remained abstract for him, and totally unconnected with real things. The knowledge he acquired floated somewhere above life and was never involved in it. It was quite different when he was in the square, though; there, he moved around with wide-open eyes and outstretched fingers, for it was an initiatory place, full of surprises and threats.

In the first place there was a whole crowd of statues which were strange both because of their nudity and because of their respective occupations. For instance, one was a horse, but where its neck should have been it had the torso of a man – a bearded man with a nasty look in his eye. He spent his time carrying off under his arm a fat, naked woman whose hair was all over the place and who was struggling without much conviction. Prickly had asked Marie to explain this scene to him. Marie was obviously at a loss, so she had appealed to the English governess of a little girl who sometimes came to the gardens and who as it so happened was there at the time. Miss Campbell had given Prickly quite a long lecture, from which he vaguely gathered that the man-horse – a scent-tar – was obliged, in order to marry, to abduct a woman by main force, precisely because of his bad smell, to which he owed his name. Remembering his father's smell, Prickly had been satisfied with this explanation.

A little farther on a young boy with hairless, chubby cheeks, dressed in a short skirt, was raising his sword against a monster, which had fallen over backwards. The monster had the body of a man of terrifying strength, and the head of a bull. There too Miss Campbell had been able to throw some light on the subject. The young boy, who was called Theseus, should have been devoured by the monster. But he had been the stronger, and he had killed the man-bull. But why did he have such a funny name, and wear a skirt like a girl? Here, Miss Campbell had no answer.

Prickly could tell the difference between the more or less regular visitors to the square and its permanent inhabitants. Among the latter, the most important character was undoubtedly the park keeper. Old Cromorne was distinguished by his uniform and képi, but especially by the left arm of his jacket which was empty, and tucked back with a safety pin. People said he was one-armed and a widower. When Prickly had asked, and been told, what a widower was, he wondered whether there was any connection between these two states. Was it because he had lost his wife that Cromorne had only one arm? Had he cut off his left arm on the day of the funeral and put it in the coffin beside his dear departed?

Much less important than Cromorne, Madame Béline and Mademoiselle Aglaia were secondary but reassuring characters. Mademoiselle Aglaia was in charge of the chairs – ninety-four chairs, she had specified to Marie and Miss Campbell with a sigh, one day when she was speaking freely. In order to fulfil her mission properly it was her duty to be discreet and unobtrusive. Cromorne had only recently said as much. Had she had his presence and uniform – to say nothing of his prestige as a disabled ex-serviceman – she wouldn't have managed to take half the money she did. For people are rather dishonest, and they would have no scruples about going off without paying for their chairs if the person responsible for collecting the money was too conspicuous. Whereas with Mademoiselle Aglaia, people were never on their guard when she came gliding down the alleyways, concealing her book of tickets in the hollow of her hand.

Pink and plump, Madame Béline sat in state behind her jars of lollipops and barley sugar in a kiosk bristling with hoops, diabolos, yoyos, kites, multicoloured balloons, skipping ropes, and musical tops. But even though she radiated goodness and *joie de vivre* this was not effortless, for she had suffered a grave disappointment. The dream of her life was to have a few tables and chairs in front of her kiosk at which she could serve lemonade and fruit juices to the public. She would thus have gone some way towards following the prestigious tradition of one of her uncles who had owned a bar in Saint-Ouen. Unfortunately, Cromorne had always opposed this project. In the first place, Madame Béline didn't have the necessary licence. As to making him an accomplice to her bending the rules of the administration, Madame Béline could no longer even dream of it after the unfortunate allusion she had once made to her bar-keeping uncle. Cromorne had been indignant. A bar-keeper from Saint-Ouen! What were they trying to do to Desbordes-Valmore Square!

If poor Madame Béline was no match for Cromorne, it was quite different with old mother Mamouse who reigned over the 'public convenience'. This was a curious construction which, though shaped like a Swiss chalet, nevertheless had something of the Chinese pagoda and the Hindu temple about it with its upturned roof, its sculptured wood, and its ceramic decoration.

What particularly interested Prickly was the division of the space inside this chalet into two strictly opposed parts. On the left was the men's domain, with its foul-smelling, parsimoniously-irrigated urinals and, behind doors that didn't close properly, Turkish latrines formed of a cynical hole framed by two soles of grooved cement to put your feet on. Nothing could be more attractive, on the other hand, than the ladies' domain. The whole place smelled of lilac disinfectant and was decorated with porcelain representing peacocks with their tails widely fanned. There was a pile of fresh, snowy white towels on a console table between two immaculate washbowls. But what especially enchanted Prickly were the little closets with their well-fitting mahogany doors, their high-perched seats, and their silky, silent toilet paper that smelled of violets.

Like the dog Cerberus, that watchful keeper of the infernal regions, Mamouse, enormous in several thicknesses of woollies and shawls, her big, flabby, impassive face framed within the confines of the black lace mantilla covering her white hair, was ensconced at a table between the two doors, that of the gentlemen and that of the ladies. On this table stood a saucer destined for offerings, and a spirit stove surmounted by a saucepan in which a broth of chicken giblets was invariably simmering.

Mamouse had explained the theory of the saucer to one of her lady clients in Prickly's presence, and he had listened with all his ears. Whatever happened, it must never be empty. The people who used the chalet were only too willing to forget to leave an offering. A few coins in the saucer are indispensable, to refresh their memories. These coins serve as a sort of bait and act like decoys, those caged birds that are supposed to attract their free congeners towards the sportsmen and their guns. Was it a good idea to add one or two notes to the coins? Mamouse's answer to this serious question was a categorical no. A note doesn't attract a note, it is more likely to discourage it by bringing into disrepute what can only be the product of exceptional munificence. Not to speak of the a hundred-times accursed day when a note left by a lady client had disappeared five minutes later under Mamouse's very nose. Coins, therefore, and the most valuable possible, of course, not those worthless little bits people call 'small change', which set a deplorable example in a saucer.

Apropos of offerings, Mamouse had a story she never failed to tell to newcomers, just as soon as she had arrived at a suitable degree of familiarity with them. The anecdote went back to a period in the very distant past, to judge by the sum in question. A very elegant gentleman, such as was to be seen in former days – light grey spats, gloves, walking stick, hat, monocle – having deposited a coin with a hole in it in the saucer, had pointed to the shut door of one of the closets with the tip of his stick.

He had taken the liberty of joking: 'You have a client in there who is treating us to some very ugly-sounding music!'

'So,' Mamouse related, once again inflamed with retrospective indignation, 'I looked daggers at him and said: "I suppose you think that for twenty-five centimes we should give you some Massenet?" For in those days,' she added nostalgically, 'I could still afford a subscription to the Opéra Comique.'

There regularly followed one of her habitual diatribes against men, with their disgusting behaviour: they're all lechers, wild boars, debauchees, and she should know, for goodness' sake, after thirty years of running a public convenience!

The stove and saucepan were an apple of discord between her and Cromorne. For the park keeper considered this vulgar stew, which so indiscreetly displayed to all eyes the culinary habits of the custodian of the chalet, to be unworthy of his garden.

'He makes out I don't have any right to it!' Mamouse muttered. 'But just let him show me the article in the regulations which forbids my broth! And how does he expect me to sit here in all this damp and all these draughts if I don't get something warm inside me?'

Prickly had of course had occasion to take a look in the battered old saucepan simmering on the stove. But the chicken necks, and livers, and gizzards, didn't arouse any echo in his mind. They weren't the sort of thing he saw in the kitchen at home. As for Mamouse's remarks, he paid very little attention to them, having other things to think about, and precisely at the moment when the fat woman was chatting to one of her customers. For his whole problem consisted in evading her attention and slipping in through the door on the right – into the perfumed domain of the ladies. At first he had succeeded in this manoeuvre more than once, but Mamouse had spotted him, and from then on she kept an eye on him. The right-hand door became more and more impassable.

This matter had been important to him since a childish drama relating to what Marie called 'doing a tinkle'. Prickly had always performed this function squatting, as if he were a girl. It was so unusual for him to pee standing up that when he tried it he experienced a difficulty that had almost become an inhibition. His family hadn't taken any notice of what at first seemed just a baby's whim. Then they'd started badgering him about it, so much so that he'd made up his mind only to urinate where no one could watch him, in a locked lavatory. Having thus found peace, he had started to observe, with disgusted curiosity, men standing up in urinals.

One day, while he was walking in the street with his mother, he tried an experiment that turned out to be unfortunate. Ahead of them walked a dog which kept stopping at every lamp post to brand it with its urine. Observing this ritual, Pickly suddenly had the idea of imitating it. He too stopped at a tree and lifted his left leg up towards its trunk. Halting abruptly, his mother caught him in this strange posture. She reacted by instinct, and a sharp smack landed on Prickly's cheek.

'Have you gone quite mad?' she asked, in a particular tone of voice that he detested.

He had been deeply mortified by this little misadventure. No one ever hit him, but now he'd been slapped because of his urinary habits. He concluded that pee-pee, and everything to do with it, constituted a source of multiple annoyances.

Things had got even worse when he started wetting his bed again. He couldn't help it. Every morning he woke up in a pool. All he knew about it was that just sometimes, when he was still half asleep, he felt the warm urine trickling down his thigh. Old Marie scolded him and put a piece of oilcloth under his sheet to protect his mattress. She threatened, if he didn't stop, to bring back the surgeon who had taken his tonsils out. This time it would be his little willie they'd cut off!

Things might well have gone no farther. But in fact, one thing followed another in diabolical fashion. One day, when he was on the look-out for a moment's inattention on Mamouse's part, he was stupefied to see his friend Dominique coming out of the chalet. The thing was, he was coming from the ladies' side and, instead of hiding from the fat woman, he exchanged a few smiling words with her and went off without leaving her an offering. Prickly was absolutely certain of this. Who was Dominique? He was the son of Angelo Bosio, the owner of the merry-go-round. Most of the time the merry-go-round slept motionless under its tarpaulins. But on Sundays, everything came to life. Bosio father and son were hard at it inside the big cream and gold top in which, peppered with a metallic sort of music, there was a confused but cheerful mixture of naiads, space rockets, rearing horses, milch cows, Formula 1 racing cars, and a dear little Far West locomotive with its cow-catcher. When Marie offered him a ride on the merry-go-round this locomotive was where Prickly liked to sit. Not that he dreamed of any adventures in the prairies, but simply because he liked the privacy of being able to shut himself into the little vehicle, to sit in an enclosed space that was his alone. Within reach of his hand there was a little chain with which he could have rung the shiny brass bell attached to the engine. He took care not to touch it.

On Wednesdays, Dominique had sole charge of the merry-go-round. As he was tall – he was at least eleven years old – big, and strong, he had no difficulty in keeping his little clientèle in order, and he was both gentle and patient as he perched some of them up on the horses, placed others in the conch drawn by the naiads, and strapped Prickly into his locomotive. Then he switched on the motor and the music and gave the merry-go-round a little push to help it get started. When he was in a good mood he undid the rope attached to the trophy and made it jiggle up and down over the children's heads. The trophy consisted of a wig made of red wool suspended on a rope that passed through a pulley. The child who caught it was entitled to a free ride. Strapped into his cab, Prickly couldn't take part in the trophy hunt. By way of compensation, Dominique sometimes treated him to a free ride.

This favour had given rise to a friendship. Prickly had found a kind of older brother in this big, calm, maternal boy. So he didn't hesitate to question him after he'd seen him come out of the ladies' side of the chalet, obviously with Mamouse's blessing. How had he managed to obtain this tremendous privilege?

That day Dominique seemed to be in a radiant mood. He started by vigorously mocking Prickly and his curiosity. 'If anyone asks you,' he said, 'you must say you don't know!' Prickly detested irony and couldn't bear to be thwarted. He stamped his foot. He was just about to burst into tears when Dominique seemed to change his mind. He cast an anxious glance around and became very serious.

'If you want to know, if you absolutely want to know, well, it'll be terrible!'

Prickly was choking with emotion.

'How d'you mean, terrible?'

'If you're brave enough to know,' Dominique declared, 'be in the centre of the maze, by yourself, in half an hour!'

Then he went off, thumbing his nose.

Prickly was appalled. The boxwood maze at the far end of the gardens had always terrified him. It was a dark, dank clump of bushes which you could edge into through a narrow opening. After that, you got lost. There were turnings, recesses, culs-de-sac, closed circuits where you went round in circles indefinitely. If you had enough patience, you managed to reach the centre. There, on a little pedestal that was green with mould, there must once have been a statue. It had disappeared, but the pedestal was still waiting, soiled by slugs.

Prickly kept an eye on the electric clock. Thirty minutes.

Would he go to the terrible rendezvous? What was Dominique's big secret? Why did he have to go to the centre of the boxwood maze to hear it? More than once he relieved his fear by giving up the idea. He wouldn't go, he wouldn't! But he was well aware that this was just a pretence. He knew that he *would* keep the tryst.

At the appointed hour he made sure that Marie was quietly chatting with her friends, then made his way over towards the maze. He was more dead than alive as he allowed himself to be swallowed up within the bluey-green bushes. But, curiously guided by an infallible instinct, with no false moves he almost immediately found himself in the centre of the maze. He was pretty sure that someone would already be there, waiting for him. Dominique. The big boy was sitting on the pedestal. He looked serious.

'You came,' he said. 'As you're my friend, I'll let you into my secret. But before I do, you must swear that you'll never tell anyone.'

'Yes,' Prickly stammered, in a whisper.

'Spit on the ground and say: *I swear.*'

Prickly spat and said: *I swear.*

Then Dominique stood up on the pedestal and started unbuttoning the fly of his short trousers, never taking his eyes off Prickly. Next, opening them wide, he pulled down the red underpants he had exposed. His smooth, white stomach ended in a milky slit, a vertical smile in which there was just a trace of pale down.

'But . . . Dominique . . .' Prickly stammered.

'Dominique is a girl's name too,' explained Dominique, who had done up her trousers again in the twinkling of an eye. 'It's Papa. He wants people to think I'm a boy when I'm looking after the merry-go-round on my own. He says it's safer. You'll understand later. And now – scram!'

Prickly started running, and soon found himself back in the midst of the other children. There was nothing apparent to distinguish him from them; but he was like none of them, for he was possessed by a burning anxiety. *You'll understand later.* This mysterious phrase gave him no respite, and he tried desperately to understand it *at once.*

Not long after, he did in fact understand. In the first place he had gone into Mamouse's chalet without trying to avoid the men's domain for once. He was coming out of the closet where he had peed squatting, as was his wont, when he saw from behind a man who was just finishing relieving himself in one of the urinals. The man turned around and Prickly couldn't believe his eyes. The quantity of swarthy, flabby flesh he was trying with difficulty to cram back into his fly was incredible. What was he going to do with all that hideous, useless meat? The answer suddenly struck him while he was dropping a coin into Mamouse's saucer. Her saucepan was simmering away as usual on its stove. Mamouse was stirring its contents with a wooden spoon. And in a flash, Prickly recognized in those anatomical bits and pieces the brown, flaccid things that the fellow had been stuffing into his trousers. It was clear, it was obvious.

Later, another obvious fact had jumped up and hit him in the face. For months now he had been hanging around the statue of Theseus and the Minotaur. In the first place, he recognized that Theseus, with his girl's skirt, was a reflection of Dominique. The resemblance was self-evident. And above all he could clearly make out, between the great muscular thighs of the Minotaur, that bunch of flabby, shapeless flesh that had so surprised him in the man at the chalet. At last, Theseus's gesture had acquired a precise meaning. His sword was aimed at the Minotaur's sex organ. The link between the brown meat of the man in the urinal and Mamouse's saucepan, was forged by Theseus's sword.

In the days that followed, Marie was pleased to observe that Prickly had stopped wetting his bed.

'I frightened you when I threatened you with the surgeon,' she told him. 'It was high time. I was just going to call him. But there's no need now.'

Prickly didn't answer. There was indeed no need.

That same day they went back to the gardens. Mamouse saw him coming up to her and standing in front of her table. She was just going to ask him what he wanted when he pulled a razor out of his pocket, one of those old-fashioned razors with a mother-of-pearl handle that are sometimes called cut-throats. He opened it and, with his free hand, unbuttoned his fly. Mamouse started howling like a wild animal when she saw him bring out his little child's willie and slash at it with the razor. Blood spurted. Then

Prickly was holding out, to Mamouse, over the table, a little bit of shrivelled flesh. Next he saw the chalet, its surrounding trees, and the entire Desbordes-Valmore gardens swaying and beginning to revolve like Dominique's merry-go-round, and he collapsed in a faint, carrying with him as he fell the saucer with all its coins, the spirit stove, the saucepan, and all the chicken giblets.

Jesu, Joy of Man's Desiring

A Christmas Story

For Danny Cowl, this invented story which will remind him of a real one

Can you make a career as a great international concert pianist when your name is Gammon? By calling their son Raphael, and thus placing him under the tutelage of the most ethereal and melodious of all the archangels, the Gammons may have been unconsciously taking up this challenge. In any case, the child soon showed signs of being gifted with an intelligence and sensitivity that sanctioned all their hopes. They put him to the piano as soon as he was old enough to sit on a stool. His progress was remarkable. Blond, blue, pale, aristocratic, he was every inch a Raphael, and in no way a Gammon. At ten, he was already famous as a child prodigy and much fought over by the organizers of fashionable soirées. The ladies went into ecstasies when he leaned his delicate, transparent face over the keyboard and, enveloped, so it seemed, in the blue shadow of the wings of the invisible archangel, sent the notes of Johann Sebastian Bach's chorale, *Jesu, Joy of Man's Desiring*, floating up to the heavens like a mystical love song.

But the child paid dearly for these exceptional moments. Each year saw an increase in the number of hours a day he was made to practise. At twelve, he was already working six hours a day, and he found himself envying boys who were blessed with neither talent nor genius, nor with the promise of a brilliant career. It sometimes brought tears to his eyes when, on a fine day, relentlessly chained to his instrument, he heard the merry cries of his schoolmates enjoying themselves out of doors.

He reached his sixteenth year. His talent was flowering with incomparable abundance. He was the star pupil of the Paris Conservatoire. On the other hand, when adolescence succeeded childhood, it didn't seem to wish to retain the slightest trace of his former angelic visage. It seemed as if the wicked fairy Puberty had waved her magic wand over him and was determined to devastate the romantic angel that he had been. His bony, asymmetrical face, his protruding eyes, his receding chin, the thick glasses he had to wear because of his galloping myopia, none of this would really have mattered if it hadn't been for his permanent expression of stubborn amazement, which was much more likely to raise a laugh than to set people dreaming. In his appearance, at least, Gammon seemed to have completely triumphed over Raphael.

Young Bénédicte Prieur, who was two years younger than he, seemed to be impervious to this lack of charm. A pupil at the Conservatoire, she simply saw him, no doubt, as the great virtuoso he was in the process of becoming. In any case, she lived only in and for music, and the parents of the two children wondered in amazement whether their relationship would ever go beyond the ecstatic intimacy they reached when playing duets.

Raphael came top in the Conservatoire examination at a record age and began to pick up a few pupils to make his modest ends meet. Bénédicte and he were engaged, but they had decided to put off their marriage until times were better. They lived on love, music, and hope, and experienced some years of divine happiness. When they were lost in a concert which each dedicated to the other, Raphael, drunk with exaltation and gratitude, brought the evening to a close by playing once again Johann Sebastian Bach's chorale, *Jesu, Joy of Man's Desiring*. For him, this was not only a tribute to the greatest composer of all time, but also an ardent prayer to God, to ask him to safeguard so pure and ardent a union. And so the notes that floated up from his fingers at the piano rippled with celestial laughter, with the divine hilarity that was none other than the Creator's benediction of his own created being.

But destiny was to put this exquisite equilibrium to the test. Raphael had a friend, like him a graduate of the Conservatoire, who earned his living by accompanying a singer in a nightclub. As he was a violinist, he didn't feel he was compromising his integrity by strumming away on an old upright piano to punctuate the inept couplets the singer was mouthing downstage. Now this Henri Durieu was about to leave for his first tour of the provinces, and he asked Raphael to stand in for him for four weeks so as not to jeopardize this invaluable pay-packet.

Raphael hesitated. It would have been bad enough to have to sit for a couple of hours in that sombre, badly ventilated place and listen to someone talking rubbish. But to have to go there every evening and, even worse, to play a piano in such ignoble conditions . . . The fee, which for a single evening was the equivalent of a good dozen private lessons, was no compensation for this sacrilegious ordeal.

He was just about to refuse when, to his great surprise, Bénédicte asked him to think again. They had been engaged for a very long time. Raphael's career as an infant prodigy had been forgotten years ago, and no one knew how long he would have to wait until he became famous. But these few evenings could provide them with the extra income they needed to enable them to get a home together. Was it too much of a sacrifice, then? Could Raphael go on putting off their marriage just because of the image – certainly worthy of respect, but nevertheless pretty abstract – he had of his art? He agreed.

The singer he had to accompany was called Gabbler. Enormous, flabby and flaccid, he trundled from one extremity of the stage to the other, relating in a whining voice all the sorrows and misfortunes that life kept heaping on him. The whole secret of his burlesque lay in this very simple observation: if you are the victim of a misadventure, you interest people; of two misadventures, you inspire them to pity; of a hundred misadventures, you make them laugh. Hence, you only have to exaggerate the pathetic and calamitous side of a character to get the audience roaring with laughter.

The very first evening, Raphael assessed the quality of the laughter. Sadism, spite, and a taste for the contemptible were cynically flaunted in it. In exhibiting his misery, Gabbler hit the audience below the belt and reduced it to its lowest common denominator. He turned these decent bourgeois, who were neither better nor worse than any others, into the vilest of criminals. His entire act was based on the infectious force of the ignoble, on the contagion of evil. In the bursts of laughter that hit the walls of the little theatre Raphael recognized the laughter of the Devil himself – a triumphal roar that is the breeding ground of hatred, cowardice, and stupidity.

And it was this ignoble merchandise that he was supposed to accompany at the piano, and not only accompany, but underline, amplify, exacerbate. At the piano – the sacred instrument on which he played Johann Sebastian Bach's chorales! Throughout his childhood and adolescence he had known evil only in its negative form – discouragement, laziness, boredom, indifference. Now for the first time he was meeting it in a growling, grimacing, positive incarnation – that of the infamous Gabbler, whose active accomplice he was becoming.

Imagine his surprise, then, one evening when he was on his way to his daily hell, to see on the bill posted on the door of the café-theatre a sticker adding, underneath the name Gabbler:

Accompanied at the piano by Gammon

He rushed into the manager's office, where he was received with open arms. Yes, the manager had felt obliged to include his name on the bill. It was only fair. His performance at the piano escaped none of the spectators and enormously enriched poor Gabbler's number – which, it was true, was a little threadbare. And in any case, the two names were just made for each other: Gammon and Gabbler. No one could have dreamed up a more sonorous, a more apt combination, or anything more delightfully daffy. And naturally his fee would be increased. Substantially.

Raphael had gone to the office to protest. He came out thanking the manager, and inwardly cursing his own timidity and feebleness.

That evening, he described the scene to Bénédicte. Very far from sharing his indignation, she congratulated him on his success and was delighted at the improvement in their finances. After all, since the whole point of the operation was that it should be lucrative, wasn't it better for it to bring in as much money as possible? Raphael felt he was the victim of a general conspiracy.

Gabbler's attitude towards him, on the other hand, became very much cooler. Up till then he had treated him with patronizing condescension. Raphael was his accompanist, an unobtrusive, useful, but inglorious role, which called for no more than abnegation and tact. But he was now attracting some of the audience's attention, hence some of their applause, and it had got to the point where even the manager had noticed it.

'Don't overdo it, old man, don't overdo it,' he told Raphael, who could bear no more.

The situation would certainly have got worse if Durieu's return hadn't put an end to it. Relieved, Raphael went back to his lessons with the feeling of having fulfilled his duty, and with the memory of an experience that was all the more instructive in that it had been so harsh. Shortly afterwards, he married Bénédicte.

Marriage didn't change Raphael's life much, but it gave him a sense of his responsibilities that he had so far been able to ignore. He had to share his young wife's worries, for she had great trouble in making ends meet, especially in finding the money they needed every month to pay the instalments on the flat, the car, the television set, and the washing machine, bought on credit. Their evenings were now more frequently spent in adding up figures than in communing in the pure beauty of a Bach chorale.

Coming home a little late one day he found Bénédicte all excited by a visit she'd had a few minutes earlier. It was Raphael, of course, whom the manager of the café-theatre had come to see, but in his absence he had told Bénédicte the reason for his visit. No, this time it wasn't a question of accompanying the lamentable Gabbler, whose contract in any case would not be renewed for the coming season. But perhaps Raphael would agree to play a few solo piano pieces between two comic numbers? This would create a pleasant diversion in the middle of the show. The audience could only be delighted by such a parenthesis of calm and beauty inserted in a programme which, for the rest, would be full of gusto and gaiety.

Raphael refused point-blank. Never again would he descend into that den of pestilence in which he had suffered for a whole month. He had had the experience of evil in his own domain, that of music and public performance. That was a very good thing, but he had no more to learn from it.

Bénédicte waited for the storm to pass. Then, in the following days, she gently returned to the attack. What he was being offered had nothing in common with accompanying the pathetic Gabbler. He would be playing solos, and whatever he chose. In short, he was being given an opportunity to practise his profession as a soloist. Certainly this début was modest, but you had to start somewhere. Had he any choice?

She returned to it every day, patiently, tirelessly. At the same time she started thinking about moving to a different district. She dreamed of an old, and more spacious, mansion flat in a residential district. But this improvement in their life style would demand sacrifices.

He sacrificed himself, and signed an engagement for six months, which could be terminated by the payment of a substantial indemnity by whichever party took the initiative in breaking the contract.

From the very first evening he realized the terrible trap he had fallen into. The audience was still vibrant and tumultuous from the previous number, a grotesque tango performed by a female giant and a male dwarf. When Raphael appeared on stage, in the black suit that was both too tight and too short for him, with his stilted, hunted air, his seminarist's face rigid with fright behind his thick glasses, everything seemed precisely calculated to form a highly comic composition. He was greeted with howls of laughter. As ill luck would have it, his piano stool was too low. He swivelled the seat to raise it, but in his agitation he unscrewed it completely and found himself facing a hysterical audience with a stool in two halves, like a mushroom with its cap separated from its stalk. In any normal situation it would probably have taken him only a few seconds to put the seat back in place. But, assailed by the photographers' flashes, the coordination of his movements impaired by panic, he had the added misfortune to drop his glasses, without which he couldn't see a thing. When he started to look for them, groping around the floor on all fours, the audience's joy knew no bounds. Next, he had to struggle for several long minutes with the two halves of the stool before he was finally able to sit down at the piano with trembling hands, and with his memory put to rout. What did he play that evening? He wouldn't have been able to say. Every time he touched the instrument the howls of laughter, which had subsided, started up again with renewed vigour. When he reached the wings he was dripping with sweat and overcome by shame.

The manager clasped him in his arms.

'My dear Gammon,' he exclaimed, 'you were admirable, do you hear me, ad-mi-ra-ble. You are the great revelation of the season. Your gift for comic improvisation is incomparable. And what a presence! You only have to appear for people to start laughing. The moment you touch the piano they go berserk. And in any case, I'd invited the press. I knew how it would be.'

Behind him, modest and smiling, Bénédicte effaced herself under the avalanche of compliments. Raphael hung on to her image as a shipwrecked mariner clings to a rock. He looked her in the face with imploring insistence. She remained sleek, radiant and unshakable, did young Bénédicte Prieur, who had this evening become Madame Gammon, the wife of the celebrated comic musician. Maybe she was thinking of her splendid mansion flat, now within her reach.

The press was indeed triumphal. It spoke of a new Buster Keaton. It extolled Raphael's sorrowful countenance, which resembled that of a frantic anthropoid ape, his catastrophic clumsiness, his grotesque manner of playing the piano. And the same photo appeared everywhere, the one that caught him on all fours, groping around for his glasses between the two halves of his stool.

They moved. Next, an impresario undertook to represent Gammon's interests. They got him to make a film. Then a second film. With the third, the Gammons were able to move once again, and this time establish themselves in a big house in the avenue de Madrid, in Neuilly.

One day they received a visit. Henri Durieu had come to pay homage to the tremendous success of his former comrade. He moved diffidently among the gilded panelling, the crystal candelabra and the old masters. As a second violin in the Alençon municipal orchestra, he couldn't get over so much magnificence. And yet he had nothing to complain about. In any case, he was no longer to be seen playing the piano in nightclubs, and that was the main thing, wasn't it. He could no longer bear to prostitute his art in that fashion, he stoutly declared.

They spoke of the years they had spent at the Conservatoire together, of their hopes, their disappointments, and of the patience each had needed to find his own way. Durieu hadn't brought his violin with him. But Raphael sat down at the piano and played

Mozart, Beethoven, and Chopin.

'What a career you could have made as a soloist!' Durieu exclaimed. 'Though it's true that you were destined for other laurels. We all have to follow the dictates of our own vocation.'

More than once the critics had compared Gammon to Grock and declared that the legendary Swiss Auguste might well have finally found his successor.

Gammon did in fact make his circus debut in Urbino, one Christmas Eve. For a long time they tried to find someone to play the supporting role of the whiteface clown. After a few inconclusive trials, Bénédicte surprised everyone by suggesting herself. Why not? Dressed in a tight, embroidered waistcoat and breeches, her face made up with chalk, one eyebrow painted black over her forehead where it formed a lofty, interrogative and mocking arc, speaking in high and mighty tones, wearing silver slippers, she did wonders, did young Bénédicte Prieur, who henceforth became the partner and indispensable foil of the celebrated musician-clown, Gammon.

Wearing a pink cardboard cranium and a false nose shaped like a sweet potato, lost in a tail coat with a celluloid shirt front teetering around his neck, and trousers corkscrewing down over enormous clodhoppers, Gammon played the part of a failed artist, a naïvely pretentious ignoramus who had come to give a piano recital. But the most dreadful cacophony came from his clothes, from the swivel stool, and above all from the piano itself. The slightest touch on any key triggered off a booby trap or a catastrophe – a jet of water, a puff of smoke, a grotesque noise, a fart, a belch, a whistle. And the audience burst into peals of laughter, raised the roof from all the tiers, and crushed him under his own buffoonery.

Deafened by these joyous catcalls, Gammon sometimes used to think about poor Gabbler, who no doubt had never fallen so low. But what protected him was his myopia, for his make-up made it impossible for him to wear his glasses and he could therefore see practically nothing, merely big pools of coloured lights. Even though thousands of torturers were driving him silly with their bestial laughter, at least he had the advantage of not seeing them.

Was there still some work to be done to perfect the diabolical piano number? Did a kind of miracle take place that evening under the big top in Urbino? The plan was that in the finale, after struggling through a piece of music as best he could, the unfortunate Gammon should witness the explosion of his piano, which would vomit out into the ring a vast array of hams, custard pies, and strings of black and white sausages. But something quite different occurred.

The savage laughs died down at the sudden immobility of the clown. Then, when the most complete silence reigned, he began to play. With contemplative, meditative, fervent serenity he played *Jesu, Joy of Man's Desiring,* the Bach chorale that had soothed his student years. And the poor old circus piano, for all its gimmicks and gadgets, obeyed his hands marvellously, and sent the divine melody floating up to the obscure heights of the big top, with its temporarily invisible trapezes and rope ladders. After the inferno of guffaws it was the hilarity of the heavens, tender and spiritual, which soared over a crowd in communion.

Next, a long silence prolonged the last note, as if the chorale were continuing in the beyond. Then, in the shimmering clouds of his myopia, the musician-clown saw the piano lid rising. It didn't explode. It didn't spew out sausages. It opened slowly like a huge, dark flower, and released a beautiful archangel with wings of light, the Archangel Raphael, the one who had been watching over him all his life and preventing him from quite becoming Gammon.

The Red Dwarf

for Jean-Pierre Rudin

When Lucien Gagnero reached the age of twenty-five he had to give up, with a broken heart, all hope of ever becoming any taller than the four feet one he had already reached eight years before. All he could do now was resort to special shoes whose platform soles gave him the extra four inches that elevated him from dwarf status to that of small man. As the years went by, his vanishing adolescence and youth left him exposed as a stunted adult who inspired mockery and scorn in the worst moments, pity in the less bad ones, but never respect or fear, in spite of the enviable position he occupied in the office of an important Paris lawyer.

His speciality was divorce and, not being able to dream of marriage for himself, he applied himself with avenging ardour to the task of destroying the marriages of other people. This was why he one day received a visit from Mrs Edith Watson. A first marriage to an American had left this former opera singer extremely wealthy, and she had then married a lifeguard from Nice who was much younger than she. It was this second union that she now wished to dissolve and, through the numerous and confused grievances she had against her Bob, Lucien scented secrets and humiliations that more than interested him. He felt personally concerned in the wreck of this couple, even more so, perhaps, after he had had a chance to see Bob. The young man was a colossus, with a sweet, naïve face – like an athletic girl, Lucien thought – a beautiful, golden, pulpy fruit on the beach, designed to arouse all kinds of appetites.

Lucien prided himself on his literary talents and was most meticulous in refining the style of the insulting letters which, according to French law, couples have to exchange in order to achieve an amiable separation. This time he surpassed himself, and Bob was horrified by the vulgarity and violence of the letters which, over several months, he dictated to him and got him to sign. They even included unqualified death threats.

Some time later, Lucien went to visit his client, who lived in a luxurious duplex apartment on the borders of the Bois de Boulogne, to get her signature to some documents. A spiral staircase joined the upper apartment, where Bob was still living, to the lower one, which was enhanced by a vast terrace. That was where he found Edith Watson, practically naked on a chaise longue, surrounded by refreshments. The radiance of that big, golden body, with its violent odour of woman and suntan lotion, intoxicated Lucien – and it seemed to intoxicate Edith herself, for she didn't care a fig about her visitor, and answered his questions in an absent-minded, far-off voice. The heat was stifling, and Lucien was extremely uncomfortable in his dark, thick, notary's clerk's clothes, and all the more so since the ice-cold beer Edith had offered him on his arrival had immediately drenched him in sweat. The last straw was that it had also made him want to urinate, and he was twisting and turning like a woodlouse in the hollow of the big deckchair he had coiled up in. Finally, in an embarrassed voice, he asked where the lavatory was, and Edith answered with a vague gesture towards the interior, and mumbled a few words, the only one of which he caught was 'bathroom'.

The room seemed immense to Lucien. It was all black marble, with a bath-tub sunk into the floor. There were various silver-plated appliances, spotlights, bathroom scales, and above all a profusion of mirrors which sent his image back to him at most unusual angles. He pissed, and then began to luxuriate in this cool spot. The bath-tub, which looked like something between a pitfall, a tomb, and a snake pit, didn't attract him in the least, but he was fascinated by the shower, which was surrounded by frosted glass. A whole battery of jets converged in it, and it seemed that you could spray yourself with water not only from above but also from the front, from the back, from the sides, and also vertically from below. There was a complicated set of taps to regulate these jets.

Lucien undressed and began to switch on the various sprinklers; their direction, violence, and temperature surprised him, like aggressive practical jokes. Then he smeared himself in a light, perfumed lather which he sprayed on with an aerosol, and remained in the multiple shower for quite a while. He was enjoying himself. For the first time he saw his body as something other than a shameful, repulsive object. When he jumped out of the shower on to the rubber mat he discovered that he was immediately surrounded by a whole crowd of Luciens imitating his movements in a labyrinth of mirrors. Then they stood still and looked at one another. Their face had an indisputable air of rather majestic gravity – sovereign was the word that occurred to Lucien – with a wide, rectangular forehead, a steady, imperious gaze, a fleshy, sensual mouth, and it even displayed that slight touch of flabbiness in the lower part of the face which suggested incipient jowls of impressive nobility. After that, everything began to deteriorate, for the neck was disproportionately long, the torso as round as a ball, the legs short and bandy, like those of a gorilla, and the enormous penis cascaded in black and purple waves down to the knees.

But it was time to think of getting dressed. Lucien glanced in disgust at the dark, sweaty pile of his clothes, then he noticed a huge crimson bathrobe hanging from a chrome peg. He took it down, draped it around him until he was completely hidden within its folds, and then, with the aid of the mirrors, he devised a dignified, casual bearing. He wondered whether he would put his shoes on. This was a crucial question, for if he relinquished the four inches of his platform soles he would be confessing, and even proclaiming, to Edith Watson that he was a dwarf and not merely a small man. The discovery of an elegant pair of Turkish slippers under a stool decided him. When he made his entrance on to the terrace, the long train formed by the outsize bathrobe gave him an imperial air.

The big sunglasses concealing Edith's face made it impossible for him to see what she was thinking, and only her sudden immobility betrayed her stupefaction when the majestic little personage appeared and with a kind of weasel leap buried himself in the depths of a canopied deckchair. The notary's clerk had disappeared and given place to a comical, disquieting creature of overwhelming, bewitching ugliness – to a fabulous monster, whose comic aspect added a negative, acid, destructive component.

'That's Bob's bathrobe,' she murmured, just for something to say, in a tone that was half protest, half simple observation.

'I can easily do without it,' Lucien replied insolently.

Throwing off the bathrobe, he slid down on to the floor like a caterpillar emerging from a flower, and in the same movement climbed up on to Edith's chaise longue.

Lucien was a virgin. His awareness of his infirmity had stifled the cries of his nascent puberty. But he discovered love that day, and the rejection of his clerk's clothing and especially of his built-up shoes, and the acceptance of his dwarf status, were in his mind inseparable from this dazzling revelation. As for Edith – who was only getting divorced because of the inadequacy of her too-handsome husband – she was enchanted to discover that such a small, misshapen body should be so fantastically equipped, and so delightfully efficacious.

This was the beginning of a liaison whose passion was entirely physical and to which Lucien's infirmity added a slightly shameful, sophisticated piquancy, for her, and a pathetic tension mixed with anguish for him. They were both agreed to throw a veil of absolute secrecy over their relationship. Apart from the fact that Edith wouldn't have had the courage to display such a strange lover to the world, he had explained to her that it was of paramount importance to her divorce for her conduct to appear irreproachable until the case came to court.

From then on, Lucien led a double life. Outwardly he was still a small man, dressed in dark clothes and built-up shoes, whom his colleagues saw pen-pushing every day at his big desk; but at certain irregular, capricious hours – determined by coded telephone messages – he disappeared into the block by the Bois de Boulogne, let himself into the duplex apartment with his own key and there, metamorphosed into an imperial dwarf, wilful, swaggering, desirous and desired, he subjected the big blonde with the sophisticated accent, whose drug he was, to the law of pleasure. His embrace sent her into ecstasies, and her love song, which usually began with guttural trills, rapturous flourishes, and vocalises extending over three octaves, always culminated in a volley of affectionate, obscene abuse. She would call her lover my plaything, my lover boy, my arse-scratcher, my dildo . . . After the storm she would make a speech from which it emerged that he was nothing but a penis with organs around it, a walking penis, and, now calling him my pendant, my lubricity belt, she played a game of going about her business in the house while carrying him around, clinging to her flank, the way female monkeys carry their young.

He let her say and do what she liked, and, while being bounced up and down by his 'dwarf-carrier' as he called her in retaliation, he would amuse himself watching her breasts wobbling above his head like a pair of tethered balloons. Yet he was terrified of losing her, and it was with anguish that he wondered whether the pleasure he gave her was great enough to make up for the satisfactions of the social life that he could not offer her. His long experience of divorce cases had taught him that women are more social beings than men, and that they can only really blossom in an atmosphere that contains plenty of human relationships. Wouldn't she one day abandon him for some prestigious – or at least presentable – lover?

Suddenly there was a period of inexplicable silence. He had been trained not to go to the Bois de Boulogne unless Edith telephoned him. For a whole, long week, she gave no sign of life. He fretted in silence, then began to vent his feelings in violent outbursts of aggression against the office juniors. Never had the letters of rupture he dictated to his clients been so venomous. Finally he simply had to find out, and went to visit his mistress on his own initiative. He did find out, and without delay. Silently opening the door with his key, he stole into the vestibule. He heard voices. He had no difficulty in recognizing them as those of Edith and Bob, who seemed to be on the best of terms – the most affectionate of terms, even.

The blow was all the more severe in that it was totally unexpected. Had the couple become reconciled? Was there now some doubt about the divorce? This reversion made Lucien feel not only that he had been rejected by his mistress, but that he was being thrust back into his former life and deprived of the marvellous metamorphosis that had changed his destiny. He was overwhelmed with murderous hatred, and it took a violent effort to force himself to hide under a shelf when Edith and Bob came out of the bedroom, laughing, and made for the door. When the sound of the lift had died away, Lucien came out of his hiding place and almost automatically went over to the bathroom. He undressed, had a shower, and then, draped in Bob's big crimson bathrobe, sat down on a stool where, stock-still, he waited.

Three hours later the door banged and Edith came in alone, humming. She called out something up the inner stairway, which indicated Bob's presence on the upper floor. Suddenly, she went into the bathroom without switching on the light. Lucien had let the bathrobe slip down off his shoulders. In one bound he was on her, clutching her flank as usual, but his two hands, powerful as a bulldog's jaws, had closed round her throat. Edith staggered, then rallied, and, weighed down by her mortal burden, took a few tottering steps.

Finally she halted, swayed, and collapsed. While she was in her death throes Lucien possessed her for the last time.

None of this was premeditated, and yet from that moment his acts followed one another as if they were part of a long matured plan. He dressed, and rushed back to his office. Then he returned to the apartment with the insulting, threatening letters he had dictated to Bob and put them in Edith's chest of drawers. Finally he went home and immediately dialled Bob's number. The telephone rang for a long time. At last a grumpy, sleepy voice answered.

'Murderer! You've strangled your wife!' was all that Lucien said, in a disguised voice. Then he repeated this accusation three times, for Bob was showing the most obtuse lack of understanding.

Two days later the papers carried this news item and went on to say that the number one suspect – the victim's husband, whose letters found at the scene of the crime left no doubt about his intentions – had taken flight, but that his arrest was no doubt imminent.

Lucien disguised himself within the character of the ill-favoured clerk, a suffering, mocked little man, but the memory of the superman he had been through renouncing the extra four inches his special shoes added to his height, haunted him day and night. Because he had finally had the courage of his own monstrosity, he had seduced a woman. She had deceived him. He had killed her, and his rival, the husband, doubling as a ridiculously tall man, was everywhere being hunted by the police! His life was a masterpiece, and there were moments when he was overwhelmed with breathtaking joy at the thought that he only had to take his shoes off to become immediately what he really was, a man apart, superior to the gigantic riffraff, an irresistible seducer and infallible killer! All the misery of the past years was due to his having refused the fearsome choice that was his destiny. In cowardly fashion he had shrunk from crossing the Rubicon into dwarfism, as he might have hesitated at the threshold of a temple. But he had finally dared to take the step. The slight quantitative difference that he had accepted in deciding to reject his platform shoes in Edith's bathroom had brought about a radical qualitative metamorphosis. The horrible quality of dwarfism had infiltrated him and turned him into a fabulous monster. In the greyness of the lawyer's office where he spent his days he was haunted by dreams of despotism. By chance, he had read a document about Ravensbrück and Birkenau, the Nazi concentration camps reserved for women. He saw himself as the Kommandant, the governor, controlling with his huge whip vast troops of naked, wounded women – and on several occasions the typists were surprised to hear him let out a roar.

But the secret of his new dignity lay heavy on him. He would have liked to adopt it in the face of the whole world. He dreamed of a conspicuous, public, devastating proclamation in front of an ecstatic crowd. He went to his tailor and ordered a dark red leotard that emphasized the curves of his muscles and genitals. Back in his office he shed the livery of the little clerk, had a shower, and put on what he privately called his evening clothes, to which he added a mauve silk scarf tied tightly around his long neck, like the old style apaches. Then, wearing moccasins with thin, pliant soles, he slipped out. He had discovered the superior comfort his height afforded him. He could pass under the lowest doorways with his head held high. He could stand upright in the smallest cars. Every seat was a spacious nest for him. The glasses and plates in bistros and restaurants offered him ogres' portions. He was surrounded by abundance in all circumstances. Soon he became aware of the colossal strength accumulated in his muscles. He quickly became known in various nightclubs, where the habitués would invite him to drink with them. He would jump up and perch on a high stool at the counter, and he could stand on his hands with his short legs crossed in the air, like arms. One night, a customer who had had too much to drink insulted him. Lucien threw him to the floor and twisted his ankle, then started jumping up and down on his face with a rage that terrified the onlookers. The same day a prostitute offered herself to him for nothing, out of curiosity, because the sight of his strength had excited her. From then on men were afraid of the red dwarf, and women submitted to the obscure fascination that emanated from him. His vision of society began to change. He was the unshakeable centre of a crowd of feeble, cowardly, stilt-walkers who were unsteady on their limbs and had nothing to offer their women but the genitals of a marmoset.

But this limited renown was to be merely a prelude. One evening, in a bar in Pigalle, after he had just won a bet by tearing in half a pack of fifty-two cards, he was accosted by a man with a swarthy face and black, curly hair, whose hands were adorned with diamonds. He introduced himself: Signor Silvio d'Urbino, the owner of the Urbino Circus, whose big top was at the Porte Dorée for a week. Would the red dwarf agree to join his troupe? Lucien grabbed a glass carafe, intending to smash it into smithereens on the head of the insolent fellow. Then he had second thoughts. His imagination had just shown him a vast crater in which the spectators' heads were squeezed together like granules of caviar, rising up in terraces around a harshly lit ring. From this crater a mighty, continuous, and interminable ovation burst over the head of a minuscule individual dressed in red, standing alone in the centre of the ring. He accepted.

For the first months Lucien was content to liven up the interludes between the acts. He would run along the circular platform round the ring, get entangled in the apparatus, run away with shrill cries when threatened by one of the exasperated men in the ring. Finally he would allow himself to be caught in the folds of the acrobats' big mats and the men would carry him off unceremoniously, a large hump in the middle of the rolled-up sheet.

The laughter he aroused in the audience elated him rather than hurt him. It was no longer the concrete, savage, individual laughter that had terrorized him before his metamorphosis. It was a stylized, aesthetic, ceremonial, collective laughter, a veritable declaration of love, expressing the deference of the female crowd to the artiste who subjugates her. And in any case, this laughter turned into applause whenever Lucien reappeared in the ring, as the alchemist's lead turns into gold in the depths of his crucible.

But Lucien wearied of this petty buffoonery, which was nothing but exercises and experiments. One day his comrades saw him wriggling into something that looked like a pair of pink plastic dungarees shaped like a giant hand. Five fingers, ending in nails, corresponded to his head, his two arms and his two legs. His torso was its palm, and sticking out behind was the stump of a truncated wrist. This enormous, terrifying organ revolved by supporting itself successively on each of its fingers, it sat on its wrist, it contracted when facing the spotlights, ran with nightmare speed, and even climbed up ladders and rotated around a pole or a trapeze, hanging on by one finger. The children roared with laughter and the women had a catch in their throats at the approach of this enormous pink-fleshed spider. The press of the entire world spoke of the 'giant hand act'.

But Lucien was still not completely satisfied by this fame. He felt there was something lacking, something was incomplete. He was waiting – not impatiently, but confidently – for something, perhaps, though more probably for someone.

The Urbino Circus had already been on tour for five months when it pitched its tents in Nice. It was to stay there for a week, and then cross the frontier back to its native Italy. The evening performance of the third day had been brilliant, and the giant hand act had been a sensation. Lucien had removed his make-up and was relaxing in the luxurious caravan he had been promoted to since his great success, when he heard a soft knock at a window. He put the light out and went over to the looped curtains framing a pallid rectangle. A tall, massive silhouette was outlined against the phosphorescent sky. Lucien half-opened the window.

'Who is it?'

'I'd like to speak to M. Gagnero.'

'But who *is* it?'

'It's me, Bob.'

Lucien was so overcome by emotion that he had to sit down. He knew now what he'd been waiting for, whom he had come to look for in Nice. He had been keeping a kind of rendezvous, a rendezvous with Edith Watson. He let Bob in, and the life-guard's awkward mass immediately filled all the space of the narrow abode in which Lucien was perfectly at his ease. Once again he despised stilt-walkers, who are nowhere in their right place.

Bob explained his situation in a whisper. Ever since Edith's death he had led a hunted existence in sunbaked attics or dank cellars, fed like an animal by his mother and a friend. He was obsessed with the temptation to give himself up to the police, but just the very idea of being held in custody terrified him, and, worse still, there were those accursed letters of rupture, full of threats to kill her, which made his case look even blacker. But Lucien could testify that it was he who had dictated these letters to Bob for the purposes of his divorce, and that the threats they contained were fictitious – purely conventional.

Lucien savoured his omnipotence over this giant with the girlish face. Curled up in the hollow of a nest of cushions, his only regret was that he didn't smoke – a pipe, in particular – for then, before replying, he would have taken infinite time in cleaning it, filling it, and finally lighting it, according to all the rules of the art. For want of a pipe, he closed his eyes and allowed himself a good minute of voluptuous, smiling, Buddhist reflection.

'The police are looking for you,' he finally said. 'It is really my duty to denounce you. I'll give some thought to what I can do for you. But I need proof that you have total, blind confidence in me. Well, it's very simple. Go back to your hiding place. Come back tomorrow at the same time. There won't be any trap. That will prove that you have confidence in me. Then we shall be united in a pact. You're quite free not to come back.'

The next day, Bob was there.

'I can't promise that I will give evidence about the letters,' Lucien told him. 'But I have something better to offer you. The day after tomorrow we'll be crossing the frontier into Italy. I'll take you with me.'

Bob fell on his knees in the caravan and kissed his hands.

It was child's play for Lucien to smuggle him over the frontier by hiding him in his bed. He insisted that he should stay hidden during the circus's stops at San Remo, Imperia, and Savone. He waited until Genoa to introduce him to Signor d'Urbino as a friend met by chance in the crowd, with whom he intended to stage a new act. They started work right away.

The enormous difference in their height in itself suggested several classic mime numbers. One was the battle of David and Goliath, to which Lucien added a finale of his own invention. After the giant had fallen to the ground, his conqueror blew him up with a bicycle pump. From then on he was an obese, docile, flabby pachyderm, rolling from one side of the arena to the other at the mercy of the dwarf who handled and manhandled him. He put him to various personal uses: as a pneumatic mattress to take a nap on, as a trampoline to leap up into the apparatus, as a punching bag. And the colossus was always ridiculed and trounced by his minuscule adversary. Finally Lucien perched himself astride his neck and put on an enormous overcoat that covered Bob right down to his ankles. And they perambulated in this fashion, having become a single man eight feet two tall, Bob blinded and obliterated by the coat, Lucien perched on high, imperious and wrathful.

It was when they reverted to the great tradition of the whiteface clown and the Auguste that their entrance took on its definitive form and crowned Lucien's triumph. The whiteface clown, made up, titivated, wearing pumps, his calves bulging in silk stockings, had formerly had the ring to himself and dazzled the audience with his wit and elegance. But he had been foolish enough to want to find a foil, to set off his beauty and éclat; and the hilarious, vulgar Auguste, with his tippler's face – invented for this purpose – had gradually supplanted him. Lucien extended this development by turning his over-refined partner into his thing, his whipping boy. And yet nothing was too splendid for Bob. The dwarf dressed him in a platinum wig, he added cascades of ribbons, embroidery, lace, swansdown, to his costume. Finally, carried away by the logic of his number, he imagined the grotesque marriage, to the strains of Mendelssohn's Wedding March, of this enormous girl decked out in snowy white, to the minute red toad who kept jumping up at her dress, croaking. At the end of the number he leaped up like a dog, circled his partner's waist with his short legs, and in this fashion she carried him off into the wings, to thunderous applause.

This final leap disturbed Lucien deeply, because it reminded him painfully and voluptuously of the stranglehold that had killed Edith Watson. Were not Bob and he united by their love for the former singer? Lucien used to speak of her to Bob in the evenings, and then, obsessed by her memory, he finally confused her with his companion. And as it was even more important to him to subjugate and humiliate the stilt-walkers than to take their wives away from them, it happened one night, then every night, that he climbed into the side-berth in which his former rival slept, and possessed him like a female.

Later, the imperial theme, first sketched out in Bob's crimson bathrobe, once again took possession of him. Nothing was more in keeping with the clown tradition than to develop the Auguste – the name itself suggested it – into a parody of a Roman emperor. Lucien draped himself in a red tunic that left his crooked, muscular thighs naked. He wore a necklet, and a crown of roses. He was no longer the Auguste, he was Nero, gag-Nero, as he was one day called by d'Urbino, who was always on the look-out for slogans and texts for his playbills. As for Bob, he quite naturally became Agrippina. The fact that Nero had had his mother murdered, after having taken her as his first mistress, seemed a good omen to Lucien (Lucius Nero) who, not having found his place among decent, everyday models, was always willing to find inspiration in the grandiose turpitudes of Antiquity. It pleased him that his life should have taken the form of a caricature of stilt-walkers' morals, highly coloured, and spattered with blood and sperm.

'The one thing that bothers me,' he said one night as he left Bob to go back to his own little bed, 'is that, whatever we do, we shall never have a child.'

This thought was certainly charged with its weight of brutal cynicism, but it was nonetheless secretly inspired by a recent discovery that was to mark a new turning point in his destiny. He had noticed that while the adulation of the ordinary public had no noticeable influence on the ball of hatred that weighed hard and heavy in his breast, a warm, springlike breath did sometimes seem to reach him from the audience, and particularly from the very top of the tiers, from the last benches hidden in the shadows of the big top. From then on he waited passionately for this breath which touched, moved and blessed him, and tried to discover in which of the performances it manifested itself. Now it was always during the matinees, and on Thursdays rather than on Sundays, Thursday being at that time the day when children didn't go to school.

'I'd like it,' he said to d'Urbino one evening, 'if once a week at least the circus refused to admit anyone over the age of twelve.'

The director showed extreme surprise at this demand, but he respected the whims of the stars whose inventive genius had led to profitable and spectacular innovations.

'We could start on December the twenty-fourth, Christmas Eve,' the dwarf added.

The date was so close and the danger of losing money so clear, that d'Urbino began to worry.

'But why, my dear Maestro, what an idea! Under the age of twelve, what does that mean?'

Once again Lucien felt himself in the grip of his old, malevolent wrath, and he advanced menacingly on the director.

'It means that for once I shall have an audience of my own size! Can't you understand? I don't want any stilt-walkers – not a single one!'

'But, but, but,' d'Urbino stammered, 'if we refuse to admit adults and adolescents it'll cost us an enormous amount of money!'

Lucien's reply rooted him to the spot – Lucien who was always so prodigiously grasping.

'I'll pay!' he announced dogmatically. 'We'll get the cashier to work out how much you'll lose and you can deduct it from my pay. And in any case, for the matinee on December the twenty-fourth it's very simple – I'll buy all the seats. Entrance will be free . . . for children.'

This Christmas performance was to remain memorable in the history of the Circus. Children flocked in from several leagues around, whole coachloads of them in some cases, because schools, reformatories, and orphanages had been notified. Some mothers who were refused entry had the idea of tying their children together so that they shouldn't get lost, and roped parties of five, six, and even seven brothers and sisters were to be seen climbing up on to the tiers.

What act the red dwarf performed that day no one will ever know, because it was witnessed by no one but children, and he swore them to secrecy. At the end of the show they gave him a tremendous ovation and he, standing squarely in the sawdust on his immovable legs, his eyes closed with bliss – he allowed himself to be submerged in this storm of tenderness, this tempest of sweetness, which cleansed him of his bitterness, justified him, illuminated him. Then, children in their thousands surged into the ring, surrounded him in a tumultuous, caressing flood-tide, and carried him off in triumph and in song.

Behind the red and gold curtains leading to the stables, the riders, the tamer, the Chinese conjurers, the flying trapeze artiste, the Nepalese jugglers, and behind them the tall, grotesque silhouette of Agrippina, all retreated, effaced themselves, amazed by this savage hymn.

'Let him be,' said d'Urbino. 'He's with his own kind, he's being fêted by his own people. For the first time in his life, maybe, he is no longer alone. As for me, I have my slogan: Lucius Gag-Nero, Emperor of Children! I can already see my playbill: the Red Dwarf in a toga with his sword and crown, and with the crowd, the immense crowd of little people, not one of whom is a fraction of an inch taller than him! But what a matinée, my friends, what a matinée!'

Tristan Vox

This story takes place only a very few years ago, though the period will nevertheless seem prehistoric to the young people of today. In those days, it is true, television did not yet exist. It was the radio that held sway over people's minds and inflamed their imaginations. It must not be thought, however, that its power was less than that of our television: quite the contrary. The very fact that radio voices had neither face nor gaze lent them even more mystery, and their magic exercised a sometimes fearsome power over listeners, whether men or women. It is to be observed that in many religions, God's decrees are made manifest through a voice descending from on high out of an empty sky. Announcers, therefore, appeared to the general public to be incorporeal creatures endowed with ubiquity – at the same time omnipotent and inaccessible. Some, who spoke over the air at the same time every day – with almost astronomical regularity – enjoyed extraordinary notoriety and held the passionate attention of enormous numbers of people. They measured this popularity by the fabulous mail they received, a mail which contained everything, absolutely everything: protests, complaints, threats, secrets, promises, offers, entreaties. Even the most narrow-minded, even the most obstinately materialistic of them, couldn't close their eyes to what they represented to their correspondents and, occasionally looking at themselves in the mirror, they would utter in a trembling voice the terrible, three-letter word that, in spite of themselves, they were forced to embody.

The most famous of them all was incontestably the pathetic Tristan Vox whose voice, emanating from a humble little studio hidden somewhere in the bowels of an enormous block in the Champs-Élysées, both soothed and exalted millions of lonely hearts, every evening from ten o'clock to midnight. How could the magic of this voice be explained? Certainly, it contained a velvety, caressing gravity heightened by a catch, a brittleness, something wounded, and which with a kind of implacable sweetness also wounded those – and especially those women – who heard it. This *Tristanian raucousness* was something quite different from the *Aznavourian raucousness* which came later, like its muffled echo, but which nevertheless turned a minor Armenian singer, a puny, hypersensitive faun, into one of the idols of the music hall.

But the physical quality of Tristan Vox's voice would not itself have sufficed to justify the extraordinary ascendancy it enjoyed. Once again – the immense advantage radio had over television was that it appealed to the eye of the soul, and not to that of the body. Television man has only the face he has. Radio man had the face attributed to him by his listeners, of whichever sex, merely on the strength of his intonation.

The strange thing was that in all the innumerable letters, to say nothing of the drawings, that Tristan Vox received, a certain consensus appeared. The image that most people had of him, judging by his voice, was that of a man in his second youth who was tall, slim, and lithe, with masses of dark, unruly hair, whose romantic waves attenuated what might otherwise have made his nobly tormented, mask-like face, with its rather high cheekbones, seem excessively sombre, in spite of the sweetness of his great, melancholy eyes.

Tristan Vox was in reality called Felix Tapp. He was getting on for sixty. He was short, bald, and pot-bellied. His fascinating voice was due to a combination of chronic laryngitis and the strange, vibratile double chin that adorned the lower part of his face. After a mediocre career as a comic actor, which had taken him on tour to all the subprefectures of France, he had been relieved to find a stable, sedentary occupation as a radio announcer.

His first job had been to read the weather forecasts and news summaries, and announce the following day's programmes. His celebrity had actually begun the day when he had lent his voice to the Speaking Clock, which anyone could hear by dialling Observatoire 8400. People had then begun to wonder about him, and an influential daily paper raised the question, as if it were a sort of detective story puzzle: Who is concealed behind the Speaking Clock? Tapp, who had chosen this profession in order to have a peaceful retirement, then surrounded himself in mystery. And thus he had brought public curiosity to its peak.

One day, the director of the radio station had come to talk to him.

'Frankly,' he said, 'you're worth your weight in gold. The audience that your slots attract is immense. You can ask me for anything you like, in material terms.'

Tapp, who repressed a grimace at the word *slot* – one of those jargon terms that he detested – was too mistrustful of his destiny to greet this preamble with unreserved joy. For him, every piece of good luck had a catch in it. He nevertheless thanked his director and promised to think over what he had said. The truth was that his needs were modest, and that he was a little embarrassed by his director's advances. Success had come to him too late. His acting career was over. Twenty years, thirty years earlier, maybe? And that wasn't even so sure. He had in fact exercised this profession as he would have exercised any other, like a nice quiet fellow who has never been troubled by ambition.

'However,' the director went on, 'for my part, I have two requests to make. We aren't here to bow and scrape to one another, are we, and I won't beat about the bush. Your listeners don't imagine you the way you are. They embroider on your voice, they idealize you, they make a great song and dance about you. It's in no one's interest to disabuse them. In the first place, then, you'd have to find a pseudonym. And in the second place, you'd have to remain absolutely invisible. No photos, no public appearances, no gala performances, cocktail parties, or anything else. Do you agree?'

These demands couldn't have suited Tapp better. Nothing was less to his taste than a dubious notoriety that would disturb his peace and comfort. His voice – which during his forty years in the theatre had never moved anyone – aroused the multitude the moment it was transmitted through a microphone. This was one of the fatuities of destiny whose effects should be limited as far as possible. Let this golden voice, then, create all possible and imaginable myths. He, Felix Tapp, would remain aloof from such follies.

Thus was born Tristan Vox, a superb assemblage of courtly romance and popular modernism. It was agreed that all communications between Vox and Tapp would be broken off. No outsider would be admitted to the studio during Tapp's slots. No photographs of him would be divulged. His relations with the outside world – mail, telephone, rendezvous – would be filtered with the greatest care. Tapp imagined that by thus cutting all the threads that linked him to Vox, the latter's inexistence would suffice to render him inoffensive. In reality he was allowing him a formidable liberty: that, for instance, of first insinuating himself into millions of lives, and then invading and creating havoc in that of his own author.

For the metamorphosis that each evening caused Tristan Vox to emerge from Felix Tapp by the simple means of a microphone, was no less mysterious than that of a pumpkin changed into a carriage by the wave of a magic wand. Tapp made no dramatic effort to resemble the saturnine hero imagined by his audience. And because it was in keeping with his character, he avoided every effect, every somewhat lively movement, every passionate accent. In between records he spoke to his listeners in confidential tones, in affectionate, slightly sad, but reassuring tones, which gave the impression of an amused and disillusioned indulgence nourished by immense experience. What did he talk about? About everything and nothing. About the seasons, his house, his garden – although he lived in a flat in the rue Lincoln – about animals, all animals, indiscriminately and inexhaustibly, he who had never possessed so much as a goldfish. On the other hand he avoided any reference to children, for he knew instinctively that his public consisted for the most part of solitary people – old bachelors and barren old maids – and that the thought of children would have cast a chill into the thousand tête-à-têtes he held simultaneously.

It could have been suggested to him that he was lying, that he was deceiving his public, that night after night he was repeatedly abusing their confidence. He would have protested in all good faith that he was merely pursuing behind the microphone the acting career that he had all his life carried on on the boards, which consisted in getting the audience to believe in a character that is not oneself. If anyone had retorted that it wasn't the same thing, he would no doubt have agreed, though without being able to say precisely what the difference was. But he did in fact play the part of Tristan Vox differently from the way an actor plays Rodrigue or Hamlet. He embodied it by affirming unequivocally that he really was the character, and at the same time he created it, at every instant, instead of taking it from the stock repertoire. Did he realize the risk he was running? For an illusion so vividly sustained must inevitably end by escaping the confines of the imaginary and encroaching on the real, thereby provoking an unpredictable tumult.

Two women formed a rampart between any incursion of the devastating Tristan Vox into the peaceable life of Felix Tapp. In the first place and in the front line was his secretary, the thin, horsey, Mademoiselle Flavia. She was the breakwater who protected him from the force of the waves of the morning mail, she was the target for the heavy artillery of presents and packets, and for the untimely assault of visitors, both male and female. She answered the letters – having first submitted to Tapp those that seemed to be of interest – she dispatched the presents to an old people's home, and, with inflexible courtesy, discouraged the people who tried to camp outside his door. Because she intrepidly faced the avid, idolatrous crowd that acclaimed and laid claim to Tristan Vox, Felix Tapp saw only what you might call her back view, and hardly knew her. She herself was permanently obsessed by the prestigious Tristan, and found it difficult to perceive the grey, peaceable Felix, who in her eyes was merely the shadow and as it were the understudy of the Other.

Moreover, the only thing Tapp wanted to do when he left the studio shortly after midnight was hurry home to the conjugal retreat where he was awaited by his wife, the gentle, buxom Amelia – née Lamiche – with her own kind of midnight snack, that is, in the Auvergne style. For Amelia was an excellent cordon-bleu cook, and they were both natives of Billom, a small town in the Puy-de-Dôme department, to which they intended to retire in a few years' time. It was even rather a pity that there was no one to witness this daily supper in which the Tapps communed in gastronomic beatitude, for their voracious yet tender air, when the lengthily concocted dish released its intoxicating exhalations under their noses, represented the very image of conjugal bliss and fidelity. On the other hand, however, it would have been difficult to imagine a picture more opposed to the melancholy, disembodied character of Tristan Vox.

It was nevertheless on this most intimate of all points – their Billom origins – that Vox was to base his first attack on Tapp.

It all began with a series of impassioned letters that a certain Isolde – obviously a pseudonym designed to go with Tristan – sent at regular intervals and which contained some rather disturbing details about the life of the Tapps. Naturally, Mademoiselle Flavia was the first to be alerted.

'It's odd,' she one day said to Tapp, when she brought him the answers she had written for him to sign. 'What exactly are the Big and Little Turlurons? I've never heard you use those words on the radio.'

Nothing, on the other hand, is more familiar to the inhabitants of Billom, since these are the names of the two big hills to the west of the town which are the destination of a favourite Sunday walk. Which Tapp explained to his secretary.

'And yet,' she persisted, 'I don't remember you ever having referred to Billom.'

She had the memory of an elephant, and Tapp could rely on her implicitly. He read the letter. In the midst of some extremely outspoken chitchat, the Big and Little Turlurons appeared to have a significance of transparent obscenity. The letter was signed: Isolde.

'Even so, it's possible that I did mention Billom, where I was born, and the two Turlurons, which everyone in the district knows,' he hazarded, without really believing it, seeing Mademoiselle Flavia shake her head energetically.

'I would never have missed that,' she asserted. 'And in any case, there's still no way we can reply to this Isolde, for the letter doesn't give an address.'

There was a short respite, and then Isolde reappeared with a salvo of epistles which this time went far beyond the bounds of decency. Perplexed, Tapp read and reread the following phrase: *Ah, my darling, if you could see me when I'm listening to you, you might well be interested!*

'What do you think she means?'

Mademoiselle Flavia adopted an outraged expression.

'How do you expect me to know?'

'A woman wrote that, and you are a woman,' Tapp said reasonably.

'You ought to know that there are different sorts of women!' the old maid said indignantly.

Tapp shrugged his shoulders and went and shut himself in his studio, after a brief telephone call to his wife. He shut the heavy door, bolted it by lowering a long-handled lever, and sat down in front of the microphone. In the old days the mikes were like big rectangular cans, riddled with little holes. There was something familiar and good-natured about those big flytraps. The new mikes looked like vipers' heads aiming at the face and mouth of the speaker. Tapp suddenly realized that it was this hostile, malicious electronic snake that was responsible for his transformation into Tristan Vox. He was particularly sensitive to the strange solitude that enveloped him every day at the same hour. The little, overheated, sound-proofed room, as impregnable as a safe, had no other opening on to the outside world than the double-glazed rectangle through which he could vaguely see the lazy silhouette of the sound recordist, bending over his consoles. They had been working together for so long that they no longer needed to use the intercom through which they could have exchanged a few words. The technician contented himself with giving Tapp the green light when he was going to put him on the air. Then the red light went on, Tapp was completely shut off from his colleagues and his private life, and his solitude opened out on to the immense, silent crowd of his listeners. From then on Felix Tapp was buried in a kind of tomb. Tristan Vox echoed like an omnipresent god in the ears of the masses. He insinuated himself into their hearts, and unfurled like a dazzling Phoenix in their imaginations.

Being a little sad and anxiety-ridden that evening, Felix Tapp reacted as usual by an increased tenderness toward the delights of gastronomy. His phone call to his wife before the programme began was simply to ask her for news of the *tripoux des Chaude-Aigues* – the tripe cooked with sheep's trotters that was now simmering on the stove and which was to be the main dish of their supper. It was totally out of the question that Tristan Vox would make even the most glancing allusion over the air to one of the most vulgar dishes in the whole of the Auvergnat cuisine, which itself had never had the reputation of being light and refined. But it can be said that the *tripoux* never stopped haunting Tapp throughout his programme.

Two days later Mademoiselle Flavia brought him another letter from Isolde and drew his attention to a phrase which she herself found totally sibylline: *My Tristan couldn't stop salivating yesterday at his microphone, he was frantically awaiting the moment when he could trot off home and stuff his stomach*!

Poor Mademoiselle Flavia! How could she possibly have suspected that that evening her boss was going to eat *tripoux*, which are neither more nor less than stuffed sheep's trotters enveloped in the stomach tissue of the same animal? The allusion was only too obvious, at least to Tapp. But was it not an illusion, due to the memory of that evening's delicious supper? Yet, if there was indeed an allusion, how could it be explained that Isolde happened to know about the Auvergnat dish that was awaiting Tapp after midnight? There was only one possible explanation: that he had involuntarily allowed something to filter through on to the air. And yet he had not the slightest recollection of having made any such blunder, and if he had now got to the point of saying into the microphone things that should be concealed, and furthermore of having no recollection of having done so, was this not good reason to be extremely worried?

Profoundly disturbed, the honest Tapp wondered whether he was still capable of continuing in this profession which after all was full of risks and heavy with responsibilities.

Isolde kept quiet for ten days. But this was apparently only in order to prepare a love letter in which perfidy and mystery formed an explosive mixture. It was in fact less a letter than a vast, coloured drawing representing an enormous cake bristling with candles. Multicoloured letters were wreathed around the cake. Rotating the sheet, one could read:

HAPPY BIRTHDAY TO TRISTAN!
And a big picoussel *with sixty candles . . .*

'What on earth is a *picoussel*?' asked Mademoiselle Flavia, as stern as a judge.

'Don't you know what a *picoussel* is?' Tapp asked her in amazement. 'It's true, though, it's only eaten in the Auvergne, and more particularly, you know, in Mur, Mur-de-Barrez, a village in the Cantal.'

And his face lit up with satisfaction.

'It's a sort of tart, yes, a tart made with buckwheat flour and filled with plums. And seasoned with *fines herbes*. For preference, you drink either a Chanturge or a Châteaugay with it.'

This idyllic evocation did nothing to cheer up Mademoiselle Flavia, who remained obsessed by a triple enigma. How did the so-called Isolde know Tapp's date of birth, his age, his Auvergnat origins? She put this question to him bluntly.

'It's someone who knows you, Monsieur Tapp. And therefore, a woman you know!'

She turned her back on him and marched out, leaving this accusatory innuendo hanging in the air. It was obvious. In the eyes of his faithful secretary, Tapp had a concubine, and he so far forgot himself as to indulge in pillow talk!

Brutally wrested from his dreams of *picoussel*, Tapp was appalled by the injustice and malignity of fate. He found he had lost his appetite as he started tucking into the *truffado d'Aurillac* that Amelia had prepared for him that evening.

'Saturday is your birthday,' she said, between two mouthfuls. 'I'm going to make you a. . .'

'A nothing!' Tapp cut her short. 'Request no flowers for my sixtieth birthday, do you hear me? Everything's fine the way it is!'

And he went off to bed, to the consternation of Amelia who was left gazing at his barely touched plate of *truffado*.

On the Saturday, a big packet in the shape of a hatbox was waiting for Tristan in the studio. The gaudy wrapping paper with drawings and letters was reminiscent of Isolde's last message. It was obvious that it contained the birthday *picoussel*.

Tapp sent it off to the old people's home without opening it.

No doubt this straight-to-the-stomach had excited Isolde. The very next day she went wild, but this time aiming very definitely below the belt. It was as if she was in the grip of a kind of frenzy of lust. And if the letter had merely contained promises, caresses, caterwaulings formulated in terms of abominable precision! But it was above all the coloured drawings accompanying the text that were of a nature to make even a Breton confessor blush.

Tapp handled this equivocal correspondence with very conspicuous repugnance.

'But after all, Mademoiselle Flavia,' he finally said one day to his secretary, 'you don't show me all the letters that arrive addressed to Tristan Vox, do you? Then why do you choose this filth?'

Mademoiselle Flavia showed signs of deep distress.

'But, because . . . that's to say . . . well, it seemed to me that this correspondent might well be of some interest to you,' she stammered.

'That is indeed possible,' Tapp admitted. 'Yes, you never know what ideas this fanatic might get into her head. We'd better keep an eye on her.'

The double life of Tapp-Vox pursued its course as best it could under a hail of letters alternating between gastronomical allusions and erotic outbursts. Oddly enough, the two themes were never combined, but seemed to constitute two distinct epistolary sources. The situation might well have lingered on, though, had not a new event come to shatter it, a fateful blow of barely imaginable violence and perfidy.

Every Wednesday a well-known radio magazine was published, *Radio-Weekly*, which, apart from the programme for the forthcoming week, contained a whole photographic supplement concerning the stars of the microphone. The editor wondered why the ordinary edition of his magazine sold out in a few hours that week. He had some more copies printed and made a few inquiries.

The key to the mystery was found in a corner of one of the pages of the supplement. In the margin by the side of the programme there was a photo of a youngish man, with rather high cheekbones, great big velvety, melancholy eyes, and an abundant, unruly, dark brown mane. And by some unbelievable blunder, the name of Tristan Vox had been printed under this photo, whereas it was in fact a picture of a certain Frédéric Durâteau, a finalist in the Borotra Cup at the Nanterre tennis club.

Tapp never so much as opened a newspaper, and it was the director of the radio station who told him about this incident. Tapp was already much affected by the daily assaults of the mysterious Isolde, and this new calamity demoralized him even further. His director, however, did his best to reassure him. The publication of a photo which didn't bear the slightest resemblance to his own could only further mislead the public and reinforce his incognito. Without any effort on his part, from now on he had a face to produce to his admirers, and this face was nothing but a mask behind which he would remain totally invisible.

His arguments were reasonable and persuasive. Tapp listened to them with the best will in the world. But in his heart of hearts he was still convinced that the horizon was heavy with menace. Worse, he had an inner conviction that his whole life was collapsing like a house of cards. From then on he began to steel himself against the next catastrophe.

It occurred on the following Monday. For the popular press had had plenty of time over the Saturday and Sunday to take up *Radio-Weekly*'s story and to reproduce, greatly enlarged, a touched-up version of the alleged photo of Tristan Vox. That Monday, then, when Tapp arrived at the studio a few minutes before the start of his programme, he saw Mademoiselle Flavia coming towards him in a state of agitation he would never have thought her capable of.

'Monsieur, Monsieur!' she cried. 'He's here!'

'Who is here?' asked Tapp.

He asked this question because it was the obvious thing to ask, but he knew only too well, alas, who it was.

'But Tristan Vox!' exclaimed Mademoiselle Flavia.

Tapp collapsed on to a chair; his knees had given way with emotion. So the moment he had been expecting with such terror for so many months had finally arrived. That of his confrontation with an imaginary character, taken from himself – and in particular, from his voice – invoked for two hours a day before an immense crowd, fertilized and charged with reality by the dreams of that crowd, summoned up by him, Tapp, and by that crowd, and hence inevitably destined to become embodied, one day or another.

He allowed a few minutes to pass under Mademoiselle Flavia's feverish, interrogatory eye.

'Where is he?' he finally managed to bring out.

'He's waiting . . . in the office.'

Tapp noticed fleetingly that she had said, not 'your office', but 'the office'. No doubt she would soon be saying 'his office'.

'Right,' he said with determination. 'I'll go and see.'

He avoided, it is true, saying more specifically 'go and see *him*', for all he wanted to do was to take a look through a crack in the door, not to get involved in a conversation which would have taken more time than he had left before the start of his programme, and which might have been too much for him.

He crept out on tiptoe, and came back in the same way two minutes later.

'It's he all right. It's the man in the photo.'

'It's Tristan Vox!' Mademoiselle Flavia specified, unkindly.

'It's the man in the photo,' Felix Tapp obstinately repeated.

He was more than half wrong, and he knew it. For the man he had seen, patiently sitting in the office, presented all the physical traits – and probably all the moral ones, too – that his enormous fan mail attributed to Tristan Vox, and if an artist had been asked to draw a photofit picture of the celebrated announcer with the aid of those letters, he would have produced the precise image of this undesirable visitor.

'What are we to do with him?' asked Mademoiselle Flavia.

'My programme starts in two minutes, and it lasts two hours,' said Tapp. 'Tell him . . . Oh, but it's all the same to me! Do what you like with him!' he shouted, and went and shut himself up in the studio.

Did the listeners to that evening's programme have any suspicion of the extraordinary circumstances that surrounded it? It is possible, for Tapp was so choked with emotion that his voice was even more compelling in its sweet, wounding raucousness. He spoke, and his soul winged its way towards thousands of other souls. But for the first time, his soul had a body. And this body was not the heavy, ridiculous body of Felix Tapp. This body was seated in a nearby office and listening 'off transmission' to what was going out over the air, missing not a single word of what Tapp dispatched into the ether. Tapp was well aware of this, and it disturbed him deeply. For the first time, he had a dreadful feeling that he was an impostor, a little as if, while acting Shakespeare's *Julius Caesar*, he had known that the real, historical Caesar was observing and listening to him in the wings.

At two minutes after midnight he emerged from the studio in a state of near prostration. He went over to his office, praying to God that the intruder would have departed. He was still there. Tapp could no longer escape the interview that 'the other' was obviously expecting. He requested Mademoiselle Flavia to let his wife know that he would be home late, and to ask her to take the barded quails out of the oven, which was quite certainly where they were as they should have been served within thirty-five minutes – the time it took him to arrive home and sit down to table. Then he took the plunge and went into the office, shook the visitor's hand – a frank, cool, muscular hand, he noticed – and sat down opposite him.

'Well?' was the sum total of his preamble.

'Well?' repeated Durâteau, a little surprised. 'Well, yes, eh . . . Well, bravo! Yes, Tristan Vox, bravo! I've been listening to you for two hours. You have never been so persuasive, so warm, so familiar without demagogy, so intimate without indiscretion, so human without exhibitionism. You want me to tell you something? Well, as I listened to you, I was proud!'

'Proud?' said Tapp in amazement. 'Proud of what?'

'Proud? But quite simply – proud of being Tristan Vox!'

'Because you are Tristan Vox?'

'Ah! my dear Monsieur, believe me, it was none of my doing! No! I didn't want anything from anybody. Only a week ago I was unaware of the very existence of Tristan Vox. And then, suddenly, my photo's in all the papers and I can't put my nose out of doors without people pointing at me, without being asked for my autograph, for money, for advice, for love – for anything you like to mention! What sort of a life do you think that is? Because personally, Monsieur though this may perhaps surprise you, I have a wife, and children, and relations, and friends, and a job. And what remains of all that, may I ask, since I have become Tristan Vox?'

'Well, now I really don't understand,' Tapp confessed. 'Have you come here to congratulate me or to complain?'

'I came, I will admit, to have it out with you. To tell you that you have no right, just like that, to devastate the life of a man who has never done you any harm. Yes, I came to talk to you about some possible arrangement – oh, I don't know – some compensation, some damages – *something*! And then, well, I've been shut in here since ten o'clock, and I've been listening to you. That is – I've been listening to Tristan Vox, and, in short, I've been listening to myself, to the very great extent to which, as everyone keeps telling me, I am Tristan Vox. And I thought I was just great! Because you see, everything you said this evening, well, I had the impression that it was my mouth it was coming out of. A strange impression, I assure you!'

'Not only for you!' Tapp remarked ironically.

There was a silence. In the distance, and coming closer, they heard the two plaintive notes of an ambulance.

'There's an angel passing,' Tapp continued, still sarcastically.

'An angel?' Durâteau repeated. 'No angel is passing between us. An angel is standing erect, radiant, incorruptible, inspired, generous – an angel of terrible purity and power. The angel Tristan Vox!'

'Oh no! I've had enough!' shouted Tapp. 'You're completely mad, and I suspect you of being contagious. You're trying to drive us all round the bend!'

It was at this point that the office door opened unceremoniously and the hirsute head of a technician appeared.

'Hey, Tapp,' he said in a hoarse voice, 'it's your secretary, she has just had an accident. They're putting her into an ambulance.'

'Mademoiselle Flavia? What sort of accident? What's happened to Mademoiselle Flavia?'

'She had a fall.'

'A fall? In her office? Down the stairs?'

'No, out of the window. From the third floor. Into the street.'

'Good heavens! But how can she have fallen out of the window?'

'No idea. Maybe she gave herself a bit of a push?'

'Good God! Will you telephone my wife? I must go to her.'

Tapp dashed out of the room, raced down the stairs, and reached the pavement just in time to see the ambulance, with its revolving roof light, disappearing, repeating its sobbing signal. He had to find out where it was making for, then look for a taxi and tell it to rush to the Neuilly clinic.

Tapp found Mademoiselle Flavia lying on a camp-bed, her

head swathed in an enormous turban of bandages, waiting to be X-rayed.

The nurse stepped aside to let Tapp pass when she saw the insistent way the injured woman was beckoning to him to come nearer. She requested him to be as brief as possible, and disappeared.

Tapp had some difficulty in recognizing his secretary in this Grand Panjandrum with the tumefied face.

'Come closer, Felix,' she murmured.

He obeyed, profoundly impressed at hearing her call him Felix for the first time.

'I don't know what's going to become of me, and I owe you an explanation. And first, a confession. Yes. Isolde – was me!'

She fell silent, to give him time to register and assimilate this fantastic revelation.

'I couldn't stand it any longer, you understand? All that life, all that work, all that correspondence devoted to a being who didn't exist. It wasn't possible any more. I thought I was going mad. I absolutely had to find a way to make him exist, to force him to exist. That was when Isolde came on to the scene. Right from her very first letters I wanted to take her place. I imitated her handwriting, and I bombarded you with violent, improper letters, which cost me tears of shame and rage while I was writing them. And it was all to oblige Tristan Vox to show himself, to come out of his hole, you understand?'

Once again she fell silent, as if to efface the memory of her epistolary labours. And whereas Tapp would never have found it possible to associate those strident, obscene letters with his idea of his secretary, the strait-laced, prudish Mademoiselle Flavia, he had no difficulty in seeing their author in this new character, beturbanned in white crêpe and covered in purplish bruises.

'I was sure he would finally appear,' she went on, 'but at the same time I felt there would soon be a catastrophe. Because I couldn't possibly face him, you understand?'

This was the third time she had asked him whether he understood. He said nothing. No, he didn't understand. And in any case, he had stopped understanding a long time ago. Was it since Tristan's photo had appeared in *Radio-Weekly*, or even before that, since the first letter signed Isolde? Which Isolde? Not

Mademoiselle Flavia who, according to her confession, had done no more than intersperse her own subsequent letters with those of the other, the first Isolde . . .

The injured woman made a desperate effort to justify herself.

'I was worried sick when he turned up at the studio. I recognized him immediately, and I was quite certain it was my fault he had come. I know it's absurd but I still can't get the idea out of my mind. And then you told me to cope with him myself, that you didn't want to see him. That implied that I was responsible for his presence in the office. And then, as the last straw, you asked me to telephone your wife. When I told her everything. . . .'

That was all he needed! Here was his wife mixed up in this imbroglio, now! As if the situation was not already sufficiently embroiled!

'Yes, and what then? What did you tell my wife? What did she say?'

But Mademoiselle Flavia had fallen back on to her pillows, with closed eyes. For a moment Tapp studied this haggard, multi-coloured clown's face, whose grotesque sadness and ugliness were the very image of his own destiny. There was no more for him to learn, here. And in any case, the nurse was signalling to him through the half-open door.

He stood up, went out, and had to walk for quite a while before he found a taxi. It was nearly two in the morning when he tried to enter his flat. The security bolt was fastened making it impossible for him to open the door with his key. He rang.

'Come on, Amelia! Open the door! It's me, Felix!'

He could hear muffled footsteps on the other side of the door.

'Is that you, Felix?'

'Yes. Open the door.'

The bolt turned noisily, the door opened, and Felix nearly fell over under the onslaught of Amelia as she threw herself into his arms.

'Felix, Felix,' she sobbed. 'Forgive me! It's all my fault!'

'Forgive you for what? What's all your fault?'

'Say you forgive me, first!'

'I forgive you.'

'Isolde – was me!'

And she started sobbing even more desperately. Whereupon

Tapp became totally convinced that the whole world was conspiring against him.

'Why don't we go to bed? We can talk it all over tomorrow,' he suggested.

Amelia choked.

'Could *you* sleep after all that? And without eating?'

Eating? Ah yes, why not? He had forgotten the barded quails envisaged for that evening. He freed himself from Amelia's embrace and went into the kitchen. An odour of burned meat was still floating in the air. At the top of the stove, the baking sheet displayed the catastrophe: four little blackened, crinkled, packages.

'But I told Flavia to telephone you to take them out of the oven.'

'Your secretary? Oh yes, she did ring me! But good heavens, not to talk about quails! Felix, what are you thinking about?'

'What am I thinking about? What do you expect me to be thinking about at two in the morning, with an empty stomach?'

'Mademoiselle Flavia told me that Tristan Vox was closeted in the office with you. She sounded worried sick. And she went on: "There's going to be a tragedy, it's bound to happen, what with Isolde's letters!" And Isolde was *me*!' Amelia exclaimed once again, once again bursting into tears.

In the end, husband and wife ate in the kitchen, without appetite, a cheese omelette which Amelia managed to make between sobs. Meantime, she retraced her calvary.

'Every day that God sends, I listened, like thousands of other people, between ten o'clock and midnight, to Tristan's voice. But that was just it – not exactly like thousands of other people. Because *I* was Felix Tapp's wife. And in theory, Tristan and Felix were the same man. In theory, yes, but how was I to know! Because I never recognized your voice on the radio, you see – never! So, obviously, I got ideas into my head. Who was this Tristan Vox who was at the same time my everyday husband and the imaginary love of a whole host of unknown women? I wanted to find out. To be in love with Tristan. I wrote some letters signed Isolde. To see what would happen. And also to try to find you again, to get you back when you became Tristan Vox.

Looking into the middle distance, with glazed eyes, Felix Tapp was thinking, while he ate. The truth was that he had lacked foresight. For years on end he had worked every evening in order to create an ideal character, endowed with every charm, every virtue, an imaginary character, true, but not – as he had believed – an inexistent one, since hundreds of thousands of listeners, both male and female, believed in his existence. In this mass credulity there was something like an accumulation of potential energy, a colossal nebula whose influence would inevitably perturb anyone subjected to it head-on – his secretary and his wife being first in the line of fire – and eventually provoke a precipitation, a human concretion which, in this particular case, was called Frédéric Durâteau. Throughout this whole business Tapp had been playing the sorcerer's apprentice, causing both unhappiness in those around him, and his own undoing, through having quite unconsciously manipulated forces beyond his understanding.

What was he to do now? Cut his losses. All things considered, Vox only existed through the daily infusion of pseudo-life constituted by his two-hourly programme.

'The tap must be turned off,' thought Tapp, with never a thought for the pun on his family name by which he had been so plagued throughout all the years he had been at school, and doing his military service.

Should he unilaterally cancel his contract with the radio station? That was out of the question. This eventuality had been foreseen, and whereas the management was entitled to dismiss him at any time with neither notice nor compensation, he, on the other hand, was under the obligation of paying a considerable sum of money as the price of his liberty. However, Flavia's attempted suicide was sufficient to justify a nervous breakdown and three weeks off.

He didn't go back to the studio, but got Amelia to write to his director to explain the state he was in. Then he waited for the answer, which arrived two days later and was just as positive as he had hoped. Taking all the events into account, he was cordially granted the time off he was requesting.

At the end of the week the Tapps took the train for Billom. They went to stay in Amelia's parents' house, which they had left after the summer holidays four months before. They found it a strange experience to discover the place on the threshold of winter – those walls and rooms, and beyond them those streets and squares, which they usually saw only in summer. It was a slightly sad and yet soothing experience, which gave them the impression that they had suddenly aged a great deal. Was it one of the effects of this ageing? – Amelia had suddenly lost all her culinary enthusiasm, and however broad the hints her husband dropped, nothing could get her to return to her pots and pans.

Tapp got into the habit of going to play billiards every evening in the big café in the rue du Colonel-Mioche. Amelia stayed at home, where she often spent the evening with a woman neighbour. Accustomed as he was to going to bed late, he frequently stayed until the café closed. One day, however, he had flu, and returned to the conjugal domicile earlier than usual. The two women, riveted to the wireless set, didn't hear the door open and close. Tapp lent an ear. The only thing that reached him was a name, that of the man whose warm, youthful and friendly voice was once again about to ring out: Tristan Vox!

That evening, Felix Tapp had the presentiment that in all probability he would never again speak into a microphone. He was confirmed in this opinion when, two days later, he saw the latest number of *Radio-Weekly* displayed at the newspaper kiosk. On its cover was Frédéric Durâteau's photograph with, in huge, boxed type, just one name: Tristan Vox.

A few days later it was with a feeling of vertiginous solitude that he discovered this same name on an envelope that Amelia was preparing to post on the sly.

Veronica's Shrouds

Every year, in July, the International Photography Festival, held in Arles, attracts a huge crowd of photographers, both amateur and professional. During the few days the Festival lasts, exhibitions proliferate at every street corner, interminable discussions take place on the café terraces, and in the evenings the distinguished guests show their work on an enormous white screen erected in the courtyard of the Archbishop's Palace, to the cheers or boos of a young, passionate, and uncompromising audience. The connoisseurs of the Who's Who of photography delight in recognizing, in the little squares and alleyways of the town, Ansel Adams and Ernst Haas, Jacques Lartigue and Fulvio Roiter, Robert Doisneau and Arthur Tress, Eva Rubinstein and Gisèle Freund. People point out Cartier-Bresson, hugging the walls because he believes he can't see when he himself is being seen, Jean-Loup Sieff, who is so handsome that you wish he would concentrate entirely on self-portraits, Brassaï, nocturnal, mysterious, never to be seen in the blazing Provençal sun without an old black umbrella.

'Brassaï, why the umbrella?'

'It's an obsession. It came over me the day I gave up smoking.'

The first time I saw Hector and Veronica they must have been together, but I am to be excused if at the start I noticed only Hector. It was on one of those narrow strips of land that run along the Camargue, and separate the sea from the last brackish ponds on which flamingos come swooping down like great red and white streaks of light. Guided by one of the organizers of the Festival, a group of photographers had assembled on this marshy ground to photograph a nude. The model, superbly curvaceous in his nudity, either ran up and down in the surf, or lay flat on his stomach on the sand, or curled up in a foetal position, or waded in the stagnant waters of the pond, warding off seaweeds and salty ripples with his sturdy thighs.

Hector was the Mediterranean type; of medium height, with powerful muscles, a round, rather childish face overshadowed by a young bull's forehead festooned with a mop of black, curly hair. He took full advantage of his natural animality which was in perfect harmony with the simple, primitive things of this region: fresh water or stagnant ponds, russet grasses, bluish-grey sands, tree stumps whitened with age. He was indeed nude, though not absolutely, for he wore a kind of necklace, a leather thong threaded through a hole pierced in a huge tooth. This savage ornament actually emphasized his nudity, and he met the incessant volleys of the photographers with naïve complaisance, as the right and proper homage due to his splendid body.

We went back to Arles in half a dozen cars. Fate had decreed that I should sit next to a slim, lively little woman in whom intelligence and a kind of feverish charm took the place of beauty, and who ruthlessly made me share the weight and clutter of the photographic equipment she had lumbered herself with. In spite of this she seemed to be in a rather bad mood, and kept muttering severely critical remarks about the working session that morning, although I wasn't quite sure whether or not her remarks were addressed to me.

'Not a single photo worth keeping. That beach! That Hector! So banal you could weep! Postcard stuff! Even though I had my forty-millimetre distagon. You can get some interesting distortions with that super-wide-angle lens. If only Hector had held his hand out towards it he would have had a gigantic hand with a small body and a sparrow's head behind it. Amusing. But after all, that's just originality on the cheap. Never mind. We can forget about the sea, and the sand, and the worm-eaten, prop-room tree trunks, but it would be nice to make something of that young Hector. Only it would take a lot of work. Work, and sacrifices . . .

At the end of that day, while I was taking a little walk in nocturnal Arles, I caught sight of the two of them – Hector and Veronica – on the terrace of the Vauxhall Hotel. She was talking. He was listening to her with an astonished expression. Was she talking about work and sacrifices? I walked slowly enough to hear him, even so, answer a question Veronica had asked him. He had pulled out of his shirt collar the necklace I had noticed that morning.

'Yes, it's a tooth,' he was explaining. 'A tiger's tooth. It comes from Bengal. The natives there are convinced that so long as they wear this fetish there's no risk of their being eaten by a tiger.'

While he was speaking, Veronica observed him with a sombre, insistent gaze.

The Festival came to an end. I lost sight of Hector and Veronica, and I even more or less forgot them during the following winter.

A year later I was once again in Arles. So were they. I found Veronica unchanged. But Hector was unrecognizable. His rather childish, puppyish behaviour, his splendid animal swagger, his sunny, optimistic efflorescence, had all disappeared. As a result of goodness knew what change in his life style he had grown so much thinner that it was almost alarming. Veronica seemed to have communicated her own feverish rhythm to him, and she kept gazing possessively at him. She didn't refuse, however – quite the contrary – to comment on his metamorphosis.

'Last year, Hector was beautiful, but not really photogenic,' she told me. 'He was beautiful, and if they wanted to the photographers could make fairly faithful copies which would therefore also be beautiful – of both his body and his face. But like all copies, photos taken that way are obviously inferior to the original.

'Now, though, he has become *photogenic.* And what does photogenesis consist of? It implies the possibility of producing photos that *go beyond* the real object. In vulgar terms, the photogenic man surprises people who, although they know him, are seeing his photos for the first time: they are more beautiful than he is, they seem to be revealing a beauty which was previously hidden. But such photos do not *reveal* that beauty, they create it.'

I learned later that they were living together in a modest farmhouse that Veronica had rented in the Camargue, not far from Méjannes. She invited me there.

It was one of those squat, thatched-roof cottages which you don't even notice in the Camargue landscape until you stumble up against the gate in their ring fence. I found it difficult to imagine the life they shared in these few, poorly-furnished rooms. Photography alone was in its element, there. The place was cluttered with electric spots, electronic flashes, reflectors, cameras, plus a developing and printing laboratory with a great wealth of chemicals in bottles, flasks, sealed cans, and individual quantities in plastic containers. One of the rooms, however, seemed to be reserved for Hector. But here, apart from a monastic table and a shower bath enclosed by a rubber curtain, there was a whole arsenal of equipment for the intensive culture of the muscles which spoke only of effort, work, and the unflagging repetition of the same movement made when painfully weighed down with iron or steel. There were rib stalls on one wall. Opposite, on racks, was a complete range of weight-lifting apparatus and a whole set of polished oak Indian clubs. The rest of the room was nothing but chest expanders, spring-grips, muscle-developers, a stomach-exercising board, a rowing machine, and bar-bells. The whole suggested both an operating theatre and a torture chamber.

'Last year, if you remember,' Veronica explained, 'Hector was still like a young, hard, ripe fruit. Very appetizing, but quite useless for photography. The light glided over his smooth, rounded forms but neither caught them nor played on them. Three hours of exercises every day have changed all that. I must tell you that since I took him in hand, all this gymnastic gear comes with us wherever we go. It's the normal complement of the photographic equipment I take everywhere with me. Whenever we travel, the station wagon is absolutely chock-a-block.'

We went into another room. On a trestle table there was a pile of enlargements – a suite of variations on the same theme.

'There!' said Veronica, with a touch of exaltation in her voice. 'There is the true, the only Hector! Look!'

Was it really Hector, that hollow mask, all cheekbones, chin, and sunken eyes, with a helmet of hair whose disciplined curls looked as if they had been varnished?

'One of the great laws of the photographic nude,' Veronica went on, 'is the paramount importance of the face. How many photos that we hoped were going to be magnificent – and which could have, and should have been magnificent – are spoiled by an imperfect face, or simply by a face that isn't in keeping with its body! Lucien Clergue, whose guests at Arles we all more or less are, has solved the problem by cutting off the heads of his nudes. But decapitation is obviously a radical procedure! Logically, it should kill the photo, whereas on the contrary, it gives it a more intense, a more secret life. You might almost think that all the soul that the head contained has flowed back from the severed head into the body represented, and that it manifests itself there by creating a host of little details that are full of life but not present in ordinary nudes: the pores in the skin, its down, contrasty grains, bristling goose flesh, and also the gentle density of the soft parts caressed and modelled by water and sun.

'This is great art. But I think it's only possible with the female body. The masculine nude wouldn't lend itself to this game of the head being as it were swallowed up by the body. Look at this picture. The head is the code to the body. What I mean is: the body itself, translated into a different system of signs. And at the same time it's the key to the body. Look at some of the mutilated statues in museum storehouses. A headless man becomes indecipherable. He can't see anything because he's lost his eyes. And he gives the visitor the unbearable feeling that it is he, the visitor, who has gone blind. Whereas a statue of a woman comes into its own, blossoms into a creature of flesh and blood far more when it has lost its head.'

'Nevertheless,' I observed, 'no one could say that the face you have given Hector radiates intelligence and interest in the outside world.'

'Of course it doesn't! An alert, inquisitive, extrovert face would be a catastrophe for the naked body. It would drain it of its substance. The body would become a negligible medium for the light that focuses on things, like a lighthouse which is itself immersed in darkness and only exists in order to illuminate the sky with its revolving light. The right face for a nude is an impassive, imperturbable face, concentrating on itself. Look at Rodin's *Thinker*. He's an animal who, with his face in his fists, is making a violent effort to extract some vague gleam of light from his miserable brain. The whole of his powerful body is penetrated and as it were transfigured by this effort, from the inward-turning feet up to the bull's neck, by way of the furniture remover's spine.'

'Yes, I was thinking about statues' eyes, with their strange gaze which always seems to look straight through us without seeing us, as if, being made of stone, they could only perceive stone.'

'Statues' eyes are sealed fountains,' Veronica agreed.

There was a silence, during which we examined three proofs printed on extrahard paper. Hector's body, seen against a uniformly black background (how well I know those huge rolls of paper of all colours that photographers use to isolate their models, just like insects pinned up in an entomologist's box), his body silhouetted by the shadows and luminous areas of one single, violent source of light, looked frozen, stripped to the bone, dissected by a kind of autopsy or anatomical demonstration.

'It isn't exactly what they call "life photography",' I said, joking in order to try to break the rather maleficent charm of these pictures.

' "Life" isn't my strong point,' Veronica admitted. 'And remember what Paul Valéry said: "Truth is naked, but underneath the naked is the *écorché*." Now there are two schools of photography. Those who belong to the first are always on the look-out for the surprising, the touching, the frightening image. They scour the towns and the countryside, the beaches and the battlefields, trying to capture the evanescent scene, the furtive gesture, the shining moment, all of which illustrate the heart-rending insignificance of the human condition, which arose out of nothingness and is condemned to return to nothingness. These, today, are called Brassaï, Cartier-Bresson, Doisneau, William Klein. And there is the other movement, entirely derived from Edward Weston. This is the school of the deliberate, calculated, immobile image that aims at capturing not the instant, but eternity. One of these is Denis Brihat, whom you may have seen here with his beard and his Hemingway glasses. He has gone off to live in the Luberon mountains, east of Avignon, and for the last twenty years he has photographed nothing but plants. And do you know what his worst enemy is?'

'Tell me.'

'The wind! The wind that makes flowers move.'

'And he has chosen to live in the mistral country!'

'This school of the immobile has four private domains: portraits, nudes, still lifes, and landscapes.'

'So in the first school you have photographs "taken from life", and in the opposite school you have "still lifes" – which is a strange term for a genre consisting entirely of inanimate objects!

But I sometimes feel that the first category is badly named too, and we should rather talk about photographs "taken from death".'

'That wouldn't bother me,' Veronica conceded. 'Death interests me – it more than interests me. One of these days I shall inevitably go and take photographs in the morgue. In a corpse – a real, raw corpse, not one that has been prettified on its bed, its hands joined, ready to be sprinkled with holy water without batting an eye – in such a corpse, yes, there is a truth . . . how shall I put it? . . . a marmoreal truth. Have you noticed, with very young children who don't want to be picked up, the way they are able to make themselves heavier, to give themselves an extraordinary *dead weight*? I've never carried a dead person. If I tried to, I'm sure *I* should be crushed to death.'

'You frighten me!'

'Don't put on airs! There's nothing more ridiculous, in my opinion, than the new form of prudery that is shocked by death and by the dead. The dead are everywhere – starting with art. And just a minute! Do you know exactly what Renaissance art is? There are several definitions of it. This is the best one, in my opinion: it's the discovery of the corpse. Neither Antiquity nor the Middle Ages dissected corpses. Greek statuary, which is absolutely irreproachable from the anatomical point of view, is entirely based on the observation of the living body.'

' "Taken from life".'

'Precisely. Praxiteles had watched athletes in action. For religious, moral, or whatever reasons, he had never cut up a corpse. We have to wait until the sixteenth century, and more precisely for the Fleming, Andreas Vesalius, for the true birth of anatomy. He was the first to dare to dissect corpses. After that, every artist went rushing off to the cemetery. And almost all the nudes of the time began to stink of the corpse. Not only are the manuscripts of Leonardo da Vinci and Benvenuto Cellini full of anatomical illustrations, but in the frequent appearance of very living nudes you can sense their obsession with the *écorché*. Benozzo Gozzoli's Saint Sebastian, Luca Signorelli's frescos in Orvieto Cathedral, seem to have escaped from some *danse macabre*.'

'That's certainly a somewhat unexpected aspect of the Renaissance.'

'When you compare it with the flourishing health of the Middle Ages, the Renaissance strikes you as being the era of the morbid and the anguished. It was the golden age of the Inquisition, with its witch-hunts, torture chambers and stakes.'

I had put down the nude photos of Hector, which all of a sudden seemed like exhibits in the trial of a witch.

'Dear Veronica, if we were transported back to those days, don't you think there might have been a great risk of your ending up being burned at the stake?'

'Not necessarily,' she replied, so quickly that I wondered whether she had already asked herself that question. 'In those days there was a very simple way of dabbling in witchcraft without running the slightest risk.'

'What was that?'

'By becoming a member of the court of the Holy Inquisition! When it comes to the stake, for all sorts of reasons I consider the best place is not *on it*, but to one side, in a dress circle box.'

'To be able to see and take photographs.'

I was getting ready to leave, but there was one last question I was dying to ask.

'Talking about seeing, I'd be disappointed to leave you without saying hallo to Hector.'

I thought I noticed that while her face had lit up for a moment at my irony, it now tautened as if I had been guilty of an indiscretion.

'Hector?'

She looked at her watch.

'He'll be asleep, at this hour. He used to have such absurd habits, but now I make him do just the opposite – eat little and sleep a lot.'

But she did smile as she added:

'That's the golden rule for health: He who sleeps forgets his hunger.'

I was on my way to the door when she seemed to change her mind.

'But even so, you can see him. I know him. It will take more than that to wake him up.'

I followed her to a little room, a kind of cell, at the end of a corridor. I thought at first that it had no windows, but then I noticed some drawn curtains which were much the same colour as the pale walls and ceiling. Everything was so white and so bare that it was like being inside an eggshell. Hector was asleep, lying flat on his stomach on a low, wide bed, in a position that reminded me of one of his poses in the Camargue the previous year. The temperature justified the fact that he had neither sheet nor covers over him. In the uniformly milky half-light, that mahogany-coloured flesh, frozen in an asymmetrical position – one knee bent, the opposite arm stretched out over the side of the bed – in which there was both total abandon and a passionate desire to sleep, to forget, to repudiate the things and the people of the outside world – even so, it was a fine sight.

Veronica gave him a possessive look, and then looked at me triumphantly. It was her creation – and undeniably a magnificent success – this golden, sculptural mass, cast into the depths of this ovoid cell.

Three days later I found her in the back room of a little bar in the Place du Forum, which was only frequented by gypsies and the inhabitants of la Roquette, the poorer part of the town. I found it difficult to believe, but it was a fact: Veronica had been drinking. Furthermore, it seemed that drink made her maudlin. We exchanged a few disenchanted remarks about the previous day's corrida, about the performance of Rossini's *Elisabetta, Regina d'Inghilterra* which was due to take place the next day at the Roman theatre, and about the Bill Brandt exhibition which had opened that afternoon. She answered in short, stiff sentences, her thoughts obviously elsewhere. There was an embarrassed silence. Then she suddenly made up her mind.

'Hector's gone,' she said.

'Gone? Where?'

'If only I knew!'

'Didn't he say anything?'

'No, well, yes – he left a letter on the table. Here!'

She threw an opened envelope on to the table. Then she began to scowl, as if to give me plenty of time to read the letter. The writing was neat and tidy, rather schoolboyish. I was struck by the tender tone, attenuated and as if refined and spiritualized by the fact that he had addressed her as *vous*.

Veronica darling,

Do you know how many photos you have taken of my body during the thirteen months and eleven days we have been together? You weren't counting, of course. You photographed me without counting. But while I was letting myself be photographed, I *was* counting. Only natural, isn't it? You have stolen my image twenty-two thousand two hundred and thirty-nine times. Obviously, this has given me time for thought, and I have come to understand a lot of things. I was so naïve last summer that I acted as a model for everyone in the Camargue. That wasn't serious. With you, Veronica, it became serious. Photography that isn't serious doesn't affect the model. It glances off him without touching him. But serious photography creates a perpetual interchange between the model and the photographer. It becomes like the system of communicating vessels. I owe you a lot, Veronica darling. You have made another man of me. But you have also taken a lot from me. Twenty-two thousand two hundred and thirty-nine times, some part of myself has been stolen from me and put into your little image trap, as you call it. You have plucked me like a hen, like an angora rabbit. I've got thinner, tougher, become desiccated, not through any diet or exercises, but because of what has been taken from me, because of the daily removal of some of my substance. Do I need to say that none of this would have been possible if I had kept my tooth? But you're no fool, you had it taken away from me, my magic tooth . . . And now I am empty, exhausted, tormented. Those twenty-two thousand two hundred and thirty-nine bits of me that you have so jealously classified, labelled and dated – you can have them. All I have left is my skin and bones, and I intend to keep them. You won't have my hide, dear Veronica! Find someone else, now, whether man or woman, someone intact and virginal, who has an unimpaired capital/image. What *I* am going to do is try to rest; I mean, I'm going to try to make myself a new face and body after the terrible mess you've made of me. Don't think I hold it against you. On the contrary, I love you dearly – in exchange for the sort of love you had for me, a devouring love. But don't bother to try to look for me. You won't find me anywhere. Not even in front of your nose, if by any chance we happen to meet, because I have become diaphanous, translucid, transparent – invisible.

With love
Hector.

P.S. I've taken my tooth back.

'His tooth? What's all that about his tooth?'

'But you know very well,' Veronica said impatiently. 'That talisman he wore round his neck on a leather thong. I had a hell of a job to get him to take it off when I wanted to photograph him.'

'Ah yes, the fetish tooth that the Bengalis believe protects them from being eaten by tigresses.'

'Tigresses? Why do you say tigresses, and not tigers?' she asked irritably.

Obviously, I couldn't justify my use of the feminine. There was a silence, heavy with hostility. But as I had started to compromise myself between Hector and her, I decided to come out with what I thought.

'Last time we met,' I began, 'you spoke at length about the anatomists of the Renaissance, and in particular about the Fleming, Andreas Vesalius. Your remarks whetted my appetite, and I had the curiosity to go to the public library to find out more about this person who was the veritable creator of anatomy. I discovered that he had lived a mysterious, adventurous, dangerous life, full of ups and downs, which was entirely motivated, from beginning to end, by one single passion – that of scientific discovery.

'"Born in Brussels in December 1514, Vesalius wasted no time in becoming familiar with cemeteries, gibbets, hospices, torture chambers – in short, with all the places where people die. He spent a good part of his life under the shadow of the gallows. His vocation seems to have been that of a necrophile, a vampire, a vulture. This would indeed have been horrible had the whole not been purified by the light of the intelligence. The emperor Charles V – also a Fleming – made him his private physician and took him to Madrid. It was here that scandal erupted. The rumour spread that Vesalius did not confine himself to the dissection of corpses . . . Certainly, the lifeless corpse reveals its anatomy. But it says nothing about its physiology, and for good reason. It is the living body that has something to say about physiology. An intrepid researcher, Vesalius arranged to have prisoners handed over to him. They were stupefied with opium, and then he cut them up. In short, after inventing anatomy, he created vivisection. This was a trifle crude, even for an age not much given to molly-coddling. Vesalius was tried, and condemned to death. Philip II just managed to save his life. His sentence was commuted into the obligation to make a pilgrimage to the Holy Land. But it would appear that fate was definitely against him. On his way back from Jerusalem he was wrecked on the desert island of Zante, where he died of hunger and exposure in October 1564".'

Aroused from her gloomy reflections, Veronica had been listening with increasing interest.

'What a marvellous life, and how marvellously it ended!' she said.

'Yes, but don't you see that for Vesalius, corpses were only the last resort. He much preferred the living.'

'No doubt,' she agreed 'but on condition that he could cut them up.'

I rarely have occasion to meet my photographer friends during the Parisian winter. I only just missed Veronica, though, at the opening of an exhibition at the Photogalerie in the rue Christine.

'She left no more than five minutes ago,' I was told by Chériau, who knew her. 'She was so sorry not to see you but she couldn't wait. Though she told me some fascinating things, you know – absolutely fascinating!'

I had nothing to be sorry about, though. Chériau is a veritable mine of information about all the gossip in the photographic world and I had only to keep my ears wide open to hear everything Veronica had told him, and a whole lot more.

'In the first place,' he began, 'she found her whipping-boy-cum-model and got him back – you know, that young Hector she picked up in Arles?'

I did know.

'Then, thanks to him, she launched out into a series of "direct photographs". That's what she calls shots taken without a camera, without a film, and without an enlarger. In short, the dream of most great photographers who consider the technical constraints of their profession to be an ignominious defect. The theory of this direct photography is as easy to formulate as it is difficult to put into practice. Veronica uses big sheets of photographic paper and quite simply starts by exposing them to the daylight. The only reaction of the sensitized paper thus exposed, without a developer, is that it begins to turn a very, very pale yellow. After this she immerses poor Hector in a developing bath (metol, sulphate of soda, hydroquinone and borax). Then, while he's still wet, she lays him down on the photographic paper, in one position or another. After that, all she has to do is wash down the paper with an acid fixative . . . and send the model off to take a shower. The result of all this is strange, flattened silhouettes, a flat projection of Hector's body rather like, as Veronica actually said in so many words, what remained on some walls in Hiroshima of the Japanese blown up and disintegrated by the atom bomb.'

'And Hector? What does he have to say about all this?' I asked, thinking of his farewell letter, which in my mind suddenly took on the aspect of a tragic, pathetic appeal for help.

'That's just it! When our dear Veronica was telling me about the marvels of "direct photography" she didn't realize that I knew the other side of the operation. Because I heard from another source – I have my spies, as you know – that poor Hector was suffering from generalized dermatitis and had had to go to hospital. What especially intrigued the doctors was that his lesions had obviously been caused by chemicals and resembled the professional skin diseases to be found in tanners, dry-salters and engravers. But whereas with such artisans they are localized on the hands and forearms, Hector had vast, toxic erythema on parts of the body – the back, for example – which are rarely exposed, and hence more vulnerable.

'To my mind,' Chériau had wound up, 'he'd be well advised to get himself out of the clutches of that witch; if he doesn't, she'll end up having his hide.'

Having his hide . . . The very expression he'd used in his letter! And yet I was still far from suspecting how it was going to be illustrated a few months later.

And indeed, a few months later the Photography Festival inevitably brought me back to Arles. It had already started when I arrived, and it was from the press that I learned that an exhibition called *Veronica's Shrouds* was being held in the Chapel of the Knights of Malta in the Musée Réattu. The paper also carried an interview with the artist. Veronica explained that after a series of experiments with 'direct photography' on paper, she had gone on to a more supple material that had greater possibilities – linen. The cloth was impregnated with silver bromide, to make it photo-sensitive, and then exposed to the light. Next it was used to enswathe the model as he came out of a developing bath still dripping wet; he was wrapped in it from head to foot: 'like a corpse in a shroud', Veronica added. Finally the cloth was fixed, and then washed. If you painted the model with titanium dioxide or uranium nitrate, you could get some interesting mordanting effects. The imprint then took on bluish or golden gradations. In short, Veronica had concluded, traditional photography has been surpassed by these new creations. *Dermography* would be a more appropriate word.

You can well imagine that my first visit was to the Chapel of the Knights. The height of its ceiling makes the nave seem tiny, and as if sunk in a pit. As a result, it is difficult for the visitor not to feel suffocated, and this impression was heightened by the 'shrouds' entirely covering the walls and floor. Everywhere, high up, low down, to the right, to the left, your gaze was overwhelmed by the black and gold spectre of a flattened, stretched, wound, unwound, corpse, reproduced in every position like an obsessive funereal frieze. It resembled a whole series of human skins that had been peeled off and then paraded, like so many barbaric trophies.

I was alone in this little chapel, which was beginning to feel like a morgue, and my anguish increased every time I discovered a detail that reminded me of Hector's face or body. I remembered, not without horror, the bloody and symmetrical imprints we used to obtain at school when we trapped a fly between two sheets of paper and crushed it with a blow of the fist.

I was on my way out when I found myself face to face with Veronica. I had only one question to ask her, and I couldn't keep it back for a single second.

'Veronica, where's Hector? What have you done with Hector?'

She gave me a mysterious smile, and with a vague gesture indicated the shrouds surrounding us on all sides.

'Hector? But he's . . . here. What I've done with him . . . is this. What more do you want?'

I was going to press the point when I noticed something that reduced me to permanent silence.

Round her neck she was wearing a leather thong threaded through the pierced tooth of a Bengal tiger.

Death and the Maiden

Hearing muffled laughter coming from the back of the classroom, the teacher suddenly broke off.

'*Now* what is it?'

The crimson, mirthful face of a little girl appeared.

'It's Melanie, Mademoiselle. She's eating lemons.'

The whole class roared with laughter. The mistress marched over to the back row. Melanie looked up at her, her face the picture of innocence, its thinness and pallor accentuated by the heavy mass of her black hair. She was holding a carefully decorticated lemon, whose peel was curled up on her desk like a snake. The teacher was perplexed.

This Melanie Blanchard had intrigued her right from the start of the school year. Docile, intelligent, hardworking, it was impossible not to consider and treat her as one of the best pupils in the class. And yet she drew attention to herself – without being provocative, it is true, and with disarming spontaneity – by ridiculous inventions and strange behaviour. In the history class, for instance, she displayed a passionate, almost morbid curiosity about all the famous people who had been condemned to death and tortured. Her eyes shining with alarming intensity, she would recite in great detail the last minutes of Joan of Arc, Gilles de Rais, Mary Stuart, Ravaillac, Charles I, Damiens, omitting no particular of their sufferings, however atrocious.

Was it merely a fascination with horror so frequently to be found in children, reinforced by a touch of sadism? Other characteristics proved that in Melanie's case it was something deeper and more complex. Right from the beginning of the autumn term she had distinguished herself by an extraordinary composition she had written for the teacher. As usual, the mistress had asked the children to describe one day in the holidays that were just over. And although Melanie's account had begun quite tritely with the preparations for a picnic lunch in the country, it came to an abrupt halt with the sudden death of the grandmother, which obliged the family to forgo their outing. Then the story resumed, but on a negative, unreal note, and Melanie went on to describe, imperturbably, and in a kind of hallucinatory vision, the various stages of the outing that had not taken place, the bird song that no one had heard, the preparation under a tree of the lunch that no one had eaten, and the comic incidents of their return during a storm which had no rhyme or reason, since no one had set out. And she concluded:

The family was assembled sadly round the bed on which the grandmother's corpse was lying, nobody ran off laughing to shelter in the barn, none of them did their hair, jostling one another in front of the only mirror in the living room, they didn't light a big fire to dry their soaked clothes, which therefore didn't steam in front of the chimney like the hair of a horse drenched in sweat. The grandmother had gone off on her own, leaving everyone else at home.

And now it was lemons! Did all the little girl's ridiculous inventions have something in common? What was it? The teacher asked herself this question, and suspected that an answer existed – for there was undoubtedly a certain 'family likeness' between all these inventions, they bore the stamp of the same personality – but she could find no answer.

'Do you like lemons?'

Melanie shook her head.

'Then why do you eat them? Are you afraid of getting scurvy?'

Melanie had no reply to these two questions. The teacher shrugged her shoulders and took a stand on more familiar ground.

'In any case, it's against the rules to eat in class. You must write out fifty times: *I eat lemons in class*.'

Melanie acquiesced obediently, relieved not to have to give any further explanation. And indeed, how could she have got other people to understand – seeing that she barely understood it herself – that she was not treating herself with lemons because she was afraid of getting scurvy, but because she was afraid of a much more profound sickness, both physical and mental, a wave of insipidity and greyness that suddenly came sweeping up over the world and threatened to submerge her? Melanie was bored. She suffered boredom in a kind of metaphysical vertigo.

Though after all – was it really she who was bored? Wasn't it rather the things, and the landscape, around her? Suddenly, a blinding light came flashing down from the heavens. The room, the class, the street, all seemed moulded out of some kind of murky mud into which their shapes were slowly dissolving. Melanie, the only living being in this nauseating desolation, was fighting desperately to save herself from being the next to be sucked down into the sludge.

From her earliest childhood she had discovered a harmless, yet impressive equivalent of this change of light which modified the very essence of things; and she had discovered it in the spiral staircase which led to the attic rooms in her parents' house. The window that lit this staircase was merely a narrow loophole containing small, multicoloured panes of glass. Sitting on the stairs, Melanie had often amused herself by looking at the garden through one particular pane, and then through another of a different colour. And each time she experienced the same astonishment, the same little miracle. For though the garden was so familiar to her that she could recognize it without the slightest hesitation, when she looked at it through the red pane it was bathed in the light of a forest fire. It was no longer the place in which she played and dreamed. Both recognizable and unrecognizable, it became an infernal cavern licked by cruel flames. Then she changed to the green pane, whereupon the garden turned into the unfathomable bottom waters of the ocean depths. Aquatic monsters must certainly be lurking in those glaucous profundities. The yellow pane, on the other hand, radiated, in a profusion of warm, sunny glints, a golden, reassuring haze. The blue one enveloped the trees and lawns in a romantic moonlight. The indigo pane made the most trivial objects look solemn and grandiose. And yet it was always the same garden, though each time with an appearance of surprising novelty, and Melanie was amazed at the magic power she thus possessed which enabled her at will to plunge her garden into a dramatic hell, a paean of praise, or a spectacular ceremony.

For there was no grey pane in the little window on the staircase, and the ashen downpour of boredom had a different origin: less innocent, but more real.

Quite early in life she had identified those elements of an alimentary order that tended to precipitate her fits of boredom and those which, on the other hand, had the power of warding them off. Cream, butter, and jam – the childish food that people were always trying to press on her – foreshadowed and provoked the advancing tide of greyness, the engulfment of life in a dense, viscid slime. On the other hand pepper, vinegar, and unripe apples – everything acid, sour, or highly spiced – exuded a breath of fresh, sparkling, invigorating air into the stagnating atmosphere. It was the difference between lemon juice and milk. For Melanie, these two drinks symbolized good and evil. In spite of the protests of her family she had adopted, as her morning drink, tea made with mineral water and flavoured with a slice of lemon. And with it, a very hard biscuit or a piece of near-burned toast. On the other hand she had been forced to give up the afternoon slice of bread and mustard she coveted because it gave rise to gales of laughter in the school playground. She had realized that with her bread and mustard she was going beyond the bounds of what was tolerated in a provincial primary school.

There was nothing she detested so much in the climates and seasons as a fine summer afternoon, with its lazy languor, with the obscene, satiated luxuriance of its vegetation which seems to communicate itself to both animals and people. The dreadful act initiated by those muggy, voluptuous hours was that of lounging in a chaise longue with one's legs apart and one's arms raised, while yawning very loudly, as if obliged to expose one's genitals, armpits, and mouth to goodness knew what kind of rape. Against this triple yawn, Melanie cultivated the laugh and the sob, two reactions which implied refusal, distance, and the human being's withdrawal into itself. The weather best suited to this rejection syndrome was a luminous frost, when all nature became denuded, frozen, hardened, brilliant. At such times, Melanie went for rapid, exalted walks in the countryside, her eyes watering on account of the glacial air, but her mouth full of ironic laughs.

Like all children, she had encountered the mystery of death. But in her eyes it had immediately taken on two completely opposite aspects. The animal corpses she had seen were usually swollen and decomposed, and exuded sanious secretions. Such beings, reduced to their last extremities, crudely avowed their basically putrid nature. Whereas dead insects became lighter, spiritual, and spontaneously attained the pure, delicate eternity of mummies. And this did not only apply to insects for, ferreting around in the attic, Melanie had found a mouse and a little bird that were equally desiccated, purified, reduced to their own distinctive essence: this was a good death.

Melanie was the only daughter of a lawyer in Mamers. She had always seemed strange to her father, who had had her late in life and whom she seemed to intimidate. Her mother had been delicate and had died prematurely, leaving Melanie alone with the lawyer at the age of twelve. She was deeply distressed by her mother's death. The first physical sign was that her chest hurt, she felt a kind of stabbing pain, as if she had an ulcer or an internal lesion. She thought she was seriously ill. Then she realized that she was perfectly well, and that it was grief.

At the same time, every so often she experienced waves of tenderness that were quite pleasant. She had only to think intently about her mother, about her mother's death, about the slim, stiff corpse lying in a box at the bottom of an icy hole . . . Her eyes filled with tears and she couldn't restrain a kind of hiccuping sob that resembled a bitter little laugh. Then she would feel uplifted, freed from the constriction of material things, liberated from the weight of existence. For one brief moment everyday reality became an object of derision, deprived of its self-importance, and no longer an obsessive burden weighing on the little girl. Nothing mattered any more, since her beloved mama was dead. The obvious truth of this irrefutable deduction shone like a spiritual sun. On the wings of funereal intoxication, Melanie discovered the hilarity in the air.

Then her grief wore off. All that was left of it was a scar which contracted when anyone mentioned the dead woman, or when she couldn't get to sleep at night and opened her eyes wide in the darkness.

After that the days passed, all identical, between an old maid-servant who was getting more and more hard of hearing and a father who only surfaced from his papers in order to talk about the past. Melanie grew up without apparently going through any difficult phases. Her family circle found her neither difficult, nor secretive, nor melancholy, and everyone would have been surprised to discover that she was swimming with the energy of despair in a dismal grey void, swimming against the insipid anguish she was caused by that affluent house full of memories, that street where nothing ever happened, and no one ever appeared.

When it looked as if a nuclear war might break out between America and the USSR over Cuba, Melanie was of an age to read the papers, and to follow the news on radio and television. It seemed to her that a breath of fresh air was sweeping through the world, and her lungs swelled with hope. For, to deliver her from her prostration, it would take nothing less than the immense destruction and appalling hecatomb of a modern war. Then the threat was dispelled, the lid of existence, which for a moment had been half lifted, closed on her again, and Melanie realized that there was nothing to be expected from history.

In the spring, the lawyer was in the habit of turning off the central heating, and lighting a fire on those evenings when the temperature was really too low. And this was why, one fine April morning, Étienne Jonchet came to deliver a lorryload of logs. He worked for a nearby sawmill in the forest of Ecouves – his fifth trade in less than a year. He was one of those handsome, downright, jovial fellows who considered the need to work to be an unfair, sordid burden. He smelled of resin and tannin, and his turned-up shirt sleeves displayed soft, golden forearms covered in obscene tattoos. Melanie had gone down to the cellar to pay him. While she was fumbling in her purse he looked at her with a strange expression which began to frighten her. It was even worse when he slowly raised his hands up to her shoulders, up to her head, and locked them round her neck. Her knees trembling, her mouth dry, all she could see were the tattooed arms, and a little farther away the young man's smiling face.

'He's strangling me,' she said to herself. 'He wants the purse and he's going to kill me to get it!'

And she felt herself weakening, going down a path towards death in which terror and voluptuousness were confused.

Finally she collapsed, but he picked her up in his arms, toppled her over a pile of anthracite, and possessed her tender, virginal body in this alcove of darkness.

When she passed her father on the stairs later she was covered in coal dust, and she amazed him by jumping up at his neck and laughing. She had lost her virginity, she was filthy, but she was happy.

They met again. A month later, pretending she was going to have a holiday with a schoolfriend, she went to live with her handsome woodcutter, taking with her nothing but the clothes she was wearing.

Étienne was not a very subtle psychologist, but even so the unusual behaviour of his new girlfriend surprised him. She turned up at the sawmill more often than was necessary. Instead of packing his lunch in his bag every morning, she chose to take it herself, and to share it with him in the midst of his workmates. He was certainly rather proud of the youth, the beauty, and especially the obvious bourgeois origins of the girl. But she ought to have disappeared when they started work again. Instead, she dawdled around the machines, running her finger over the serrated blades, calculating their sharpness, their cutting edge, the width they sawed, the tension of the steel bands, whose sides were rendered infinitely smooth and shiny by the terrible friction they were subjected to. Then she would pick up a handful of sawdust, feel its fluffy, elastic freshness, hold it close to her nose in order to appreciate its forest odour, then let it trickle down through her fingers. That this velvety snow could be made from compact tree trunks was a miracle that enchanted her.

But nothing fascinated her so much as the brief howls of the circular saws as they cut into the heart of a log, and the crazy, heaving movement of the great frame-saw as its twelve blades danced up and down in the soft wood.

The equipment was kept in repair by an old man named Sureau. A former cabinet-maker, he had known better days, but after his wife died he had taken to drink and he made a precarious living sharpening the blades in the sawmill. Melanie decided to win him over. She visited him in his hovel, did little favours for him, insinuated herself into his good graces. In actual fact she knew what she wanted, but no one would have understood the grandiose project she was determined to use him for. She finally got him to take up his tools again – he called them his 'clarinets' – to sharpen them, and to return to his trade. True, it might well take him years to produce what would no doubt be his all-time masterpiece.

The summer went by in a nimbus of sun and love, with the underlying mystery of the Sureau project. It seemed as if Melanie's and Étienne's embraces would never come to an end. They continued through the autumn mists, through the nocturnal clatter of the rain on the shingle roof of their hut, and under the white mantle of the snow, which that year was heavy.

At the beginning of March Étienne was given the sack, after a row with his boss. He went off to look for work. He had heard some talk of vacancies at a nearby stud farm. He promised to come back and fetch Melanie as soon as he was settled. But she was never to see him again. Since it never rains but it pours, old Sureau went into hospital with pleurisy. It is so true that spring is often fatal to old men.

However, Melanie had no intention of returning to her father, with whom she kept up a parsimonious correspondence. For the moment, the marvellous surprise of her love life, the superb folly of the sawmill, and the Sureau project, which was a direct consequence of them both, erected a wall between her present life and the grey waters in which the paternal house seemed to have run aground, like a worm-eaten Ark, in the eyes of her memory.

And yet the void was inexorably closing in on her again, in the piercing, humid breezes of a spring which seemed as if it was never going to end. The shack was invaded by the desolation of the forest as it made its black, haggard way out of the thaw. One day, Melanie surprised herself in the fateful act: she yawned, and recognized with dread the sign that at the same time greeted and summoned up the plashing tide of boredom. The time for childish little gimmicks – lemons, mustard – was well and truly past. Since from now on she was free, she should have run away. But where would she run to? For such is the pernicious force of boredom: it surrounds itself with a kind of universal contagion and sends out its malefic waves over the whole world, over the entire universe. Nothing, no place, and no thing, seems to escape it.

Rummaging around in the toolshed where hatchets, axes, wedges and saws were awaiting the improbable return of Étienne, Melanie found the solution. It was a rope, a beautiful new rope, still as bright and shiny as it had been when it left the rope factory, and it terminated – on purpose, so it seemed – in a loop. If you passed the end of the rope through this loop you produced a slip-knot, which was the very thing to hang yourself with.

Trembling with excitement, she fastened the rope to the main roofbeam. The slip-knot swung two and a half metres above the ground, the ideal height, for all you had to do was stand on a chair to put your head through it. And indeed, Melanie placed the best chair she possessed underneath the knot. Then she sat on the only other chair in the house – which was wobbly – and admired her handiwork.

It wasn't that those two objects – the rope and the chair – were particularly admirable in themselves. It was more a question of the perfection of the combination of that seat and that sort of hempen wire, and of its fatal significance. She lapsed into a state of blissful, metaphysical contemplation. In preparing her own death, in raising a visible, palpable barrier against the barren prospect of her life, in building a dam to halt the stagnant waters of time, at one stroke she was putting an end to boredom. The imminence of her death, made concrete by the rope and the chair, conferred an incomparable density and warmth on her present life.

She then experienced several weeks of sinister happiness. The charm had already begun to wear off, however, when the postman, whom she rarely saw, appeared one day. He brought her a letter from her best friend, Jacqueline Autrain, a schoolteacher who had been appointed to a nearby village for the coming third term of the school year, and who was going to live alone in the flat over the school. She would be so happy if Melanie would agree to come and spend a few days with her to help her settle in.

Melanie packed her bag, hid the key to the hut in a hole known to Étienne, and went off to stay with her friend.

Jacqueline's welcome, and the springlike radiance of the village, made her forget her obsessions and their funereal remedy. True, she had left her beautiful rope hanging above the chair in the darkness of the locked hut, as if in anticipation, as a kind of pledge against an obligatory return. While her friend was teaching, Melanie took care of their flat. Then she began to get interested in the children. She started giving private lessons to ones who found it difficult to keep up. After the love she had experienced all through the summer and winter, in this way, with the coming of spring, she discovered friendship. Between these two celebrations of life was the vast expanse of a bleak desert peopled with exorbitant, nauseating shadows that only a rope ending in the loop of a slip-knot rendered habitable.

Jacqueline was engaged to a young man who was at the time serving his apprenticeship with the riot police. Twice during the spring, when she had had a few days off from her job, she had visited him at his barracks in Argentan. One day he turned up with his helmet, his cap, his truncheon, and his big, bulging holster. The two young women were amused by all this paraphernalia.

His leave lasted three days. The first was nothing but a succession of laughter and caresses between the fiancés. When the spectacle became too demonstrative Melanie tried to slip away unnoticed. On the second day, the young man insisted on going for an outing with the two women, although it was obvious that Jacqueline would have preferred to stay at home and get the full benefit of such rare hours. On the third day she picked a violent quarrel with Melanie and accused her of trying to divert the too naïve policeman's attentions to herself. Coming in unexpectedly, the young man darted into the fray, and by tactlessly trying to defend Melanie he completed his fiancée's despair. When he departed for Argentan he left behind him an accumulation of emotional debris.

Melanie couldn't possibly go on living with Jacqueline. She settled in Alençon, and taught in a private school for the last two terms of the school year.

Then the holidays emptied the schools, the streets, and the whole town, and Melanie found herself alone once again under a white, merciless, piercing sun. On the dusty branches of the plane trees, between the uneven cobblestones of the squares, on the flaking walls tortured by the light, there emerged the livid, bloated face of boredom.

Feeling herself sinking, Melanie clung to her most recent memories. When she thought about Jacqueline's fiancé, strangely enough it was always the image of the bulging holster containing his pistol that first entered her mind. She wrote to him at the Argentan barracks and asked him to meet her. He replied, suggesting a day, an hour, and a café.

If he had imagined that this was going to lead to an affair, he was disappointed. Melanie explained that on the contrary, what she wanted was to clear up any misunderstanding and try to restore the good relationship between Jacqueline and him that she might unintentionally have helped to damage. She begged him to get in touch with his fiancée again as soon as possible, and to let her know that their reunion had been a success. This would be a great relief to her.

Then she had an inspiration. Why shouldn't he telephone Jacqueline right now, from the café? Then she would know that every attempt had been made.

He put up a feeble argument, then shrugged his shoulders, stood up, and made his way to the telephone booth. He left his cap, his helmet, his truncheon, and his bulging holster on the table.

Melanie waited for a moment. He must be having difficulty in getting through, because the young man was taking his time coming back. Actually, she couldn't take her eyes off the bulging holster which was innocently swelling on the table. Suddenly she yielded to temptation. She slipped the object into her handbag and rapidly reached the door.

Back in her little room in Alençon, the satisfaction of duty accomplished gave her a few days' peace. But she couldn't forget that by reconciling the fiancés she had permanently excluded herself from their friendship. The pistol, on the other hand, was a source of great comfort. Every day, at a certain hour – she always trembled with impatience and anticipated joy as she awaited it – she brought out the magnificent, dangerous object. She had no idea how to use it, but she was lacking in neither time nor patience. Placed on the table, naked, the pistol seemed to radiate an energy that enveloped Melanie in voluptuous warmth. The compact, rigorous brevity of its contours, its matt and almost sacerdotal blackness, the facility with which her hand embraced and grasped its form – everything about this weapon contributed to giving her an irresistible *force of conviction*. How good it would be to die by means of this pistol! Furthermore, it belonged to Jacqueline's fiancé, and Melanie's suicide would unite her friends, just as her life had nearly separated them.

The pistol was not loaded, but the holster contained a magazine and six bullets, and Melanie soon found the orifice in the butt where it should be inserted. A click apprised her that the magazine was in place. Then the day came when she felt she could no longer wait to try it out.

She went off very early in the morning into the forest. When she came to a clearing, a long way from any path, she took the pistol out of her bag, and, holding it with both hands, as far away from her as possible, she pulled the trigger with all her might. Nothing happened. There must be a safety catch. For a moment she ran her fingers over the butt, the barrel, and the trigger. Finally a kind of protuberance slid towards the barrel, leaving a red spot exposed. That must be it. She tried again. The trigger yielded under her fingers and the weapon, as if seized by a sudden fit of madness, kicked in her hands.

The explosion had seemed tremendous to Melanie, but the bullet had left no trace in the trees or thickets into which it must have vanished.

Trembling all over, Melanie put the pistol back in her bag and resumed her walk. Her legs felt weak, but she didn't know whether this was the result of fear or of pleasure. She now had a new instrument of liberation at her disposal, and how much more modern and practical this one was than the rope and the chair! She had never been so free. The key to her cage was there, in her bag, next to her make-up remover, her purse, and her sunglasses.

She had gone about a hundred metres when she saw, coming striding towards her, an old man dressed as a cross between a fisherman and a mountaineer, and carrying a cylindrical botanist's box slung across one shoulder. He approached her right away.

'What's going on? Didn't you hear an explosion?'

'No,' Melanie lied. 'I didn't hear anything.'

'Odd, odd. All the more so as it seemed to come from your direction. And I had been afraid I was becoming hard of hearing! Ah well. Let's say I had an illusion, then, yes, how shall I put it, an auditory hallucination.'

He had pronounced these last two words with a kind of ironic emphasis, and he ended his phrase in a grating little laugh. Then, noticing Melanie's bag:

'Were you looking for mushrooms, too?'

'Yes, that's right, for mushrooms,' Melanie lied again, eagerly.

Then, carried away by a sudden inspiration, she added:

'I'd especially like to know how to recognize the poisonous ones.'

'Pah! poisonous! For a real mycologist they're so rare they're practically non-existent! Do you know that my friends in our learned society and myself often invite each other to dinners in which a whole course consists of mushrooms reputed to be lethal? You only have to know how to prepare them, and also perhaps how to eat them without fear. Apprehension makes the organism more vulnerable, everyone knows that. A game for specialists, that's what it comes down to.'

'Then poisonous mushrooms are as harmless as that?' asked Melanie, with a touch of disappointment in her voice.

'For us – for us mycologists! But for the profane – hold on! It's rather like the big cats in a menagerie, isn't it! Their trainer can go into their cage and tweak their whiskers. But woe betide the visitor who allowed himself any such liberty!'

'You're absolutely fascinating!'

Aristide Greenhorn, who owned an antique shop in the rue des Filles-de-Notre-Dame, not far from the house where Saint Teresa of Lisieux was born, belonged to the race of those erudite men, curious about everything, who flourish discreetly in the shade of small provincial towns. He reserved the best part of himself for the learned Society which he regaled with eclectic communications, ranging from the miracles of botany to books of magic spells written by obscure mystics.

He was too delighted at having found a virgin ear to let Melanie go so soon, and for quite a while they walked side by side, chatting. When she got back to her modest lodging, the pistol in her bag was hidden under a perfumed provender of ceps, chanterelles, and parasol mushrooms that they had picked together. But she had also insisted on bringing back – isolated in a plastic bag, it is true – three livid entoloma and two death caps, the most fearsome killers of the undergrowth.

That evening, she laid out on her table the pistol, stripped of its holster, and a plate containing the five poisonous mushrooms. A dusky silence enveloped her solitude, but these lethal objects radiated an invigorating warmth with which she was more than familiar. Once again she experienced the same voluptuous excitement that she had felt in the hut in the presence of the rope and chair. But she was now going much farther in her intimate relations with death.

She was worried, at first, by the mysterious affinity that seemed to link these two kinds of object. They had a concise strength in common, a dormant, languid energy seemingly lurking in forms which could only contain it with difficulty, but which were inspired by it. The massive bulk of the pistol – a hand-held weapon – and the muscular curves of the mushrooms, also reminded her of a third object that had been hidden at the back of her mind for a long time but which she finally flushed out, not without blushing: Étienne Jonchet's sex organ, which had given her so much pleasure for so many weeks. And thus she discovered the profound complicity between love and death, and that it was the sordid, threatening emblems tattooed on Étienne's delightful arms that had given their embraces their real meaning. Thus Étienne found his proper place in the forest landscape whose centre remained the rope and the chair.

The mushrooms, the pistol, and the rope, were three keys which each opened a door to the beyond, three monumental doors, whose aspect and style were certainly very different.

The mushrooms were the soft, tortuous keys to a door which displayed the smooth rotundity of a gigantic belly. It was like a vast anatomical altar of repose erected to the glory of digestion, defecation, and sex. This door would only begin to open slowly, lazily. In eating and assimilating these mushrooms, Melanie would have to edge her way through a narrow slit with the obstinate cunning of a baby determined to be born the wrong way round.

The second door was cast in bronze. Black and tabular, unshakeable, it stood in front of a blazing secret whose disquieting glow could be glimpsed through the keyhole. Only a terrible explosion, a detonation resonating against Melanie's ear, would open it at one stroke and expose a landscape of flames, the incandescent cleft in a furnace, thick clouds of sulphur and saltpetre.

The third key – that of the rope and chair – concealed beneath its rusticity the abundant richness of a direct affinity with nature.

If she put her head through the hempen necklace, Melanie would discover the secret depths of the forest humus, fertilized by rainstorms and hardened by Christmas frosts. This was a beyond which smelled of resin and log fires, which resounded with the rumbling organ sounds the wind made when hurling itself against a cluster of tall trees. In becoming the human weight that would ballast the rope, itself fastened to the main beam of the woodcutter's hut, Melanie would take her place in that vast architecture of balanced treetops and swaying branches, of vertical trunks and entangled foliage, that was called: the forest.

Greenhorn had invited Melanie to visit him. One evening, she triggered off the silvery music of a cluster of tubes that the opening door set in motion. A whole paradise of polychromatic plaster saints welcomed her, either with open arms or with a right arm upheld in blessing. Little Sister Teresa, in a hundred copies of different sizes, clutched a crucifix to her Carmelite uniform as she raised her eyes up to the mouldings on the ceiling.

'She was born just a couple of steps from here, you see,' Greenhorn explained with fervour. 'At number 42 rue Saint-Blaise. If you like, we'll visit her birthplace together.'

He couldn't help noticing Melanie's air of consternation as she thanked him. He realized that he was on the wrong track, and that in this instance the pious antique dealer had to give place to the philosopher. He needed to keep a wary eye open and show signs of humility, if he wanted to pin down the personality of this strange girl who went for solitary walks in the woods shooting pistols, and who had a predilection for collecting poisonous mushrooms. She was certainly someone out of the ordinary. Unfortunately, it turned out to be difficult to make conversation, because she was more interested in learning simple, precise things from him than in talking about herself.

She left him after a quarter of an hour, but she came back two days later, and they gradually became more at ease with each other. With increasing amazement, Greenhorn pieced together the scraps of information Melanie gave him about her brief fate. For the difference in their ages and the soothing atmosphere of the shop reassured Melanie, and encouraged her to reveal herself. He couldn't help giving an involuntary start the day she told him that she taught small children. For she had hinted at the basic elements of her adventure with the handsome, tattooed Étienne, and at her fascination for the rope and its slip-knot. 'Poor children!' he thought. 'Though after all, people who are completely normal rarely go in for teaching, and it may well be natural and preferable that children, those semi-lunatics whom we tolerate in our midst, should be brought up by eccentrics.'*

Later, she told him about the spiral staircase, the narrow window, and the multicoloured panes of glass that made it possible for her to see her garden under profoundly different aspects. 'Kant!' he thought. 'The a priori forms of sense-impressions! At the age of ten, without either wanting to or realizing it, she discovered the basic essentials of transcendental philosophy!' But when he tried to initiate her into Kantianism he soon saw that she wasn't following him, and that she wasn't even listening.

Going back even farther in her memories, she alluded to the likes and dislikes she had had as a little girl – liking lemons, disliking cakes – to the boredom that had sometimes submerged her like a grey, greasy tide, to the sparkling and invigorating relief she had found, at first in a small way in corrosive food and drink, and later, in grandiose fashion, in her mother's death.

At this point he no longer doubted that she had an innate metaphysical vocation, which was accompanied by a spontaneous rejection of anything to do with ontology. He tried to get her to understand that she embodied, in the rough, the ancient antagonism between two forms of thought. Since the most distant dawn of occidental humanity, two currents had crossed and opposed one another, the first dominated by Parmenides of Elea, the other by Heraclitus of Ephesus. For Parmenides, reality and truth combine in the motionless Being, single, solid, and unchanging. This fixed vision horrified the other thinker, Heraclitus, who held that flickering, rumbling fire is the primordial substance of the universe, and that the limpid current of singing water is the symbol of life in perpetual flux. Ontology and metaphysics – Being in repose, and Being surpassed – have always, since the beginning of

* This definition of children is to be found in Jean Paulhan's preface to *The Story of O*. Here it is obviously just a vague recollection, and after all it is not so surprising that Greenhorn should have read Pauline Réage's novel.

time, opposed two kinds of wisdom and two kinds of speculation.

While he was speaking thus, carried away by his sublime subject, Melanie was staring at him with her huge, dark, passionate eyes. He might have thought she was listening to him, captivated by the amazing portrait of herself that he was drawing. But he was shrewd and lucid, he knew that he had a long, red, curly hair growing out of a wart on his cheek, and he only had to look at Melanie to realize that she had no eyes for anything other than this minute blemish, and that she hadn't taken in a single word of his discourse.

No, decidedly, he had to face facts, Melanie did not have a philosophical turn of mind, in spite of her prodigious talent for spontaneously involving herself, though crudely and quite unconsciously, in the great problems of eternal speculation. The facts of philosophy, by which she was possessed and which were the supreme guidelines of her destiny, could not be translated into concepts and words that she would understand. A metaphysician of genius, she would remain a primitive and never rise to the level of the Word.

Her visits ceased. Greenhorn was not particularly surprised. Since his arguments had had no effect on the girl's mind, he knew that his relationship with her was at the mercy of fortuitous, obscure, and unforeseeable influences. Nevertheless, he finally went and knocked on the door of the little room where she lived. A neighbour told him that she had moved.

What instinctive warning had decided her to return to the cabin in the forest of Écouves? No doubt, a thought that had imposed itself upon her had a great deal to do with it.

The prospect of death – of a certain kind of death, made concrete by a particular instrument – was the only thing capable of rescuing her from being engulfed in the nausea of existence. But this liberation was only temporary and gradually lost all its potency, like a stale drug, so she had to wait until a different 'key' came along and promised her a new death, a younger, fresher, more convincing promise, whose credibility was still intact. Now it was obvious that this game couldn't go on much longer. Sooner or later all those unkept promises, all those missed rendezvous, would have to be followed by the day of reckoning. Threatened once again by shipwreck in the quagmires of Being, Melanie had therefore decided on Sunday, 1 October, at noon, as the date and hour of her suicide.*

The idea of this commitment had at first frightened her. But the more seriously she envisaged it, and as the decision ripened in her mind, the more she felt warmed and sustained by successive and increasingly intense waves of energy and joy. It was this above all that had dictated her behaviour. Death, even when it was still distant, by its very certainty, by the precision of its date and occurrence, was already beginning its work of transfiguration. And once this date was fixed, every day, every hour, increased this salutary influence, as each step that brings us nearer to a great bonfire enables us to participate a little more in its light and warmth.

And this was why she had gone back to the forest of Écouves where, first in Étienne's tattooed arms, and then in the contemplation of the rope and the chair, she had experienced a happiness that presaged the great final ecstasy.

On 29 September a divine surprise was to crown her joy. A small van stopped outside the hut. An old man sitting beside the driver got out and knocked on the door. It was old Sureau, whose illness had been only a fairly severe warning sign. The two men got out of the vehicle and carried into the living room a tall, heavy, fragile object, completely enveloped in black veils, like a great widow, stiff and solemn. . .

'If I wasn't afraid of being paradoxical,' said the young doctor, putting down his stethescope, 'I would say that she died of laughter.'

And he explained that in its first stage, laughter is characterized by a sudden dilation of the orbicular muscle of the lips, and the contraction of the musculus risorius, of the canine, and the buccinator, and, at the same time by a discontinuous expiration, but that in its second stage the muscular contractions could spread to the whole of the network subordinate to the facial nerve and even reach the muscles of the neck, in particular, the platysma. And that in its third stage it undermines the whole

* October 1 is the feast day of Saint Teresa of Lisieux. Melanie no doubt considered this a touching tribute to her old friend Greenhorn. But we are entitled to wonder whether he appreciated it at its true worth.

organism, causes tears and urine to flow, and the diaphragm to contract in painful spasms, to the detriment of the intestines and the heart.

For those gathered round Melanie Blanchard's corpse, this lecture in comic physiology had very different meanings. Knowing Melanie, they were even more aware than the doctor himself that this apparently extravagant theory of death by laughter was pretty well in keeping with the eccentric character of the deceased. Her father, the shy, absent-minded old lawyer, remembered her on that spring day, with her clothes in disarray, her face and arms covered in coal dust, throwing herself at his neck and laughing like a madwoman. Étienne Jonchet recalled her strange and profound smile when she was stroking the most terrifying blades in the sawmill. The schoolmistress thought of the voluptuous grimace that the little girl could not suppress as she took a big bite out of a lemon. Meanwhile Aristide Greenhorn was trying to apply to this special case the theory developed by Henri Bergson in *Laughter,* according to which the comic is a mechanism overlaying a conscious being. Jacqueline Autrain was the only one who didn't understand a thing. Sobbing on her fiancé's shoulder she was convinced that Melanie, consumed with love for the young man, had sacrificed herself for their happiness. As for old Sureau, he had no thought for anything other than the masterpiece of his career as a craftsman, and, under the peak of his cap, he was keeping a close eye on its funereal outlines which encumbered the far end of the room.

Before she died, Melanie had sent them a kind of anthumous invitation informing them of the day and hour of her suicide, taking care to post the envelopes too late for anyone to intervene. Thus they met, one after the other, in the living room of the forest hut, after Étienne Jonchet – the only one not to have received an invitation – had discovered the corpse when he came to fetch his tools.

The rope still hung from the ceiling, the beautiful new, waxed rope that ended in an impeccable slip-knot. On the bedside table were the pistol – with just one bullet missing from its magazine – and a saucer containing five mushrooms that were beginning to dry out. Melanie was lying intact on her big double bed, carried off by a devastating heart attack which had done nothing to obscure the radiant, even hilarious, expression on her face. And in fact this dead girl, who had needed no violent expedient in order to cross the threshold, seemed to be floating in the joy of not living.

'And what is that?' the doctor finally asked, pointing to the 'widow'.

Old Sureau moved, and, with the careful, tender gestures of a young bridegroom undressing his bride with his own hands, he began to strip the object of its enveloping black lustre veils. They all recognized, with stupefaction, a guillotine, a drawing room guillotine, made with loving care out of the wood of a fruit tree, delicately dovetailed, waxed, polished, weathered – a real masterpiece of cabinet-making, to which the brightly shining blade with its relentless profile added a cruel, glacial note.

Greenhorn, as an expert antique dealer, noticed that the two uprights along which the blade slid were decorated in the antique fashion with eurythmic foliage, and that the crosspiece above them was in the form of a Hellenic architrave.

'And what's more,' he murmured, lost in admiration, 'it's in the style of Louis XVI!'

The Woodcock

On that morning at the end of March, the rain was crashing down on the glass roofs of the Alençon fencing academy where the best swordsmen of the First Cavalry Regiment were confronting each other in courteous but impetuous bouts. The uniformity of their knickerbockers, gathered below the knee, of their quilted plastrons, and above all of their wire mesh masks, obliterated titles, ranks, and even ages, and the two fencers who held the attention of their confrères could have passed for twin brothers. And yet, at a closer look, one of them seemed to be more incisive, more sinewy, more agile, and in any case he was at that moment putting his opponent in a difficult situation, and the latter broke, riposted to no avail, broke again, and finally lowered his arms, touched by a long lunge from his opponent.

Applause rang out. The fencers removed their masks. The loser was a lad with a pink complexion and curly hair. He took off his gloves and himself joined in applauding his victor, a lean, greying man in his well-preserved, youthful sixties. People surrounded him. There was sympathy, amused admiration, and respectful familiarity in the exclamations and congratulations converging on him. Modest and happy, he beamed at these companions, all of whom could have been his sons.

And yet he could still not accept without bristling the role of the prodigious old man into which these young men were pushing him. There was indeed good reason for irritation in all this fuss over a long lunge. He had pinned down young de Chambreux. So what? Why did they keep on reminding him of the forty odd years' difference in their ages? How difficult it was to grow older! This was clearly revealed when he took his leave an hour later. Through the open door they could see the grey, shifting curtain of a heavy downpour which would probably continue for some time.

He was about to plunge into the deluge without any protection. De Chambreux rushed up, holding an umbrella.

'Take this, Colonel! I'll send someone to fetch it tomorrow.'

He hesitated. Not for long.

'An umbrella? Never!' he protested. 'An umbrella is all right at your age, young man. But I! What would I look like under that?'

And heroically, without even bending his head, he dashed out into the downpour.

Colonel Baron Guillaume Geoffroy Étienne Hervé de Saint-Fursy was born with the century in the family manor house in the eponymous Norman village. In 1914 he had suffered the double disgrace of being too young to enlist and of being called Guillaume, like the Prussian Kaiser. Nevertheless, he entered the military academy of Saint-Cyr, following the hallowed tradition of his father and grandfather. He passed out as a cavalry lieutenant, in spite of a weakness in mathematics that no private lessons had been able to remedy. But he shone in salons, in fencing academies and in show-jumping. He owed his principal equestrian trophies to a mare who had had her hour of celebrity. For a long time Phyllida had won the Colonel a silver medal in every event he had entered. 'I love her more than any woman,' he sometimes used to say. But this was merely a quip, for he loved women more than anything else. His three foibles – the foil, Phyllida, and philandering – were his whole life. Though to these should be added hunting and shooting, and indeed the Baron was one of the best shots in the whole region. What was more, he used to mix up all these elements in his peremptory remarks, explaining, for instance, that a woman is to be conquered as a horse is controlled – the mouth, first, and then the croup will follow of its own accord – or that she is to be hunted like the woodcock. ('The first day I flush it, the second day I tire it, the third day, I shoot it.') He was affectionately known as 'the Woodcock' on account of these observations, and also because of the curve of his calves and his permanently out-thrust chest.

He had married young, very young – too young, some of his friends thought – for he was only twenty-two when he married Mademoiselle Augustine de Fontanes. She was appreciably older than himself but a rich heiress – at least in prospect. To their great regret they had no children. A major with the regular army in

1939, he had a magnificent war record, but the 1940 debacle had left him seriously injured both physically and psychologically. For him there had been only one recourse: Marshal Pétain. So he retired prematurely, as soon as the war was over.

Since then he had devoted his energies to the estate his wife had inherited. He escaped provincial boredom through his horses, his foil, and various little affairs, which became less and less easy to come by, it is true, with the passing years. Because for this man who was such a complete extrovert, withdrawal could only mean abdication, and old age could only be disaster.

This story is that of the Baron's last spring.

In front of the window looking out on to the garden, the back of the Baroness de Saint-Fursy and that of the Abbé Doucet made two disparate shadows – the one square, the other rounded – which expressed with surprising eloquence their respective characters.

'The end of the winter has been exceptionally humid,' said the Abbé. 'It's a real blessing for the pastureland. In my village they say: February rain is as good as manure. But it's true, everything is still very black, very wintry!'

The Baroness seemed to take a healthy delight in contradiction, and the Abbé Doucet was such an agreeable man to contradict!

'Yes, spring is late this year,' she affirmed. 'Well, that's a good thing! Look how neat and tidy that garden is. Everything is still orderly, just as we left it in the autumn. You see, Abbé, when you clean up a garden just before winter sets in, it's rather like laying out a corpse before you put it in its coffin!'

'I don't follow you,' protested the Abbé, who dreaded the flights of fancy in which the Baroness occasionally indulged.

'From one week to the next,' she continued imperturbably, 'the weeds will invade it, the grass will spill over on to the paths, the moles will wreck everything, and we shall have to chase out the swallows who every year insist on making their nests in the eaves and in the stable.'

'Certainly, but it's so beautiful when life breaks out again! Look at those first crocuses making that yellow patch under the plum tree. The presbytery garden contains nothing but white flowers.

First the narcissi, then the lilacs, then, naturally, the roses, *rosa mystica*, and finally and above all, the lilies, St Joseph's lilies, those dedicated to the very chaste husband of Mary, the flower of purity, of innocence, of virginity. . .'

As if discouraged by these remarks, the Baroness turned away from the window, leaving the Abbé to meditate on the garden, and went and sat down on the settee.

'Purity, innocence, virginity!' she sighed. 'It really takes a saintly man like you to see all that in the spring. Celestine! Celestine! Where is that tea? Poor Celestine, she's become so terribly slow. And deaf, of course. One has to shout oneself hoarse in order to get any service. I sometimes wonder whether you don't confuse saintliness with naïvety, and whether the young guttersnipes to whom you teach the catechism are not more wide-awake than you, Abbé! It's true that the young people of today . . . Even your Children of Mary. There is one of them . . . What's her name, now? Julienne . . . Adrienne . . . Donatienne . . .'

'Lucienne,' the Abbé murmured in a faint voice, without turning round.

'Lucienne, that's right. Then you know what I'm talking about. Well, anyone might have thought you were the only one not to have noticed that even her mother's dresses aren't big enough for her stomach, and that in a few weeks' time your Child of Mary . . .'

The Abbé left the window abruptly and marched over to her.

'If you please! You are talking of a scandal. Scandal is very often to be found in the unloving way in which we regard our neighbour. Yes, young Lucienne will be a mother this summer, and I know the man responsible for her condition. Well, I have decided not to notice anything. Because if I did notice, I would have to hunt him down, and even go to the police, and the consequences would be disastrous for several people, and above all for her.'

'You must forgive me,' the Baroness conceded, though without relenting. 'I am afraid there is never enough love in the way I regard people.'

'Then shut your eyes!' said the Abbé severely, with surprising authority.

Celestine's entry with the tea tray provided a diversion. Very clumsily, she put down the teapot, the cups, the sugar bowl, the milk, and the jug of hot water, and withdrew, aware of how much her awkwardness exasperated the Baroness.

'Poor old Celestine!' she said, shrugging her shoulders. 'Thirty years of good and faithful service in the same family. But she's of retiring age now.'

'What will become of her?' asked the Abbé. 'Would you like me to recommend her to the Mother Superior of the Hospice of Saint Catherine?'

'Later, perhaps. For the moment she's going to live with her daughter. We shall still send her her wages. It remains to be seen whether she can stay there. That would be the best solution. If she doesn't get on with her children, then I'll have another word with you about her. I am more worried about who is going to take her place.

'Have you someone in mind?'

'Absolutely no one. I have made preliminary enquiries at the employment agency run by the diocesan charitable organization. But though their girls are completely unskilled, their demands are extravagant. Ex-tra-va-gant! And then,' she added, in lower tones, 'there's my husband.'

Surprised and uneasy, the Abbé leaned over towards her.

'The Baron?' he asked, in a whisper.

'Alas, yes. I have to take his penchants into account.'

The Abbé opened his eyes wide.

'When you choose a maid, you have to take account of the Baron's penchants? But . . . what sort of penchants?'

The Baroness whispered in his ear:

'His penchant for maids . . .'

Even more astounded than shocked, the Abbé straightened up to his full – though short – height.

'I hope I don't understand!' he exclaimed, in normal tones.

'But in order to thwart his penchants!' the Baroness boomed indignantly. 'It is absolutely out of the question for me to have a pretty young girl on the premises. It only happened once, when was it . . . let me think . . . fourteen years ago. It was infernal! The house became a veritable bordello!'

'The Devil!' exclaimed the Abbé, relieved.

'I have put an advertisement in the local paper. I imagine that the applicants will begin to appear next week. Ah, here is my husband.'

The Baron had, in fact, just made a noisy entry into the room. He was wearing riding breeches, and playing with his whip.

'Good afternoon Abbé, good afternoon, my dearest!' he called out gaily. 'I have two wonderful pieces of news for you. In the first place, my little filly has just jumped the French hurdle without turning a hair. The rascal! She's been jibbing at it for the last week. Tomorrow I shall put her over the big ox-fence.'

'You'll end by breaking your neck,' the Baroness predicted. 'and it won't help matters when I'm pushing you in a wheelchair.'

'And what is the other wonderful piece of news?' enquired the Abbé, with polite curiosity.

The Baron had already forgotten.

'The other? Ah yes! Well, it's that spring is knocking at our door. There's something . . . something . . . in the air . . . Don't you think?'

'Something a little intoxicating, yes,' the Abbé rounded off. 'I was just now remarking that the meadow is studded with crocuses.'

The Baron had sunk back in an armchair with his cup of tea. He sang under his breath:

If every crocus had a bell
To hear ourselves we'd have to yell.

Then, with a crafty look at his wife:

'As I was coming in I heard you mention the word "applicant". Would it be indiscreet if I were to ask: An applicant for what post?'

The Baroness made a vain attempt at denial:

'*I* – I spoke of an applicant?'

'Yes, yes, yes – and would it not be a question of Celestine's successor?'

'Ah yes,' the Baroness conceded, 'I was speaking of the difficulty I was having in finding a girl with all the qualities that . . . that . . .'

The Baron cut her short. 'I,' he said, 'will tell you the two most important qualities she must have. She must be young, and she must be pretty!'

For some of the little jobs on which his noble occupations depended, the Baron had had an extension built on to his study, in which he kept a work-bench, his tools, and his technical library. Here he maintained his shotguns, his fencing blades, and his horses' saddles and harnesses. This particular day he was engaged in turning some cartridges when he heard his wife enter his office and sit down at his desk. Having donned his number 0 uniform, as he called it to himself – military cap, old fatigue jacket and corduroy trousers – he considered that he had cut himself off from family and domestic life, and he bitterly resented this incursion by the Baroness into a domain that was almost as closed to the feminine element as the military club. Nevertheless, he forced himself to remain in a good humour when her voice came through the open door.

'Guillaume, I'm preparing the guest list for our dinner in April. Will you come and go over it with me?'

'My dearest, I'm making some cartridges. But carry on; I'm listening.'

The Baroness's voice began to filter through the door.

'Deschamps, Conon d'Harcourt, Dorbec, Hermelin, Saint-Savin, de Cazère du Flox, Neuville . . . We'll invite them as usual, of course.'

'No problem, no. Only, the thing is, I'm not going to have enough wads. Gadzooks! – what an idiot I was not to have bought some from Ernest yesterday!'

The Baroness's voice was becoming impatient.

'Guillaume, don't swear, and concentrate on our dinner.'

'No dearest, yes dearest!'

'The Bretonniers are out. We can no longer receive them.'

'Really? – why not?'

'Oh come now, Guillaume, what are you thinking of? You know very well that there's talk of their building firm becoming bankrupt.'

'Pah, there's talk of it, yes.'

'I won't have dubious people in my house.'

'In any case, it has nothing to do with his wife . . . and she's charming.'

'If she spent less on her wardrobe, her husband might perhaps be a little less ruined!'

'Just a very little less, maybe. But from now on, a number 6 is incompatible with snipe for me. Number 6 is forbidden for snipe! It's efficient, oh yes, no doubt about that, it's efficient all right! But what slaughter! Last time, I picked one up and it was nothing but a rag, a tatter, a bit of lace. Huh, that's rather nice, a lace bird . . .'

'Not the Bretonniers, then,' the Baroness continued inexorably. 'It's a more delicate question when it comes to the Cernay du Locs. Should we or should we not invite them?'

'Oho! What's happening to the Cernay du Locs now?'

'My dear friend, sometimes one wonders what planet you live on. You seem unaware of the fact that that couple shows all the signs of having adopted a somewhat, er, peculiar moral code.'

'Well, well, well, well,' the Baron crooned, energetically turning the handle of his crimping machine. 'And may one know in what the peculiarity of this moral code consists?'

'You must surely have met that Flornoux, or Flournoy, who hasn't left them all winter.'

'No; but what about him?'

'It would appear that that gentleman, who seems to be on the most excellent terms with Anne du Loc, has been of the greatest aid to Cernay du Loc in obtaining certain contracts for his architect's office.'

'The Devil! And in return for this push in the right direction, the husband may well have shut his eyes a little. That *is* it?'

'That is what people are saying, at all events.'

The Baron suddenly stopped work, as if he had just had a revelation.

'Anne du Loc . . . A lover. Well I'll be damned! But that's incredible! But my dear, have you ever looked at Anne du Loc? Do you know how old she is?'

There was the sound of a chair being moved in the study, and all of a sudden the Baroness's silhouette appeared in the door-frame, imposing and tragic.

'Anne du Loc? She is ten years younger than I! You might weigh your words!'

Seeing his wife facing him, the Baron turned away from his work and made as if to stand up, without, however, doing so.

'Oh come now, Augustine, that has nothing to do with it. You surely aren't going to compare yourself with that . . . with that . . .'

'With that woman? And why not? Really, anyone might think that I belonged to a different sex!'

'In one sense,' declared the Baron, as if suddenly interested in the problem of the sex of his spouse, 'in one sense, that is so! You are not *a* woman, you are *the* woman who is my wife.'

'I do not greatly like that kind of nuance.'

'Ah, but it's an important nuance – it's even fundamental. In this nuance there is all the respect I have for you, for the Baroness Augustine de Saint-Fursy, née de Fontanes.'

'Respect, respect . . . I sometimes think that in a sense you exploit this feeling you have for me.'

'There there, my dear, let us avoid misunderstandings between us. It is a long time since you gave me to understand that . . . that certain aspects of conjugal life inconvenienced you, and that you wished my . . . nocturnal visits to become less frequent.'

'I have always thought that there was a time for everything and that, as one gets older, well, there are certain things that are no longer appropriate. I was far from suspecting that when I requested you, as you put it, to make your nocturnal visits less frequent, you would obey me with such docility, and that you would make your nocturnal visits to others.'

Embarrassed at remaining seated beneath his wife's tall silhouette, the Baron got to his feet, not foreseeing that he was going to make their conversation even more serious.

'Augustine, shall we both make an effort to be sincere?'

'Say straight out that I am insincere!'

'I say what I say. And I say this: those things you were speaking of, you must admit that for you they were *never* appropriate. I admit that for me, they have *never ceased* to be appropriate.'

'You are a satyr, Guillaume, you have to admit it!'

'I recognize very humbly that chastity is not my strong point.'

'But my goodness, you are no longer a young man!'

'That, my dear, is in the lap of the gods. So long as I am still fit and my eye is good, so long as I have both the appetite and the means with which to satisfy it . . .'

He said this with a sort of naïve conceit, drawing himself up to the full height his short stature permitted, passing a finger over his moustache, looking for a mirror that wasn't there.

'But what about me?' the Baroness protested vehemently. 'Is it by making a laughing stock of me in the eyes of the whole town with your . . . nocturnal visits, that you claim to respect me?'

'Ah, but we would need to know what kind of respect you want! No, no, we aren't going to revive yet again an argument that has neither rhyme nor reason.'

He seemed suddenly overcome by fatigue, and he looked round him as if bewildered.

'What I would like to tell you once again, Augustine, is that . . . Ah, it's so difficult. All of a sudden I'm twenty years old, I can't find the words, I'm stammering as if it were my first declaration of love. Well, the thing is, whatever happens, whatever I do, you are someone very important to me, Augustine. When I speak of respect, it isn't really the right word. But I haven't forgotten those words my mother pronounced when we went to ask her to approve our plan to marry. We were holding hands, we were so young, so confident, in the presence of that affable, lucid old lady. In our eyes it was she, rather than the curé and the mayor, who ought to bless our marriage. She said: "Little Augustine, I am happy that you wish to accept our Guillaume. Because you are a thousand times wiser and more intelligent than he. We entrust him to you, Augustine. Look after him, and be very patient and very indulgent with him . . ."'

'". . . and, for our little Woodcock," the Baroness continued, '"be the quietude, the strength, and the light he needs in order to live, to live *well.*"'

'That's right, she stressed the word *well,*' the Baron recalled.

There was a silence during which, moved and meditative, they looked at each other. Then the Baron abruptly sat down again at his work-bench and feverishly returned to his cartridges.

'By the way,' asked the Baroness, 'what is this shooting party you are preparing for? The winter is coming to an end, the season is over, is it not?'

'Now there, Augustine, it's my turn to ask you what planet you live on! Well, let me tell you that it has always been like this every year. At the end of the winter we celebrate the new year, and we fire a few shots to keep our hand in. Oh, naturally, we don't kill anything. It's more for the sound. It's a tradition.'

'In other words,' the Baroness concluded, 'you fête the close of the hunting and shooting season?'

'That's right, the close of the season.'

'Well, here's to the close of the hunting season!'

The Baroness withdrew into the study, leaving her husband absorbed in his cartridges. But after a moment he raised his head, a perplexed look in his eye, and passed his hand over his chin.

'But what does she mean with her close of the hunting season?' he murmured.

The advertisement of the post of maid of all work with a well-to-do retired couple which appeared in the local paper produced results within two days.

The Baroness held continuous court in her salon, seated at a table piled high with slips of paper. 'You look like a fortune-teller,' the Baron observed sourly; he was in a bad mood. Each time she heard the doorbell, whose insistent or timid ring constituted a preliminary piece of information, she put on her spectacles while poor Celestine went to open the door. After a few minutes' psychological wait, the applicant was shown in. There was a preliminary silent, visual examination directed towards the candidate's appearance and physical characteristics.

The Baroness was torn between two contradictory exigencies. She wasn't perverse enough to seek out ugliness per se. Like everyone else, she would have preferred to be served by a comely girl who was not too disagreeable to look at. But the Baron must not be tempted – a categorical imperative that took precedence. So she dreamed of a creature who was not really ugly, but vapid, colourless, insipid, unequivocal. Or of a woman who was *bifrons* – pretty and graceful in the eyes of her mistress, but downright repugnant in those of her master. An unrealizable dream, as was proved by the procession of applicants whom the circumstances rendered either stupid and paralysed with shyness, or arrogant and pretentious.

As for the Baron, he had finally decamped, in order not to have to be present any longer at an operation he felt was directed against him. Ah, if *he* had only been in charge of engaging 'the new one'! It wouldn't have taken long, in this lovely Normandy spring! And as he went up the rue du Pont-Neuf towards the

Champ du Roi, the piquant and adorable scene of the entrance examination came to life like a film in his imagination. 'There, there, come closer, don't be afraid, my child. That little forehead, that little nose, that little chin, yes yes, not bad. And that chest, my goodness, it could be a little higher, a little more rounded, more welcoming. And the waist, the waist, the waist, my two hands could almost join round it, what am I saying, they *do* join round it! And now, my little bird, step back, back a little farther, show me your legs, more than that, come now, good Lord!, when we have such pretty legs we aren't afraid to show them.' Then, suddenly coming down to earth, he began to envy the people who had lived in the days of the slave markets.

Apropos of films, huge posters were in fact advertising the one being shown at the Rex that week: *Bluebeard*, with Pierre Brasseur and Cécile Aubry. Pierre Brasseur? Pah, he thought. A spineless man, a bogus tough guy, a loud-mouth, but no character. Just look at his chin. A receding chin, a cowardly chin that destined him to play nothing but half-witted roles. Until the day when he had the brilliant idea of growing a beard. It's always the same: the ornament is there to hide the flaw. It's like horses with swan necks that painters admire so much but which in actual fact are the sign of a broken-winded animal.

But Cécile Aubry . . . Heh heh! A little small, true, her head a little too big for her body, her face with the sulky expression of a Pekingese. But all the same, all the same – what a pretty little slip of a girl, in this flighty spring! That was the type he would have liked to see engaged as a maid of all work at his place. A maid of *all* work, really? Cécile Aubry, delightful at all work, exquisite at all work! And the Baron imagined Cécile – oh yes, you always call maids by their first name – waltzing around in his office, feather duster in hand, laughing merrily as he chased her with his caresses that she both provoked and eluded.

When he arrived home two hours later, the act had been consummated. He discovered this when he just avoided bumping into a big wicker trunk cluttering up the hall. The new maid came from Pré-en-Pail, a little village twenty-four kilometres away, on the road to Mayenne. She was fifty years old, had the shadow of a moustache, the physique of a furniture remover, and her name was Eugénie.

At first, Eugénie gave the Baroness every satisfaction. With her hefty build she could move even the heaviest furniture with ease. And in any case, the Baroness took advantage of her arrival to embark on one of those vast spring-cleaning enterprises that turned the house upside down and inside out, and caused the Baron infinite exasperation. This was really the moment when the women of the house took possession of its space and left him no choice but to seek safety in flight. And in these circumstances, Eugénie turned out to be even more fearsome than poor Celestine. As the Baron discovered to his cost, the day she accidentally sent him flying while she was walking backwards with a chest of drawers wedged on her stomach.

In the eyes of the Baroness, Eugénie had another quality. She was laconic, as was only right and proper for people of her station, yet she knew how to listen and to indicate her attention and approbation by just the right number of words. Their dialogues rested on the complicity of women vis-à-vis men, but she always knew how to re-establish the social gulf that separated her from her mistress by claiming to be less experienced than she in these delicate matters.

That morning she was got up like a real domestic soldier: a turban round her head, swathed in an apron, her sleeves rolled up, with the regulation panoply of brooms, feather dusters, ceiling brushes and polishing brushes. The Baroness followed her, preceded her, directing her manoeuvres.

'In the winter,' said the Baroness, 'one doesn't see the dust. But the moment the first ray of sunlight appears, one realizes how much work there is to be done.'

'Yes Madame,' Eugénie agreed.

'I want my house to be impeccable. Yet I am not fanatical about cleanliness. Certainly I would not tolerate bits of fluff under the beds. But my grandmother insisted on her maid removing the dust from the grooves between the floorboards with a hairpin. I don't go as far as that.'

'No, Madame.'

'You are not to touch the frames, the bibelots, or the porcelains. I see to them.'

'Yes, Madame.'

'My husband's study is somewhat complicated. No one must

enter it when he is there, it disturbs him. And even when he isn't there, if one went by what he says, no one would set foot in it either. Everything must be cleaned without him being aware of it.'

'Yes, Madame.'

'When I was a little girl, the Mother Superior of my convent school used to say: "A clean, well-kept house is the reflection of a soul dedicated to the holy angels." '

It was at this moment that Eugénie moved a stack of files and sent a cascade of erotic photos and pornographic magazines flying all over the carpet.

'That filthy stuff again!' exclaimed the Baroness. 'I knew he was hiding it somewhere!'

She picked them up, piled them up again, and gave them a disgusted glance.

'All that naked flesh flaunted – it is so ugly!'

'It certainly is,' agreed Eugénie, leaning over her shoulder.

'And so boring! It is only men, with their dirty male desires, who can see anything in it.'

'Ah yes, talk of dirty, men certainly are dirty!'

'If you please, Eugénie! It is a question of the Baron!'

'Excuse me, Madame.'

'Men are as they are,' the Baroness argued. 'So be it. But what I cannot understand is the creatures who lend themselves to their caprices.'

'Maybe it's for the money,' Eugénie ventured.

'For the money? That would be the lesser evil. But I doubt it. The trouble is that there are some who are vicious enough to like it, you know.'

'Only too true, alas!'

The Baroness was on her feet again and she took a few steps towards the mantelpiece, which was covered with equestrian trophies.

'When I became a boarder at the convent school run by the Sisters of the Annunciation,' she said dreamily, with a vague smile, 'I was nine years old. There were bathrooms. Four bathrooms for the whole school. Each girl was allowed to take a bath once a week. Near the bath-tub there hung a sort of cape made of unbleached linen. It was to allow us to undress, wash, and dress again, without seeing our own bodies. The first time, I didn't know what it was for. I washed, without putting it on, without anything. When the supervisor noticed I hadn't veiled myself, do you know what she said?'

'No, Madame.'

'She said: "What, my child, you stripped naked in full daylight! Don't you know, then, that your guardian angel is a young man?"'

'Goodness me! I'd never thought of that.'

'Nor had I, Eugénie,' the Baroness concluded. 'But since then, I have never stopped thinking of it. Yes, I have never stopped thinking of that very gentle, very pure, very chaste young man who is ever by my side, like a faithful companion, an ideal friend . . .'

As the Baroness had rightly said to the Abbé Doucet, spring, with its germinations and burgeonings, was a season of troubles and turbulence. Barely had Eugénie completed the spring-cleaning, barely had she laid down the arms – her brooms, feather dusters, ceiling and polishing brushes – of her panoply, barely was her turban unwound and her apron ungirded, than she received a telegram from Pré-en-Pail. Her sister was about to be confined and her seven children couldn't be left in the house alone, even though Mariette, the eldest, was eighteen.

Eugénie explained the situation to the Baroness. The sister in question was hopeless. What was more, she had married a drunkard who was no good at anything except fathering children. As for Mariette, she was a spoiled, scatter-brained girl who spent all her time dolling herself up or reading true love stories, it was no use relying on her. In short, Eugénie asked for twenty-four hours off, to go and size up the situation on the spot.

The twenty-four hours went by, and became thirty-six, forty-eight hours. Finally, on the evening of the second day, when the Baroness was out – *someone* had to do the shopping – the doorbell rang. The Baron called his wife and perceived with irritation that she wasn't there. Firmly decided not to move, he sank back into his armchair and held up a newspaper between the outside world and himself. Then the doorbell rang again, and this time its sound was imperious, intolerable, and almost threatening. The Baron got up and ran into the hall, all set to heap deserved insults on the lummox. He opened the door violently, and immediately retreated as if bedazzled. Whom did he see before him? Cécile

Aubry, in the flesh. He was flabbergasted, he couldn't believe his eyes. It was true, though, it really was that obstinate, puerile little face under the enormous mass of hair, with its sulky lips, its insolent green eyes, with the addition of a country awkwardness and the outrageous odour of a cheap perfume that smelled of the nearby Norman earth.

'I'd like to see the Baroness de Saint-Fursy,' said she forthwith.

'That's me . . . Well, that's to say, I am the Baron de Saint-Fursy. My wife is out for the moment.'

'Oh, good,' said the girl, with a sigh of relief.

Then she gave the Baron a big smile, entered without being invited, and cast a circular, possessive glance around the hall.

'Well, the thing is,' she said, 'I'm Mariette, Madame Eugénie's niece. My aunt can't come back yet. No. My mother's still ill. In hospital. The birth of the last one, you understand. He'd have done better to stay where he was. Especially as in the village, there's no one to lend a hand. So I reckoned that to help you out, I could come and stand in for her in the meantime.'

'You? Replace Eugénie? Well well . . . but why not?'

The Baron had regained all his assurance, and, confronted with this cascade of miracles, he had once again become the Woodcock.

'At least that would make a change for us. But . . . Did Eugénie send you?'

'Well, er . . . yes and no. I suggested it. She shrugged. She said I certainly wouldn't suit you.'

'Goodness, what an idea!'

'Yes, isn't it? And from my point of view, you know, life at Pré! Eighteen years it's lasted!'

'Eighteen years?' The Baron was astonished. 'But where were you before that?'

'Before that? I wasn't born!'

'Ah, so that's why!'

'I jumped at the opportunity. I came away without saying anything. I just left a note on the kitchen table that I'd gone to help the Baroness.'

'Excellent, excellent.'

'But do you think Madame's going to want me?'

'Certainly. Well, certainly not. But I'm the one who decides here, aren't I? Then that's settled, it's agreed, your appointment is guaranteed. Bring your bag, I'll show you to your quarters. Or rather, no, I'll show you round the house first. This is my study. They always insist on cleaning it. They move my papers and then I can't find anything. That, yes, that's a photo of my father, General de Saint-Fursy. This one is me as a lieutenant. I was twenty.'

Mariette had grabbed hold of the photograph.

'Oh, how Monsieur has changed! Well I never! I'd never have recognized him. Wasn't he young and fresh-looking!'

'Well, yes, naturally, at that age.'

'How years change people!'

'All right, all right, that's enough.'

'Yes but you know,' Mariette hastened to add, 'I think you're better-looking now.'

'That's kind.'

'What I think, a man that's too young, he isn't a man.'

'That's exactly what I think, too. Bravo, bravo. Come on, we go back through the hall to get to the dining room.'

He had gallantly stepped aside to let her pass, but he nearly bumped into her because she had stopped short in front of a tall, sombre silhouette. In his intoxication, the Baron had almost forgotten his wife.

'Ah, good evening my dearest,' he said hurriedly. 'This is Mariette. Her aunt Eugénie still can't leave her mother. So she has come to help us. That's kind, isn't it?'

'Very kind,' the Baroness agreed, with a glacial air.

'And then, it'll make a change to have someone young in the house, don't you think?'

'Thank you very much, Guillaume.'

'But my dearest, I wasn't thinking about you! I was thinking . . . well, I was thinking about Eugénie.'

'And you were also perhaps thinking a little about yourself?'

'About myself?'

Allowing the two women to precede him, the Baron stopped in front of a mirror.

'Thinking about myself?' he murmured. 'Change. Get young. Become the twenty-year-old lieutenant again? Why not?'

During the following weeks, the Baron adroitly exploited this first and facile success that Chance had offered him. His task was all the easier in that Mariette, treated with a kind of sacred horror by the Baroness and constantly menaced by the return of Eugénie, had no other refuge than him. No doubt the Baroness would have been far better advised not to have thrown the girl totally on to her husband's side, and she may well have realized this. But her feelings toward 'that little slut' were too strong for her even to begin to think of bringing a little psychology into play.

The Woodcock, on the other hand, had kept his wits about him sufficiently to be able at least to keep up appearances. Obviously, Mariette often took much longer than necessary when she went shopping and, as if by chance, the Baron was always out at the same time. Nevertheless, his advances remained discreet, when they didn't explode in his wife's face like a time bomb. This was what happened after he had taken the young country girl to Roger, the only hairdresser in the region who was also a beautician, with, as model, the photograph of Cécile Aubry in *Bluebeard*. The Baroness was staggered when she saw this dream creature arrive at her house, manicured, made up, her hair styled and lacquered, and she immediately understood who had been the *deus ex machina* of this metamorphosis.

Nevertheless, one day she resolved to muster enough wisdom and patience to have a serious and affectionate talk with her husband. The best moment would be after dinner, when Mariette, after a brief *Bonsoir M'sieur Dame*, had withdrawn. She waited, then, until the door on the first floor had closed, and then opened her mouth to start her attack on the Baron, who was sitting opposite her reading his paper, his scrawny thighs nervously crossed. Whereupon the cacophonous strains of a jazz record began to erupt from Mariette's room and invade the whole house.

'What on earth is that?' the Baroness exclaimed.

'New Orleans jazz,' replied the Baron, without raising his eyes from his paper.

'I beg your pardon?'

'New-Orleans-jazz,' the Baron repeated more slowly, and with an even more impeccable Oxford accent.

'Is that another of your inventions?'

'Do you really think the child needs my help to buy a record player and some records? They belong more to her generation than to mine.'

'Yes, I *do* really think so!' she exploded. 'She needs you or your money! No no, really, I can stand it no longer! I can stand it no longer!' she repeated as she left the room, a handkerchief pressed to her lips.

Nibbling at his moustache, the Baron let a moment go by. Then he too stood up and took a step in the direction of his wife's room. He owed her at least that. She was his wife. The priest who had married them had entrusted her to him for life. Nevertheless he stopped short, and took a couple of steps in the direction from which the music was coming. Mariette. Cécile Aubry. Their fresh little bodies mixed up in this musk-scented spring. He went back to his armchair. Sat down again. Picked up his newspaper. The volume of the music increased. They had chosen the recorder and the records together. Was that music really intended to be listened to alone in a celibate bedroom? He threw his paper down. Stood up. Then, with furious strides, he went and took his hat off the hook, threw his loden cape over his shoulders and went out, deliberately slamming the door for everyone to hear.

Why did the Woodcock finally decide on flight? Certainly because, rather than mere principles, he had an acute sense of what was and what was not elegant, and to deceive the Baroness on her own premises, almost in her presence, could be reconciled only with great difficulty with the honour that constituted half the motto of the First Cavalry Regiment: HONNEUR ET PATRIE. And yet he had already done that, yes, there *had* been occasions when he had carried his extramarital affairs so far as to consummate them under his own roof. Hence, there must be something else, and it was the feeling, which was quite new to him, that with Mariette it was a much more serious affair than with the others, it was a rather pathetic presentiment that it was the conclusion, the finale, the sort of farewell performance that, whatever the cost, he must not miss. It was advisable, then, not to rush things, and to have the courage, the application, and the tact necessary to end with a flourish the amorous career of a man who all his life had been far more seduced than vulgarly seducing.

The Baroness, on the other hand, had decided to act, with all the assurance bestowed by the knowledge that her prerogative coincided with the general good. For she had devised a theory about Mariette, according to which this innocent and rather stupid country girl was becoming rapidly and seriously perverted by the wicked ways of the town. She needed no further proof than the metamorphosis of the girl who, in the space of a few days, had developed in the most dubious direction.

And yet Mariette remained totally submissive and respectful towards the Baroness, and she made not the slightest objection when the latter informed her of her decision to send her back to Pré-en-Pail, without awaiting Eugénie's return.

'But you know, Mariette,' she added, mellowed by so total a victory, 'I am still extremely grateful to you for having come to my aid while Eugénie was helping your mother. Only, you see, it seems to me that the atmosphere of the town is detrimental to you. Everyone in his or her place, isn't that so? When one is born in the countryside, it is preferable to remain there.'

'Too true,' mumbled Mariette, swaying her hips.

'And what do you think you will do, at Pré-en-Pail?' continued the Baroness, with the greatest indifference.

'Well . . . pff! . . . Milk the cows, plant beans, pick potatoes – seeing that I'm a peasant girl.'

The Baron, who had just come in, felt that both women were taking this a bit far.

'I hope, Mariette,' he added, in a light-hearted, sophisticated tone of voice, 'that you also know how to plough, and to fell trees?'

'Guillaume, you are not amusing,' the Baroness said curtly.

But before she left, she gave Mariette a rattle for her baby brother and a little crucifix on a chain for herself. She insisted on driving her to the station and seeing her into her carriage, while the Baron had taken out his old Panhard to go and look at a horse at the Carrouges stud farm.

The train's first stop was Saint-Denis-sur-Sarthon, where Mariette got out with her suitcase. The Baron's old Panhard was parked outside the station. There were laughs and embraces. Then they returned to Alençon. The Baron installed his inamorata in a delightful little apartment that he had just rented in the Boulevard of the First Cavalry Regiment.

There followed three days of euphoria, a fragile, light-weight gangway thrown over abysses of misunderstanding. For while the Baroness never stopped congratulating herself on having managed to dispose of Mariette with such ease, the Baron was basking in the joy of having brought her back. After a while, however, the Baron's air of radiant happiness began to intrigue the Baroness. No matter how hard he tried to concentrate on dark thoughts that would cast a shadow over his face, and to invent equestrian successes to justify the sudden fits of good humour that escaped him willy-nilly, the Baroness began to look for ways to fathom the mystery. Eugénie's return finally convinced her that the Mariette affair was by no means so much in the past as she had believed, for, on hearing of her niece's return to Pré-en-Pail, Eugénie opened her eyes wide. No, the girl hadn't been seen in the village for the last ten days. Where was she, then? The Baron's frisky air answered the question. And in any case, a personality as well known as the Baron de Saint-Fursy would never have been able to dissimulate his second life for long from the restricted circle of Alençon society. The rumour spread, slowly but surely, that he was keeping a young female in a delightful little love nest. He was well liked. At all events he was more popular than the Baroness, who was considered arrogant and self-serving. People regarded him with sympathetic and amused indulgence. The Baroness, on the other hand, was soon surrounded by a circle of right-thinking acquaintances whose scandalized expressions and pitying remarks wounded her cruelly. This was not the Baron's first escapade. But it was the first time he had openly set up as an adulterer.

Naturally, the Baroness confided her misfortune to her spiritual adviser. Once again the Abbé Doucet recommended resignation. She must take the Baron's age into account. He was reaching the stage when the passions are all the more imperious in that they have only a short time left in which to flourish. This flare-up was more intense than the others because it would no doubt be the last. The very fact that the culprit had for the first time lost all sense of proportion proved that he was undergoing the Devil's ultimate assault. It was only a matter of a very short time, and the calm, serene light of old age would be upon him.

'Shut your eyes,' the Abbé repeated, like a litany. 'Shut your eyes. When you reopen them, the storm will have passed.'

Shut her eyes? This advice outraged both the conscience and the pride of the Baroness, who saw in it both complacency and humiliation. And how was she to put up with the soothing hypocrisy that coagulated around her every time she mixed with the bourgeoisie of Alençon? For a moment she thought of going away. She owned an old seaside villa at Donville. Why should she not go and spend the summer months there, leaving Eugénie in charge of her Alençon residence? But to her mind, this solution too involved abdication, rout, and desertion of duty. No, she would stay, and in spite of the Abbé's exhortations she would keep her eyes wide open on to the truth, however cruel it might be.

Shut her eyes. If the conscience of the Baroness de Saint-Fursy rejected this too facile recommendation, it might still have been thought that someone in her had heard it and put it into practice without further ado. Someone on a deeper and more elementary level than her conscience. For in fact one evening, coming home in an extremely good humour, the Baron found his wife dabbing at her eyes with a piece of gauze moistened with eye lotion. He was taken aback and politely showed his concern.

'It's nothing,' she said. 'Probably an allergy caused by all the pollen there is in the air at this time of year.'

'Ah yes,' he exclaimed, 'the spring! Pollen! Pollen gives some people asthma. But you – it makes your eyes ache. It has a very different effect on other people!'

But he suddenly fell silent and became serious when his wife turned towards him and he saw tears streaming down her contorted face from two dead eyes.

Two days later she began to wear a pair of spectacles with grey lenses that made her look old, poor, and pathetic. Then she got into the habit of having all the shutters in the house closed, thus obliging everyone to live with her in a lugubrious twilight.

'These eyes of mine!' she complained. 'I can no longer stand anything but filtered light, and that only for a few minutes a day.'

Next, she changed her grey lenses for black ones. She seemed to be possessed by a calm, patient demon who hated the light and who was gradually dismissing it from her life.

At first the Baron took advantage of this apparent retreat of his wife. Now Mariette could venture out into the town without being afraid of meeting her former employer. Certainly, there was still the risk that she would one day find herself face to face with her aunt. But then, at least, it was likely that there would merely be a private family discussion, whose echoes would not necessarily reach the Baroness's ears. As for the Woodcock, he had never been so happy. Not only was Mariette the most delightful little mistress he had ever had; she also took on the role of the child who had been refused him. He had her taught to drive. He ordered her a pair of riding breeches which would adorably mould her firm, rounded little crupper. He dreamed of a holiday in Nice or Venice, of a hunting costume and a charming little gun for the opening of the shooting season. He even began to teach her English. But what delighted him most was the whispered chorus of flattering allusions that surrounded him like sonorous incense at the club, the mess, the riding school, and the fencing academy. The rumours increased his pleasure tenfold.

All this made it easier for him to bear the poisoned, funereal atmosphere that the Baroness, vigorously seconded by Eugénie, maintained in the house. The situation seemed to be moving towards an inevitable estrangement. What happened was the opposite.

It was very fine, that day, and the Baron went home in sprightly mood. The windows on the ground floor were open, but the shutters were half-closed, following the Baroness's instructions. As he approached, the Baron stopped humming to himself and hazarded a jocular glance through the shutters of the small salon. He could see the Baroness sitting at her work table with a book in her hand. Hearing some slight sound, no doubt, she closed the book, hid it in her sewing basket, stood up, and left the room.

The Baron laughed silently at having caught his wife *in flagrante delicto*, in the inadmissable process of reading. 'Well well,' he thought, 'so she's started again. And high time too!' He crept into the small salon on tiptoe, went up to the table, extracted the book from the basket and – still laughing – took it over to the window to read it.

His smile froze. He couldn't understand a thing. Little raised dots arranged in squares replaced the words. He still didn't understand, but a terrible suspicion came over him. He rushed out into the corridor, calling his wife. He finally found her in their bedroom. She formed a tall, sombre silhouette against a white wall adorned with a crucifix.

'Ah, here you are at last! What on earth is this?'

He put the book into her hands. The Baroness sat down, opened the book, and hid her face in it as if she was going to cry.

'I so wished you wouldn't discover the truth! Well – not until you had to.'

'What truth? What are you doing with this book?'

'I am learning to read. The Braille alphabet. For the blind.'

'For the blind? But you're not blind!'

'Not entirely, not yet. I still have two-tenths of the sight in my left eye, and one-tenth in the right. In less than a month it will all be gone. Pitch black. My doctor is categorical. You see, then, that I must waste no time in learning Braille! For it does make it easier if one can still see a little.'

The Baron was shattered. His goodness, his rectitude, his sense of honour, his fear of the way he would be judged by the mess, the riding school, and the fencing academy, all coalesced to make the situation shattering.

'But it's insane, it's incredible,' he stammered. 'And I hadn't the slightest idea! Your glasses, your eye drops, the darkness in which you enclosed yourself. Confounded idiot! Ignoble egoist! And all that time . . . My goodness, but I was purposely refusing to understand! Ah, there really are some days when one detests oneself!'

'No no, Guillaume, it was because I was hiding it. You understand – I am ashamed of this horrible infirmity which will make me a burden on everybody.'

'Blind! I simply can't believe it. But what does the doctor say?'

'I went to consult our old friend Dr Girard, first. Then I saw two specialists. Naturally, they tried to keep the facts from me. But really! Of course I realized the truth. All their comforting words are contradicted by the cruel truth: my sight is diminishing daily, and already I can barely see at all.'

The Baron was never at a total loss when faced with the blows of fate. He was not the man to go in for renunciation, for resignation. He straightened up, he pulled himself together, he made up his mind. It was once again the Woodcock who spoke:

'Augustine, we shall fight this together. It's all over. I shall never leave you again. I shall take you by the hand, like this, and we shall walk gently together towards a cure, towards the light.'

He took her in his arms and cradled her.

'My Titine, we shall find one another again, as we did before, just the two of us, we shall be happy again. Do you remember, when we were young, how I used to infuriate you by singing, to the tune of *Come, Poupoule*: "Come, Titine, come, Titine, come!"'

The Baroness abandoned herself to her husband's arms. She clung to him, she smiled through her tears.

'You will never be serious, Guillaume!' she reproached him tenderly.

No, one does not deceive a blind person. One does not take advantage of the cecity of one's spouse. The very next day, the Baron employed just as much zeal in destroying his happiness as he had in constructing it. He saw Mariette once more, but only to bid her adieu. He would continue to pay the rent of her little apartment. He would contribute to her living expenses until she found a job – for it never occurred to him that instead of finding work she might find another protector. But they would never see each other again. She wept copiously. He managed to remain dry-eyed. But it was with a broken heart that he left for ever the love nest of his last spring.

During the following weeks he showed all the signs of touching devotion to the sick woman. He cut up her meat. He read aloud to her. He took her for leisurely walks on his arm, pointing out any obstacles, and naming their acquaintances whom they were passing or approaching. The whole of Alençon was edified.

The Baroness's life was one of unadulterated bliss. She stopped shutting herself up in the darkness for days on end. More and more frequently she left off her dark glasses. Sometimes she even surprised herself leafing through a newspaper or opening a book. Indeed, it seemed as if she was slowly reascending the slope from the nadir into which her unhappiness had plunged her.

One day she sent for the Abbé Doucet with the greatest urgency, and the moment he arrived she closeted herself with him.

'I asked you to come because I have something to say to you. Something serious,' she began, without preamble.

'Something serious, my goodness! I hope no new misfortune . . .'

'No – it is even rather a piece of good fortune. A serious, a very serious piece of good fortune.'

Then she turned to face him, and abruptly took off her dark glasses. After which, puckering up her eyes, she stared at him.

The Abbé stared back at her.

'No . . . I . . . How strange!' he stammered. 'You do not have the look of a blind person. What life there is in your eyes!'

'I can see with them Abbé! I am no longer blind!' she exclaimed.

'Lord! – it's a miracle! It's the reward for your resignation, for the care the Baron has taken of you – and for my prayers, too! But since when . . .'

'At first, I was living a kind of vague twilight, which was occasionally shot through by rays of light that lasted only a moment. And which moments were they? Those when I felt that my Guillaume was particularly close to me. And then, very gradually, the day dawned.'

'So what caused – or at least accelerated – your cure. . .'

'Yes, what I am saying would provoke a smile in anyone other than you, it is so very . . . edifying.'

'Edifying? It's true, though, the edifying does make people laugh these days, it even frightens them, it frightens them more than does scandal. Strange times!'

'Well, Abbé, you will be able to recount our story to your flock, for I have never heard one that is more wonderful. My cure has but one name – one first name, even. And that first name – is Guillaume.'

'The Baron?'

'Yes, my husband. And to think that we will have to keep it secret in order not to make people laugh!'

'It's wonderful! I am overjoyed to have experienced this in the course of my humble ministry! What did the Baron think when you told him the marvellous news?'

'Guillaume? But he knows nothing of it! You are the first to whom I have confessed my cure. I am speaking of it, am I not, as if it were an evil deed!'

'But the Baron must be told immediately,' said the Abbé

impatiently. 'Would you like . . .'

'No, anything but that! We must not be too hasty. It is not so simple.'

'I don't follow you.'

'Just think. Guillaume has a liaison with that creature. I fall ill . . . well, I lose my sight. He breaks with her and devotes himself to me. A few weeks later I recover my sight.'

'What a marvel!'

'Precisely. What I am telling you is very wonderful and perfectly true. But is it not a little too wonderful to be *believable*?'

'The Baron cannot deny the facts.'

'What facts? For him, could it not be a fact that he has been hoaxed? I cannot bear the idea that he may consider my illness to have been feigned. Not everyone believes, as you do, in miracles.'

'And yet you will have to . . .'

'And there is another point of view. It was only my infirmity that removed Guillaume from the clutches of that creature. Should we not fear that my cure might cause him to relapse into his vice? I need your advice, Abbé, and perhaps even your complicity.'

'This does indeed give one food for thought. Hence, for the Baron's own good, it might be necessary to conceal your cure for the time being. To stretch the truth a little in this way would, I think, be justified by the excellence of our intentions.'

'It is not merely a question of dealing with him in the correct fashion. But also of preparing him progressively for the good news of my cure.'

'Of gaining time, in short; no more than that.'

'The time necessary for him to forget his creature.'

'So that it would be less a lie, than a truth kept in abeyance – postponed, gradually revealed.'

'Naturally, however, no one must suspect the truth. In any case, I have spoken of it only to you, and I know I can rely on your discretion.'

'You can, my child. The secrets of the confessional have accustomed us priests to hold our tongues. Yes indeed, for it would be a disaster if the Baron were to learn from a third party that you are no longer blind! And some people are so garrulous!'

'Worse – some people are so malevolent!' the Baroness added.

The Baroness and the Abbé may well have planned a progressive revelation of the truth. Alas, the truth does not always allow itself to be tamed. It erupted one fine Sunday afternoon on the Demi-Lune Promenade with brutal indiscretion.

During the summer months, a walk along this Promenade constitutes one of Alençon's sacred rites. Everyone in polite society is to be seen there, strolling arm in arm up and down an elm-lined avenue, greeting one another, ignoring one another, halting for very precisely measured moments, according to the subtle network of social relations and precedences. The Saint-Fursys had occupied a privileged place on this chess board since the Baron had fully assumed his obligations as the husband of a gravely handicapped lady. They were surrounded by an aura of sympathetic respect. Why did the drama have to occur in these privileged circumstances?

The Baron nearly stopped short when he saw something unusual, something extraordinary, under the trees – or rather, *someone*, a young woman. Mariette, yes, looking prettier and more spring-like than ever. But that was not all. The little country lass from Pré-en-Pail had a companion. No one ever walks alone on the Demi-Lune. She was hanging on to the arm of a man, a young man. And how they suited each other, with their common youth, and how happy they looked!

The vision had lasted no more than a moment, but the Baron had registered the shock so acutely that it was impossible for his wife, pressed so tightly against him, not to have noticed anything. But in that case, why did she not question him, she who never stopped asking him about everyone they met? He looked up at her in dismay. And what he saw staggered him even more than the apparition of Mariette in the midst of the burgers of Alençon: the Baroness was smiling. She was not smiling at anyone in particular, like all the rest of the people meeting and greeting one another. It was a private smile, irrepressible, no doubt, and it was a smile that was spreading all over her dark-spectacled face, broadening, and – something unheard-of for so long – she laughed, she couldn't restrain a silvery, ironic little laugh.

Why the smile, why the laugh? And in the first place, why had she asked no questions when she felt her husband tremble all over at her side? Why? Because she had seen the same thing as he –

Mariette on the arm of a young man – Because she could in fact see as well as he!

The Baron had received a double shock. In accordance with his temperament, he reacted immediately. He turned to face his wife, scrutinized her for a moment, and then, with an abrupt gesture, he snatched off her glasses and let them fall to the ground.

'Madame,' he said, in a colourless voice, 'I have just been twice wounded. By you and by someone else. In so far as you are concerned, I intend to get to the bottom of the matter. And I have a strong suspicion that you are quite capable of going home without my aid.'

And he departed with rapid strides.

Once home, he telephoned Dr Girard. The doctor gave him the name and address of an ophthalmologist, and then some information about a specialist in psychosomatic medicine, in Paris. It was the latter whom the Baron went to see the very next morning, on the advice of Dr Girard.

He detested Paris, where he had not in fact set foot for several years. Dr Stirling's waiting room put the finishing touches to his sense of disquiet, with its amorphous furniture and its abstract paintings. He sank into an armchair with the feeling of having allowed himself to be swallowed whole by a gigantic jellyfish. He could still just manage to reach up to a low table covered with magazines. He pulled one down on to his knees. Its title jumped up at his face like a cobra: *Conversion Hysteria and Organic Neuroses*. He pushed it away in disgust. Finally a nurse came and invited him into the doctor's room. He was a ridiculously spindly man, a mere boy, the Baron thought. His long hair, and minute, snub nose that had great difficulty in supporting a pair of enormous spectacles, were the last straw. 'I'll wager he stammers,' thought the Baron.

'What may I do for you?'

No, he doesn't stammer, the Baron observed, disappointed.

'May I introduce myself. Colonel Guillaume de Saint-Fursy. I have come to see you about my wife, who is your patient,' he explained.

'Madame de Saint-Fursy?'

'Obviously!'

The doctor switched on an automatic filing system, and placed the ejected file in front of him.

'Madame Augustine de Saint-Fursy,' he mumbled. Then, after a few unintelligible phrases that he read very quickly: 'That's right. Your family doctor sent her to a colleague, an ophthalmologist, and he advised her to come to me. What exactly do you want?'

'Well, it's very simple, isn't it,' said the Baron with some animation, relieved to be able to return to his preoccupation. 'My wife was blind. At least, I believed she was. Well – she made me believe she was. And then, all of a sudden, she's cured, she can see as well as you or I. The question I asked myself, then, and that I am asking you, is very simple: My wife – is she or is she not a fraud?'

'In the first place, may I ask you to sit down?'

'To sit down?'

'Yes. Because, you see, while your question is indeed simple, the answer is not.'

Scowling, the Baron agreed to sit down.

'What it comes down to,' the doctor continued, 'is that Madame de Saint-Fursy was suffering from a visual disorder which might have resulted in total blindness. Naturally, she started by consulting your family doctor, who, equally naturally, sent her to an ophthalmological specialist.'

'And all this without my knowledge,' protested the Baron.

'What followed, then, was that the ophthalmologist proceeded, with all necessary care and with the help of the most advanced instruments, to an examination of Madame de Saint-Fursy's eyes. And what did he find?'

'Yes, what did he find?'

'Nothing. He found nothing. Anatomically and physiologically, Madame de Saint-Fursy's eyes, optic nerve and pineal body were in perfect order.'

'Then she's a fraud,' the Baron concluded.

'Not so fast! What did the ophthalmologist do? Realizing that he was confronted with a case that went beyond the bounds of his speciality, he sent his patient to a specialist in psychosomatic medicine – myself. I repeated the examinations, and I finally arrived at the same conclusions as my colleague.'

'My wife's eyes are perfectly healthy – therefore her blindness is simulated. There's no escaping that fact.'

'Listen to me,' the doctor went on patiently. 'Let me take an extreme example, which, fortunately, has no connection with Madame de Saint-Fursy's case. Every day, in psychiatric hospitals, schizophrenics die. Death occurs after a long and protracted disintegration of the personality of the subject. Well, when an autopsy is performed on a man who has died of schizophrenia, what is found? Nothing! According to all the medical rules, the corpse is that of a man in perfect health.'

'That's because they didn't look properly!' the Baron concluded. 'And in any case, you said yourself that that example of schizo . . . schizo . . .'

'. . . phrenia . . .'

'. . . phrenia, fortunately had no connection with my wife's case.'

'Yes and no. The connection is that there are some illnesses whose effect is obviously physiological – the death of the schizophrenic, Madame de Saint-Fursy's blindness – but whose cause is psychological. We call them psychogenic ailments. And I may add that your wife's visit gave me the greatest joy.'

'Delighted to hear it,' said the Baron ironically.

'Yes yes, Colonel. Just think: a case of psychogenic blindness! I've had all the rest of them here in my office: psychogenic ulcers, psychogenic gastritis, psychogenic anorexia, psychogenic cardiospasm, psychogenic constipation and diarrhoea, psychogenic mucus or ulcerative colitis, psychogenic bronchial asthma, psychogenic tachycardia, psychogenic hypertension, psychogenic eczema, psychogenic thyrotoxicosis, hyperglycaemia, metritis, osteoarthritis . . .'

'That's enough!' the Baron yelled furiously, standing up. 'For the last time I am asking you this question: My wife – is she or is she not a fraud?'

'I could answer your question if human beings were all of a piece,' said the doctor very calmly. 'But they are nothing of the sort. There is the ego, the ego which is conscious, lucid, thoughtful – the one you know. But *beneath* this conscious ego there is also a cluster of unconscious, instinctive, and emotional tendencies, the id. And above the conscious ego is the super-ego, a sort of heaven inhabited by ideals, moral principles, and religion. So you see: three levels,' he explained, with gestures, to the Baron who in spite of himself had been listening, 'the id in the basement, the ego on the ground floor, and the super-ego in the upper storeys.

'And now, just suppose that a sort of relationship develops between the basement and the upper floors without the knowledge of the ground floor. Suppose that the super-ego issues an order to its underlings but that this order, instead of reaching the ego, short-circuits it, and influences the id directly. The id will obey, but in its own animal fashion. It will obey to the letter, absurdly. This is when psychogenic disorders occur, that is to say disorders whose origin is psychological, but in which the conscious will of the ego plays no part. And not only illnesses, but also accidents which are suicidal acts carried out by the id in accordance with a decision not properly understood by the super-ego. For instance, out of the several thousand people who get run over by cars every year, a considerable number – this has been proved – have unconsciously caused themselves to be run over in response to a condemnation pronounced by their super-ego. This is a very particular kind of suicide; a suicide that is intentional and yet unconscious.'

The Baron seemed to be won over.

'In short,' he translated, 'it's like this. General Headquarters gives a strategic order which in the ordinary way would be converted into tactical terms by the General Staff, who would pass it on to the men. But the General Staff knows nothing of it, and the order goes straight down to the NCOs, who interpret it wrongly.'

'Precisely. I'm glad to see that you follow me.'

'That's the mechanism, then. But – but why?'

'Why? That is indeed the great question that psychosomatic specialists ask themselves. To answer it correctly is to cure the patient. In our case, this question may be formulated in the following terms: Why did Madame de Saint-Fursy's super-ego command her id to become blind?'

Feeling himself suddenly incriminated, the Baron became aggressive again.

'I should be interested to learn why.'

'Unfortunately, you are the only person who can answer that

question,' the doctor went on. 'I am merely a third party. Madame de Saint-Fursy is trapped in the process. You, Colonel, are at the same time an actor in the drama and its most important witness.'

'What do you want me to say? After all, I'm not the doctor!'

'What I would like you to tell me is this: Is there something in Madame de Saint-Fursy's life that she does not wish to see?'

Once again the Baron stood up and turned his back on the doctor, thus facing the mirror over the fireplace.

'What are you insinuating?'

'Something ugly, immoral, low, degrading, abject – an ignominy so close to her which there is only one way not to see: to become blind. Yes, Madame de Saint-Fursy has converted her anxiety into *somatic* symptoms, you understand, in this way she has converted an unbearable misfortune or humiliation into blindness. Thus converted, the humiliation disappears, but the only way in which it can disappear is by being metamorphosed into an infirmity – in this case, into blindness.'

The Baron had continued staring at himself in the mirror throughout the doctor's explanation. Finally he turned and faced the speaker:

'Monsieur,' he said, 'I came here with the suspicion that I was being taken for a ride. And now I am quite certain that I am being hoodwinked.'

And he left abruptly.

Back in Alençon, he made his adieux to his wife in a way that left her speechless:

'I've just come from your nincompoop. And what haven't I learned! It would appear that your super-ego is plotting with your id, without the knowledge of your ego. And what is the purpose, if you please, of this magnificent plot? To convert an infamy into psychosomatic symptoms – an infamy, an ignominy – in other words, my love affair, Madame! Yes! And what is the result of all this? A case of psychogenic blindness. Psychogenic – that's to say, something that happens by fits and starts. My husband is behaving badly, so bang! I go blind. My husband comes back to me, and bingo! I recover my sight! How extremely convenient! Decidedly, there's no stopping progress! Well, personally, I say no! No to the id, no to the super-ego, and no to the plot! As for converting this and that into somatic symptoms – from now on you can do your somatizing on your own. Adieu, Madame!'

After this exit line, the Baron made a beeline for the little apartment in the Boulevard of the First Cavalry Regiment. Mariette, sitting at her dressing table in her négligée, was more than startled at his incursion, which was all the more unceremonious in that he still had his key. He poured out the whole story in one breath, the Baroness's blindness, her cure, his lightning trip to Paris, and his final adieux.

'Again!' she remarked simply.

'Again what?' asked the Baron, disconcerted.

'Again your final adieux. Because you have already made them. To me. Six weeks ago.'

For the last twenty-four hours the Baron had been living as a soldier does before an attack – without a backward look. Mariette's first word – the word again – brought him back with a jolt. It was true, though, that he had broken with this pretty little thing in order to devote himself body and soul to his wife's blindness! What had she been doing since then? Why should she have been waiting for him like a good little girl?

He started to walk round the room, both out of embarrassment and in order to try to repossess Mariette's surroundings. Finally he decided to wash his hands and charged into the bathroom. He came out again immediately, brandishing an electric razor.

'What's this?'

'My razor. For under my arms,' explained Mariette, and with a charming gesture she raised her hand above her head, revealing a smooth, moist, provocative armpit. It gave the Baron quite a turn. He knelt by her side and leaned over towards the milky, odorous cavity, from which he drank fervently.

Mariette squirmed, laughing.

'Guillaume, Guillaume, you're tickling me!'

He took her in his arms and started to carry her over to the bed, in spite of her protests. An ashtray got knocked over, and dark Gauloise butts spilled over on to the carpet. He decided to see nothing, and for a few minutes he once again became the famous Woodcock that he had always been. It was so good!

Life began again. The Baron kept up all his old habits. He was still to be seen clashing swords at the fencing academy, and doing a clear round over all the obstacles in the horse shows on his little chestnut mare. Naturally everyone knew about his break with his wife and his liaison with Mariette. He merely avoided the circles in which he would have been censured – the salons of the Prefect and the Bishop, for example – and only showed his face in places where he was sure of admiring indulgence. To the few intimate friends who ventured to allude to Mariette, he always said: 'Perfect happiness!' putting on a greedy, vulgar act, winking, his hand affectedly pressed against his waistcoat.

It wasn't true. Certainly he experienced intense, violent, even startling pleasures, such as he would never have thought possible at his age. 'She'll kill me,' he sometimes thought, with sombre satisfaction. But as for happiness, perfect happiness . . .

Baron Guillaume didn't want to admit it to himself. His understanding with Mariette merely hung on the thread of the permanent effort made by them both to conceal the presence of a third party. Mariette was not short of free time to devote to *the other.* But how careful she had to be to avoid the vestiges of one of her lives spilling over on to the other, what good will the Baron had to contribute not to notice the traces the phantom inevitably left behind him! One evening he exceeded all limits. A pair of shoes, an enormous pair of wagoner's clodhoppers, muddy and very much the worse for wear, showed their rounded snouts under the wardrobe. However hard the Baron sniffed, he could smell nothing. This irritated him. He was convinced that those filthy things stank! And how was it possible to leave them behind like that? Had 'the other' left in his socks, or was it to be supposed that he was still there, three metres away, in the wardrobe or in the lavatory?

See nothing, shut your eyes, blindfold your eyes with Mariette's fragrant hair, Mariette's tiny breasts, Mariette's triangular little pussy . . . Shut your eyes? In spite of himself, these three words reminded him of something, a painful episode in his past life, the Baroness's blindness. Was he too going to make himself blind, *to convert into somatic symptoms* his absolute necessity not to see *the other*?

Summer came, and gradually emptied the town. The gloriously sunny days were like an invitation to go on holiday. The Baron occasionally talked of escape, in Mariette's presence. To Vichy, to Bayreuth – maybe to Venice? These prestigious traditional names, however, did not seem to ring a bell with the girl. She would pout, shake her head, and then, snuggling up to him like a pussy cat, she would say: 'Aren't we fine here, just the two of us?'

After an evening in the mess of the First Cavalry Regiment, he returned to his love nest to find that she wasn't there. He waited for her. Then, as she still didn't appear, he glanced in the wardrobe. All her clothes had gone. So had her great big country suitcase. The bird had flown. Perhaps she had left a letter? He inspected all the furniture, and the pockets of his own suits. Nothing. Finally he noticed a bit of paper screwed up into a ball in the waste-paper basket. He unfolded it. Obviously. The poor little thing really had tried to write. He imagined the scene. Her sucking her pen and laboriously stringing her words together. *The other*, on his feet, all ready to go, getting impatient, cursing and swearing. In the end it was too difficult, she had given up. When you're leaving, why write: 'I'm leaving'? Isn't it clear enough? He deciphered a few lines in her quirky, childish handwriting:

Mon Cherry,
(this was a relic of her English lessons)
This hide-and-seek life couldn't go on. Really, I couldn't bear it, always having to lie. And then, you know, I realized that there was a great big gap between us when you talked about us going to Vichy and goodness knows where else. Me, it's Saint-Trop, what do you expect! But you at Saint-Trop, well, it just isn't on! So we're going there, me and Guillaume. Yes, he's called Guillaume too, that's a laugh isn't it? It even stopped me making a lot of goofs! We'll be back. Why shouldn't we get on okay together, the three of us? Why shouldn't you be our

The letter stopped there, and the Baron tried in vain to decipher the three scribbled words she had struck out.

Why shouldn't he be their . . . their what, exactly? Their cuckold, their grandpa, their backer, their go-between? Each of these words inflicted a cruel wound on him, and he couldn't stop hearing in the background, like a mocking, vengeful, Greek chorus, the members of the First Cavalry Regiment, their laughter and comments. And yet he did not experience the invigorating, refreshing anger that would have shaken him a few years earlier. The difference in their ages, no doubt. Mariette's youth, and his own maturity, moved him to something more like pity. He was touched by the awkward efforts of the child – as exemplified by the style of her letter – to deal with a situation which was beyond both her strength and her intelligence. Was it her fault that everything was so complicated? Was it not rather he – who was both wise and well-off – who had failed in his duty to provide her with a simple, happy life, without snags?

Once again – and for the last time – he was equal to the situation. He won all the trophies in the end of season equestrian events. In the fencing academy he immobilized the most agile, the most mettlesome blades. Never had the Woodcock been so flamboyant! This was only too apparent when he was to be seen, during the fourteenth of July review, caracoling on his little chestnut mare, the one that he had always said had such a feminine temperament that he loved her like a woman. What he did not avow was that this mare was the only remaining feminine element in his life – a cruel derision.

Then everything came to halt. During the last days of July the whole of Alençon languished, in preparation for the total torpor of August. The Baron abhorred a vacuum, and solitude. He wandered round in the deserted, sun-drenched town 'like a lost soul', as the woman who ran the haberdashery on the rue Desgenettes was to say later.

Finally, one day, his steps led him irresistibly to his house, to his wife's house. Was Augustine there? Or had she moved to her place in Donville during the dog days? The house appeared completely abandoned, the garden gate padlocked, the shutters closed, the garden overgrown with weeds. There was even, sticking halfway out of the letter box, the handful of leaflets and circulars that are the sort of scum of a non-existent mail.

The sun was beating down on the street, carving up the buildings into distinct black and white masses. There was something dreadful, overpowering, funereal, about all that light in all that void. The Baron experienced a vague feeling of nausea. It seemed to him that his blood was beating against his temples with mortal violence. And then, in the silence of this architecture that was at the same time familiar – his own house – and belonging to another world, he distinctly perceived a sort of clicking sound, like distant castanets, or like the faint tapping of sticks on the outer edge of a drum. The sound came nearer and became even more sinister. Now it was like the chattering of teeth in an epileptoid tremor. And suddenly the two tall black silhouettes towered up in front of him.

The intertwined shadow of two women in deep mourning, very close together, slowly advanced on him, like a wall toppling over. The taller of the two was masked by dark glasses and kept tapping the curb with the tip of a white stick, which was what was making the clicking sound. The wall continued to advance on the Baron, menacing and inexorable. He retreated, lost his footing, and collapsed into the gutter.

The doctors could not say whether he had fallen as the result of an apopleptic fit, or whether on the contrary it was the impact of his forehead on the cobblestones that had caused a stroke. When the Baroness and Eugénie picked him up, he was unconscious. He gradually regained consciousness, but the whole of the right side of his body was paralysed. They cared for him with admirable selflessness. In the Baroness's mind, her husband's hemiplegia and her own blindness combined in a sort of edifying diptych to the glory of conjugal fidelity. Mariette, who was nevertheless the cause of both the one and the other, had completely disappeared from the picture.

This, however, was the image that also imposed itself on the strollers on the Demi-Lune, when they observed the spectacle of the Baroness, definitively cured of her blindness, stiff, grave, and as serene as Justice, pushing the Baron's wheelchair. The Woodcock, reduced to the moiety of himself, was a sad, shrivelled figure, hunched up in his chair. He was now no more than a half-person made up of paralysed flesh, a cruel caricature of what he had been, with half his face frozen in a ribald grin, his eye winking, his hand affectedly pressed against his waistcoat, as if he were repeating, indefinitely and silently: 'Perfect happiness! Perfect happiness!'

The Lily of the Valley Lay-by

❦

'Time to get up, Pierre!'

Pierre was sleeping with the obstinate calm of the twenty-year-old who has blind confidence in his mother's vigilance. No danger of his old woman letting him oversleep, she who was so nervous and slept so badly herself. He turned over heavily to face the wall, taking refuge behind his powerful back and the nape of his shaven neck. She watched him, remembering the so recent dawns when she had had to wake him to send him to the village school. He looked as if he had fallen fast asleep again, but she didn't insist. She knew that for him the night was over, his day had started, and that from now on his routine would follow its inexorable pattern.

A quarter of an hour later he joined her in the kitchen and she poured out his chocolate into a big flowered bowl. He gazed at the black rectangle of the window in front of him.

'It's still dark,' he said, 'but even so the days are getting longer. I'll be able to switch off the headlights in less than an hour.'

She seemed to be dreaming – she who had not left Boullay-les-Troux for the last fifteen years.

'Yes, spring's almost here. Down there on the Riviera, you may even find the apricot trees in blossom.'

'Well – the Riviera! We don't go any farther south than Lyons on this trip. And in any case, even if there were any we'd hardly have time to look at them.'

He stood up and, out of pure respect for his mother – for according to peasant tradition no man ever washes the dishes – he rinsed out his bowl under the tap in the sink.

'When will I see you?'

'The day after tomorrow, as usual. In the evening. A straight-forward round trip to Lyons, sleeping in the cab with my pal Gaston.'

'As usual,' she murmured to herself. 'I still can't get used to it. Well, since you seem to like it . . .'

He shrugged his shoulders:

'No choice!'

The monumental shadow of the articulated lorry could be made out against the horizon as it whitened with the dawn. Slowly, Pierre walked round it. It was the same every morning, his reunion, after the night, with this enormous toy that warmed the cockles of his heart. He would never have admitted it to his old woman, but he would really have preferred to make his bed in it and sleep there. It was all very well to lock everything up, but as the lorry was so gigantic it had no real defence against attacks of all kinds – someone might run into it, it could be dismantled and some of its removable parts stolen. It wasn't even unthinkable that the vehicle itself might be stolen, with all its load; such a thing had been known, however unlikely it might seem.

But this time too, everything seemed to be in order, though there was a washing job to be done straightaway. Pierre rested a little ladder against the radiator grille and began to clean the huge windscreen. The windscreen is the conscience of the vehicle. All the rest of it can remain muddy and dusty, if need be, but the windscreen must be absolutely impeccable.

Next he went down on his knees, almost religiously, in front of the headlights, and wiped them. He blew on their glass and polished them with a white rag as carefully and tenderly as a mother cleaning her baby's face. Then he returned the little ladder to its place against the slatted sides of the lorry and climbed up into the cab, threw himself on to the seat and pressed the starter.

On the Quai du Point-du-Jour, in Boulogne-Billancourt, at the corner of the rue de Seine, there is an old, lopsided block of flats whose decrepitude is in startling contrast to the café on the ground floor with its flamboyant neon lighting, its nickel-plating and its multicoloured pinball machines. Gaston lived by himself in a tiny room on the sixth floor. But he was ready and waiting outside the bistro, and the lorry barely had to stop to pick him up.

'Okay, Pop?'

'Okay.'

It was always as regular as clockwork. Gaston would observe a ritual silence for three minutes. Then he'd start to unpack the travelling bag he'd hauled up on to the seat between Pierre and himself, and spread out his thermos flasks, knapsacks, mess tins, and parcels with a speed that revealed a long-established routine. Gaston was a wiry little man, not so young any more, with a calm watchful face. He gave the impression of being dominated by the pessimistic wisdom of the weak man accustomed since childhood to warding off the blows of a world which he knows from long experience to be fundamentally hostile. After he had sorted everything out, he would follow on with an undressing session. He swapped his shoes for felt slippers, his jacket for a thick, polo-neck sweater, his beret for a balaclava helmet, and even tried to take his trousers off, a delicate operation because there was very little room and he was on shifting ground.

Pierre didn't need to watch him to see his manoeuvres. While keeping his eyes fixed on the labyrinth of congested streets leading to the outer boulevards, he missed nothing of the familiar commotion taking place on his right.

'Look, you've only just got dressed to come down, but you have to undress again the moment you're on board,' he commented.

Gaston didn't condescend to reply.

'I wonder why you don't come down from your room in your nightshirt. That way you'd kill two birds with one stone, don't you think?'

Gaston was perched on the back of his seat. When the lorry started off again at a green light, he let himself gently topple over on to the bunk fixed up behind the seats. His voice was heard one last time:

'When you have any intelligent questions to ask me, you can wake me up.'

Five minutes later the lorry was hurtling down the slip-road leading into the outer boulevards, where there was already a good deal of traffic even at this early hour. For Pierre, this was merely an uninspiring preliminary. The real motorway travellers were indistinguishable in this stream of delivery vans, private cars and workers' buses. You had to wait until they were filtered out at the exits to Rungis, Orly, Longjumeau and Corbeil-Essonnes, and at the turn-off to Fontainebleau, before, with the Fleury-Mérogis tollgate, you finally reached the threshold of the great concrete ribbon.

When he later stopped behind four other big lorries waiting to go through the barrier, he had two reasons to be pleased. Not only was he driving, but as Gaston was asleep he wouldn't make him miss the entry to the A 6 motorway. He solemnly held out his card to the attendant, took it back, got into gear, and started rolling along the smooth, white road leading to the heart of France.

Having filled up at the Joigny service station – this too was a ritual – he drove off again at cruising speed until the Pouilly-en-Auxois exit, then slowed down and pulled into the Lily of the valley lay-by for their eight o'clock snack. Hardly had the vehicle come to a halt under the beeches in the little wood than Gaston shot up from behind the seats and began to collect the components of his breakfast. This too was immutable routine.

Pierre jumped out. Wearing a tight-fitting blue nylon track-suit and moccasins, he looked like an athlete in training. Moreover, he tried out a few exercises, hopped about boxing with an imaginary opponent, then ran off in impeccable style. When he came back, hot and panting, Gaston had just got into his 'day clothes'. Then, no hurry, he laid out a real French breakfast on one of the tables in the lay-by – coffee, hot milk, croissants, butter, jam and honey.

'What I like about you,' Pierre observed, 'is the way you go in for comfort. It's as if you always travel with either your mother's kitchen or a bit of a three-star hotel.'

'There's an age for everything,' replied Gaston, pouring a trickle of honey into the half-opened side of a croissant. 'For thirty years, every morning before work, I kept to a diet of dry white wine. White Charentes, and nothing else. Until the day I realized that I had a stomach and kidneys. Then that was that. No more alcohol, no more tobacco. Coffee with milk for yours truly! Plus toast and marmalade. Like an old granny at Claridges. And I'll tell you something worth hearing . . .'

He interrupted himself to bite into a croissant. Pierre sat down next to him.

'What about it, then, that something worth hearing?'

'Well, I'm wondering whether I'm not going to give up coffee with milk, which isn't so easy to digest, and switch to tea with lemon. Because, well, tea with lemon, you can't beat it.'

'In that case, while you're about it, why not eggs and bacon, like the English?'

'Oh no! Anything but that! Nothing salty for breakfast! No – breakfast, you understand, needs to be . . . how can I put it? It needs to be pleasant, no, affectionate, no, maternal. That's it, maternal! Breakfast should somehow take you back to your childhood. Because the start of the day isn't all that amusing. So we need something soft and reassuring to wake us up properly. Something hot and sweet, then, that's what we need.'

'And what about your flannel belt?'

'That's just it! That's maternal, too! Do you see the connection, or did you just say that without thinking?'

'I don't see it; no.'

'Babies' nappies! My flannel belt is a return to nappies.'

'Are you having me on? And what about the feeding bottle, then, when do you have that?'

'My dear fellow, look at me and take a leaf out of my book. Because I have at least one advantage over you. I have been your age, and nobody, not even the good Lord, can take that away from me. Whereas you, you can't be absolutely sure of getting to be my age one day.'

'Well, what *I* have to say is that all this guff about age, it leaves me cold. I believe people are either dim or bright, once and for all, and for life.'

'Yes and no. Because, you see, there are degrees of dimness, and I believe there's a special age for it. After that, things tend to get better.'

'And in your opinion, what is that special age, as you call it?'

'It all depends on the person.'

'For me, for example, it wouldn't be twenty-one, would it?'

'Why precisely twenty-one?'

'Because I *am* precisely twenty-one.'

Gaston gave him an ironic look as he sipped his coffee.

'Ever since we've been on the road together, yes, I've been observing you and looking for your dim side.'

'And you can't find it, because I don't smoke and I don't like everlasting little glasses of white wine.'

'Yes, but don't you see, there's a difference between being dim in little ways and in big ways. Tobacco and white wine, that's just little ways. They can kill you, but only in the long run.'

'Whereas when you're dim in a big way, that can kill you at one fell swoop?'

'Yes, that's right. Me, when I was your age, no, I was younger than that, I must have been eighteen, I joined the Resistance.'

'And that was being dim in a big way?'

'In an enormous way! I didn't give a single thought to the danger. Obviously, luck was on my side. But my best pal, who was with me, he didn't come out of it. Arrested, deported, missing. Why? What was the good of it? I've been asking myself that for the last thirty years.'

'Well, I'm not in any danger in that direction,' Pierre observed.

'No, not in that direction.'

'Which means that you're still looking for my way of being enormously dim, and you haven't found it yet?'

'I haven't found it yet, no. I haven't found it yet, but I'm beginning to get a whiff of it . . .'

Two days later, Pierre and Gaston and their lorry were once again at the same matutinal hour at the Fleury-Mérogis tollgate. This time it was Gaston who was holding the joystick and Pierre, sitting on his right, felt as always slightly frustrated at starting the day in the role of second in command. He wouldn't have allowed such an unreasonable feeling to show for anything in the world; in any case, he barely even admitted it to himself, but that was why he was in a slightly sour mood.

'Hi, Bébert! You on duty again today?'

It was so strange, Gaston's need to fraternize with that race apart, the somewhat mysterious, somewhat despicable race of tollgate attendants. In Pierre's eyes, the official entry to the motorway was invested with a ceremonial value that should not be disturbed by useless chat.

'Well yes,' the employee explained. 'I switched with Tiénot, he's gone to his sister's wedding.'

'Ah,' Gaston concluded, 'then we won't see you on Friday?'

'Well no, it'll be Tiénot.'

'See you next week then.'

'Okay, have a good trip!'

Gaston passed the toll card to Pierre. The vehicle started rolling along the motorway. Gaston changed each gear placidly, without any frantic acceleration. They settled down into the euphoria produced by the cruising speed of the enormous vehicle and the dawn of a day that promised to be superb. Pierre, firmly ensconced in his seat, was fiddling with the toll card.

'You know, those chaps who work at the tollgates – I don't understand them. They belong, and yet they don't belong.'

Gaston could see he was going to launch out into one of those lucubrations in which he refused to follow him.

'They belong, they belong – they belong to what?'

'To the motorway, of course! They stand on the threshold! Then, in the evenings, when they're off duty, they get on their motorbikes and go back to their farms. But then – what about the motorway?'

'The motorway – what of it?' Gaston asked irritably.

'Oh hell, make an effort, can't you! Don't you feel, when you come through the gate, when you have your toll card in your hand, don't you feel that something's happened? After that you belt along the concrete line, it's straight, it's clean, it's quick, it doesn't do you any favours. You're in another world. You're in something new. That's the motorway, hell! You belong to it!'

Gaston persisted in his incomprehension.

'No, for me the motorway's just a job, that's all there is to it. I might even say I find it a bit monotonous. Especially with a crate like ours. Of course, when I was young, I wouldn't have minded racing down here at two hundred kilometres an hour in a Maserati. But chugging along with forty tonnes behind you, I find the ordinary main roads much more amusing, with all their level crossings and little bistros.'

'Okay,' Pierre conceded, 'I agree about doing two hundred in a Maserati. As a matter of fact, I've already done that.'

'*You*'ve done that? You've done two hundred on a motorway in a Maserati?'

'Well, it wasn't exactly a Maserati. It was an old Chrysler, Bernard's you know, the one he souped up. We got up to a hundred and eighty on the motorway.'

'That's not the same thing at all.'

'Oh come on, you aren't going to quibble over twenty kilometres!'

'I'm not quibbling, I'm just saying: it's not the same.'

'Okay, but I'm telling you: I still prefer our crate.'

'Explain.'

'Because in the Maserati . . .'

'In the souped-up Chrysler . . .'

'It's the same thing, you're stuck down on the ground. You're not in control. Whereas our contraption, it's high up, you're in control.'

'And you need to be in control?'

'I like the motorway. So I want to see. Here, look at that line running straight off into the horizon! That's really nice, isn't it? You don't see that when you're flat on your stomach on the ground.'

Gaston shook his head indulgently.

'What you ought to do, you know, you ought to fly a plane. Then you really would be in control!'

Pierre was indignant.

'You haven't understood a thing, or else you're getting at me. A plane's no good. It's too high. With the motorway, you have to be on it. You have to belong to it. You mustn't leave it.'

That morning the Lily of the valley lay-by was bathed in such smiling colours under the young sun that the motorway in comparison might have seemed a hell of noise and concrete. Gaston had started cleaning up the cab and had brought out a whole panoply of cloths, feather dusters, brushes and polishes, watched ironically by Pierre, who had got out to stretch his legs.

'I reckon this cab is where I spend most of the hours of my life. So it might just as well be clean,' he explained, as if talking to himself.

Pierre wandered off, attracted by the atmosphere of living freshness in the little wood. The farther he went under the budding trees, the fainter the roar of the traffic became. He felt in the grip of a strange, unknown emotion, his whole being moved to a tenderness he had never yet experienced, unless perhaps when, many years before, he had approached his baby sister's cot for the first time. The delicate foliage was humming with bird song and insect flight. He took a deep breath, as if he had finally emerged into the open air from a long, asphyxiating tunnel.

Suddenly, he stopped. Not far away he perceived a charming tableau. A blonde girl in a pink dress, sitting in the grass. She didn't see him. She had eyes only for three or four cows peacefully grazing in the meadow. Pierre felt he had to see her better, to speak to her. He walked on. Suddenly, he was stopped. A fence loomed up in front of him. A menacing wire fence, almost like that round a prison or concentration camp, its top bristling with rolls of barbed wire. Pierre belonged to the motorway. A lay-by is no place for escapism. The distant hum of the traffic woke him from his dream. Nevertheless, he stayed there mesmerized, his fingers gripping the wire, staring at the blonde patch over by the foot of the old mulberry tree. Finally a well-known signal reached his ears – the lorry's horn. Gaston was becoming impatient. He must go back. Pierre dragged himself out of his contemplation and returned to reality, to the articulated lorry, to the motorway.

Gaston was driving. He was still absorbed in his spring cleaning, was Gaston.

'At least it's cleaner, now,' he observed with satisfaction.

Pierre said nothing. Pierre wasn't there. He was still gripping the wire fence on the perimeter of the lay-by. He was happy. He smiled at the angels floating invisibly in the pure sky.

'You're very quiet all of a sudden. Haven't you got anything to say?' Gaston finally marvelled.

'Me? No. What do you want me to say?'

'No idea.'

Pierre shook himself, and tried to come back to the real world.

'Well, you know,' he finally sighed, 'it's spring!'

The trailer had been detached and was resting on its prop. The lorry was free to leave the Lyons depot while the warehousemen unloaded the cargo.

'The good thing about an articulated lorry,' Gaston, who was driving, said appreciatively, 'is that we can clear off with the tractor while they're loading or unloading. Then it's almost like a private jalopy.'

'Yes, but there are times when we ought each to have our own tractor,' Pierre objected.

'Why do you say that? You want to go off on your own?'

'No, I say that for you. Because we're heading for the cafeteria, now, and I know you don't like that much. If you had your own jalopy you could go on to old mother Maraude's hash house; you always say there's nothing like her special little dishes.'

'It's true that with you, we always have to eat like greased lightning in a place like a dentist's surgery.'

'The cafeteria's quick, and it's clean. And there's a choice.'

They joined the queue, pushing their trays along the shelf below the display of waiting food. Gaston's scowl expressed his total disapproval. Pierre chose raw vegetables and a grill, Gaston a pâté de campagne and tripe. Next they had to find a table where there was a bit of room.

'Did you see the variety?' said Pierre triumphantly. 'And we didn't have to wait a second.'

Then, noticing Gaston's plate, he said, astonished:

'What's that?'

'In theory, it's supposed to be tripe,' said Gaston prudently.

'Only natural, in Lyons.'

'Yes, but what isn't natural is that it's going to be cold.'

'Shouldn't have had that,' said Pierre, and he pointed to his raw vegetables. 'These don't get cold.'

Gaston shrugged his shoulders.

'Your famous rapidity, then, is going to make me start my lunch with the plat de résistance. Otherwise my tripe's going to turn into solid fat. And cold tripe is impossible. Im-pos-sible. Never forget that. If that's the only thing you learn from me, you won't have wasted your time. That's why I prefer to wait a while, having a drink with my pals in a little bistro. The patronne herself brings you her special dish of the day, hot and perfectly cooked. That's what I think about speed. As for the cooking, the least said the better. Because in these cafeterias, I've no idea why, they don't dare season the grub. For instance, tripe, it's supposed to be cooked with onions, garlic, thyme, bay leaves, cloves, and a lot of pepper. Very hot and highly seasoned. Whereas this! – just taste it – you'd think it was boiled noodles for someone on a saltless diet!'

'Should have had something else. You had a choice.'

'A choice! Don't talk to me about choice! I'll tell you something worth knowing: in a restaurant, the less choice you have, the better it is. If you're offered seventy-five dishes, you'd do better to leave, it'll all be bad. The good cook only knows one thing: her dish of the day.'

'Have a coke then, that'll make you feel better!'

'Coke with tripe!'

'Make up your mind! You've been telling me for the last ten minutes that it isn't tripe.'

They ate in silence, each following his own train of thought. It was Pierre who finally expressed his conclusion:

'Basically, you know, we don't exactly see the job in the same way. I obviously belong to the motorway, I'm the A 6. Whereas you're still living on the main roads – you're the N 7.'

The fine weather seemed indestructible. More than ever, the Lily of the valley lay-by deserved its name. Gaston was lying not far from the vehicle, sucking a bit of grass and looking at the sky through the delicate branches of an aspen tree. Pierre had headed swiftly for the far end of the lay-by. His fingers gripping the wire fence, he scrutinized the meadow. Disappointment. The cows were there sure enough, but there was no cowgirl to be seen. He waited, hesitated, and then decided to pee through the fence.

'Make yourself at home!'

The young voice with the Burgundy accent came from behind a bush to his left. Pierre hastily covered up.

'If there's a fence, it's for a good reason. It's to keep out the motorway filth. All that pollution!'

Pierre was trying to reconcile the somewhat distant and idealized image he had been carrying round in his head for the last ten days with the very concrete image of the girl in front of his eyes. He had imagined her taller, slimmer, and above all, not so young. She was a real adolescent, a bit rustic at that, and without a trace of make-up on her freckled little mug. He immediately decided that he liked her even better, that way.

'Do you come here often?'

That was all he could find to say, in his embarrassment.

'Sometimes. So do you, I think. I recognize your lorry.'

There was a silence full of the rustle of spring.

'It's peaceful here, so close to the motorway. The Lily of the valley lay-by. Why's it called that? Are there any lilies of the valley round here?'

'There used to be,' the girl said. 'It used to be a wood. Yes, it was full of lilies of the valley in the spring. When they built the motorway, the wood disappeared. Swallowed up, buried under the motorway, as if by an earthquake. So the lilies of the valley – they've had it!'

There was a further silence. She sat down on the ground, leaning her shoulder against the fence.

'We pass this way twice a week,' Pierre explained. 'Only, of course, every other time we're going back to Paris. So we're on the other side of the motorway. To come here we'd have to walk across both carriageways. It's dangerous, and anyway you aren't allowed to. What about you, have you got a farm round here?'

'My parents have, yes. At Lusigny. Lusigny-lès-Beaune. It's five hundred metres away, maybe less. But my brother's gone to live in town. He's an electrician in Beaune. He doesn't want to cultivate the soil, as he puts it. So we don't know what'll happen to the farm when our old man's too old.'

'Obviously; that's progress,' said Pierre with approval.

The wind floated gently through the trees. The lorry's horn sounded.

'I must go,' said Pierre. 'See you soon, maybe.'

The girl stood up.

'Goodbye!'

Pierre started off, but came back immediately.

'What's your name?'

'Marinette. What's yours?'

'Pierre.'

Shortly afterwards, Gaston thought that something had changed in his companion's way of thinking. He was suddenly worrying about married people!

'There are times,' Pierre said, 'when I wonder how our married pals get on. All week on the road. So, when you're at home, obviously all you want to do is sleep. And naturally, no question of going for a run in the car. So the little woman is bound to feel neglected.'

Then, after a silence:

'But you were married in the old days, weren't you?'

'Yes, in the old days,' Gaston admitted without enthusiasm.

'And?'

'And – she did the same as me.'

'What the same as you?'

'Well yes of course, I was always away. She went away too.'

'But *you* came back.'

'And she didn't come back. She went to live with a chap who owns a grocery. A chap who's always there!'

And after a meditative pause he concluded with these words, heavy with menace:

'Basically, the motorway and women, you know, they don't go together.'

According to custom, Gaston should have washed the vehicle every other time. This is standard practice with every team of lorry drivers. But it was almost always Pierre who took the initiative, and Gaston took the theft of his turn philosophically. Clearly, they took a different view of aesthetics and hygiene, in regard to both themselves and the tool of their trade.

That day Gaston was lounging on the seat while Pierre aimed such a solid, deafening sheet of water on to the bodywork that it interrupted the few remarks they exchanged through the open window.

'Think you've given it enough?' asked Gaston.

'Enough what?'

'Enough elbow grease. Do you think you're in a beauty parlour?'

Without answering, Pierre turned off the hose and brought a dripping sponge out of a bucket.

'When we teamed up, I quite understood that you didn't like dolls, lucky charms, transfers, and all the stuff other men stick on the lorries,' Gaston went on.

'No, you're right,' Pierre agreed. 'I don't think it suits the lorry's type of beauty.'

'And in your opinion, what is that type of beauty?'

'It's a useful, suitable, functional beauty, you might say. A beauty that's like the motorway. Nothing extraneous, you see, nothing that dangles, or that doesn't have a use. Nothing to make it look pretty.'

'You must admit that I took it all off straightaway, including the gorgeous Veedol girl with the naked thighs who used to skate on the radiator.'

'You could have left that one,' Pierre acknowledged, picking up his hose again.

'Well well,' Gaston marvelled. 'Would Monsieur be becoming more human? It must be the spring. You ought to paint some little flowers on the bodywork.'

In the din made by the water lashing the metal, Pierre could barely hear.

'What on the bodywork?'

'I said: you ought to paint some little flowers on the bodywork. Some lilies of the valley, for instance.'

The jet was aimed at Gaston's face, and he hastily cranked up the window.

This same day, during the customary stop at the Lily of the valley lay-by, there was an incident that worried Gaston more than it amused him. Pierre, who thought he was asleep in the bunk, opened the back of the trailer and took out the little metal ladder they used when they wanted to climb up on to the roof. Then he went over to the far end of the lay-by. An evil genie sometimes seems to take charge of events. The scene that followed must have been visible from some point in the road, which describes a wide curve at that spot. What happened was that two motorway cops on motor bikes appeared just at the moment when Pierre had leaned the ladder against the fence and was beginning to climb up it. Confronted, questioned, he had to come down. Gaston intervened. They had it out, with exaggerated gestures. One of the cops spread out the whole paraphernalia of the perfect bureaucrat on one of the wings of the vehicle and buried himself in paperwork, while Gaston put the ladder away. Then the cops went off on their mounts like two horsemen of the Apocalypse, and the lorry continued on its way to Lyons.

After a very long silence, Pierre, who was driving, spoke first.

'You see that village over there? Every time I pass it I think of my own village. That dwarfish church, and the houses huddled all around, it's like Parlines, near Puy-de-la-Chaux. Now that really is the sticks, even for the Auvergne, which is a place full of cows and coal merchants who keep little cafés. Not more than twenty years ago, the people and the animals used to sleep in the same room. At the far end, the cows; on the left, the pigsty; on the right, the hen house, even though it did have a sort of cat-flap to let the birds out. By the window, the dining table, and on either side of it two big beds which had to accommodate the whole family. So that not a scrap of heat was wasted in the winter. But the atmosphere when you suddenly came in from outside! You could cut it with a knife!'

'But you don't know anything about that, you're too young,' Gaston objected.

'No, but that's where I was born. It's what you might call hereditary, and I sometimes wonder whether I ever really got free of it. It's like the floor. Just mud. No question of tiles or wood. But then – no need to wipe your feet when you came in! The mud from the fields that was sticking on to your soles, and the mud inside the house, it was all the same, no harm in mixing it. That's the thing I particularly appreciate in our job: to be able to work in moccasins with flexible soles. And yet it wasn't all bad in our village. For example, they used wood for heating and cooking. Say what you like, that's not the same thing as the gas and electricity we had later, when my old girl got widowed and we moved to Boullay. It's a living heat. And the decorated Christmas tree . . .'

Gaston was becoming impatient.

'But why are you telling me all this?'

'Why? No idea. Because I was thinking about it.'

'You want me to tell you? That ladder business. You think it was to go and chat up Marinette? Not only that. It was more to get away from the motorway, and back to your Parlines-by-Puy or whatever!'

'Ah, hell! You wouldn't understand.'

'Just because I was born in Pantin, I wouldn't understand that you're suffering from the typical nostalgia of the hayseed?'

'How should I know? You think I understand it myself? No, really, there are times when life becomes too complicated!'

'And Saturday nights, do you sometimes go dancing?'

Pierre would have preferred to sit down with Marinette and just be there with her in silence, but that barrier, that wire fence his fingers were gripping, created a distance between them which forced them to talk to each other.

'Sometimes, yes,' Marinette replied evasively. 'But it's a long way. There's never any dances at Lusigny. So we go to Beaune. My parents don't like me to go alone. The neighbours' daughter has to come with me. Jeannette, she's a serious-minded girl. They trust me with her.'

Pierre was dreaming.

'One Saturday I'll come and fetch you at Lusigny. We'll go to Beaune. We'll take Jeannette with us, since that's the way it is.'

'Are you going to come and fetch me with your forty-tonne lorry?' the realistic Marinette asked, amazed.

'Oh no! I've got a motor bike, a 350cc.'

'Three on a motor bike won't be very comfortable.'

There was a despondent silence. She didn't seem too keen, Pierre thought. On the other hand, though, could it have been the fact that she wanted it to happen right away that made her immediately see all the material obstacles?

'But we can dance here,' she said suddenly, as if she had just made a discovery.

Pierre didn't understand.

'Here?'

'Yes, I've got my little transistor,' she said, bending down and picking up the radio from the tall grass.

'With this fence between us?'

'Some dances, you don't touch each other. The jerk, for instance.'

She switched on the radio. Some sweet, rather slow music began to fill the air.

'Is *that* the jerk?' asked Pierre.

'No, that'd be more like a waltz. Shall we try, even so?'

And without waiting for his answer, holding the transistor, she began to gyrate, under Pierre's mesmerized gaze.

'Aren't you going to dance, then?'

Awkwardly at first, and then with more abandon, he followed suit. Thirty metres away, Gaston, coming to fetch the companion who seemed to have grown deaf to all his signals, stopped in amazement at the sight of that strange, sad scene, the boy and the girl, both radiating youth, dancing a Viennese waltz *together*, separated by a barbed wire fence.

When they set off again, Gaston took the wheel. Pierre stretched out his hand to the dashboard radio. Immediately, Marinette's waltz came on the air. Pierre leaned back, as if lost in a happy dream. It suddenly seemed to him that the landscape he saw going by all round him was in marvellous accord with this music, as if there were a profound affinity between this flowering Burgundy and the imperial Vienna of the Strauss family. Attractive, noble old residences, harmonious undulations, soft green meadows, succeeded each other before his eyes.

'It's funny how beautiful the countryside is round here,' he finally said. 'I've been through it dozens of times but I never noticed it before.'

'It's the music that does that,' Gaston explained. 'It's like in the movies. When they play the right sort of music with a scene, it has much more effect on you.'

'There's the windscreen too,' Pierre added.

'The windscreen? What d'you mean?'

'The windscreen, you know, the glass that protects the landscape.'

'Ah, because you think that's what the windscreen is for – to protect the landscape?'

'In a way, yes. And by that very fact it makes the landscape more beautiful. But I couldn't tell you why.'

Then, after a moment's thought, he corrected himself.

'I could, though; I do know why.'

'Come on, then. Why would the windscreen make the landscape more beautiful?'

'When I was little, I used to like going to town and looking in the shop windows. Especially on Christmas Eve. Everything in the windows was nicely arranged on velvet, with tinsel and little branches of Christmas trees. But the window, it's forbidding, it won't let you touch. When you went into the shop and got them to show you something they took out of the window, it was never so nice. It had lost its charm, if you see what I mean. So here, with the windscreen, well, the landscape's like a shop window. Nicely arranged, but impossible to touch. Maybe that's why it's more beautiful.'

'In short,' Gaston concluded, 'if I understand right, the motorway is full of beautiful things, but only to look at. No point in stopping and holding out your hand. Don't touch, forbidden, hands off!'

Gaston fell silent. He wanted to add something, to follow his idea through to its conclusion, but he hesitated. He didn't want to be too unkind to this Pierrot, who was so young and so awkward. Even so, he finally made up his mind:

'The thing is,' he said in a low voice, 'it isn't only the landscape that the motorway makes it impossible to touch. It's the girls, too. The landscape behind a windscreen, the girls behind a fence – everything in a shop window. Don't touch, forbidden, hands off! That's what the motorway is.'

Pierre hadn't moved. His passivity irritated Gaston. He exploded:

'Isn't that right, Pierrot?' he yelled.

Pierre jumped, and gave him a distracted look.

The enormous, immobile shadow of the vehicle rose up against the star-spangled sky. There was a faint light inside the cab. Gaston, in his night clothes but with a pair of steel-rimmed spectacles on his nose, was immersed in a novel. Pierre, lying on the bunk, was worried by this prolonged vigil.

'What're you doing?' he asked in a sleepy voice.

'You can see perfectly well: I'm reading.'

'What're you reading?'

'When you're talking to me and when I'm talking to you, I'm not reading any more. I stop reading. You can't do everything at the same time. So, before we started talking, I was reading a novel. *The Venus of the Sands*, it's called.'

'*The Venus of the Sands*?'

'Yes, *The Venus of the Sands.*'

'What's it about?'

'It takes place in the desert. In the Tassili, to be precise. That must be somewhere in the south of the Sahara. It's caravaneers. Men who cross the desert with camels carrying goods.'

'Is it interesting?'

'Contrary to what anyone might think, it has a certain connection with us.'

'Meaning?'

'My caravaneers, they walk all day long across the sand with their camels. They transport goods from one place to another. In a way, they're the lorry drivers of that time. Or else, we're the caravaneers of today. You simply substitute the camels for the lorry and the desert for the motorway, and it becomes the same thing.'

'Mmm,' murmured Pierre, half asleep.

But Gaston, engrossed in his subject, continued:

'And then, there's the oases. The caravaneers' lay-bys are the oases. There, there's springs, palm trees, and girls waiting for them. That's why the book's called *The Venus of the Sands*. She's a fantastic girl who lives by an oasis. So, obviously, the caravaneers dream of her. Here, listen to this:

"*The young tribesman had got down from his white mehari* – that's what we'd call a camel – *from his white mehari and was looking for Ayesha* – that's the girl's name – *in the shade of the palm grove. He couldn't find her because she was hiding near the well, watching the young man's efforts through the slit in her veil, which she had pulled down over her face. At last he caught sight of her and recognized her indistinct silhouette through the branches of a pink tamarisk tree. She stood up when she saw him approach, for it is not correct for a seated woman to speak to a man.* You see, in these countries they still have a sense of hierarchy.

' "*Ayesha,*" *he said,* "*I have travelled for a week across the sandstone of the Tassili, but every time my eyes closed under the burning furnace of the sun, your tender face appeared to me. Ayesha, flower of the Sahel, have you once thought of me in all that time?*"

'*The girl revealed the mauve gaze of her dark eyes and the white radiance of her smile.*

' "*Ahmed, son of Dahmani,*" *she said,* "*that is what you say tonight. But with the first glimmering of the dawn, you will bid your white mehari to arise, and you will depart towards the north without a backward glance. In truth, I believe you love your camel and your desert more than you love me!*"

'What do you say to that, eh?'

Pierre turned over in his bunk. Gaston heard a sort of groan in which he thought he could make out a name: 'Marinette!'

They were approaching the Lily of the valley lay-by; Pierre was at the wheel. Gaston was dozing behind him on the bunk.

The vehicle entered the turn-off and stopped.

'I'm going to get out for a moment,' Pierre explained.

'I'm not budging,' came the answer from the bunk.

Pierre walked ahead under the trees. Grey skies had obliterated the colours and the bird song. There was a kind of disenchanted, morose, almost menacing expectancy in the air. Pierre reached the fence. He could see neither cows nor cowgirl. He stayed there for a moment, disappointed, his fingers gripping the fence. Should he call out? There was no point. Clearly, no one was there, and that was why the charm had been broken. Suddenly, as if he had come to an abrupt decision, Pierre turned round and strode back to the lorry. He took his place and drove off.

'You didn't waste any time,' the bunk commented.

The lorry went hurtling along the turn-off and rejoined the motorway, regardless. A Porsche coming up like a meteor swerved violently to the left, flashing indignant headlights. Stepping savagely on the accelerator, changing gear like a virtuoso, Pierre brought the lorry up to its maximum speed, though unfortunately it was fully loaded. Then came the Beaune exit. The vehicle charged into it. Gaston's flabbergasted head, wearing its balaclava, shot up from behind the seats.

'What the fuck are you doing? Have you gone raving mad?'

'Lusigny, Lusigny-lès-Beaune,' Pierre muttered through clenched teeth. 'I have to go there.'

'But you realize what that's going to cost us? *You* don't care. What time shall we get to Lyons this evening? After that business with the ladder, do you really think you can go on playing the fool?'

'A little detour, that's all! Let me have just half an hour.'

'Half an hour my foot!'

The lorry stopped at the tollman's window. Pierre handed him his card.

'Lusigny, Lusigny-lès-Beaune? You know where that is?'

The man made a vague gesture and replied with a few unintelligible words.

'What?'

Another, even vaguer, gesture, accompanied by obscure sounds.

'Okay, okay!' Pierre concluded, driving off.

'Look,' said Gaston, 'you don't even know where you're going?'

'Lusigny. Lusigny-lès-Beaune. That's clear, isn't it? Five hundred metres away, Marinette said.'

The vehicle went on for a while, and then stopped by a little old woman holding an umbrella in one hand and a basket in the other. Scared, she jumped aside.

'Excuse me, Madame – which way to Lusigny-lès-Beaune?'

'To the industrial zone? Which one do you mean?'

'No, Lusigny. Lusigny-lès-Beaune.'

'Which way to the Rhône? But that's nowhere near here!'

Gaston thought it was time for him to intervene, so, leaning over Pierre's shoulder, he pronounced distinctly:

'No, Madame. We are looking for Lusigny. Lusigny-lès-Beaune.'

The old woman waxed indignant. 'Well! I'm a silly old crone, am I! Huh! The modern generation!' And she marched off.

'Shit!' muttered Pierre, letting in the clutch.

The lorry crawled on for almost another kilometre, then slowed down even more when a man pushing a cow in front of him came into view through Gaston's window. Gaston immediately questioned him. Without stopping, without a word, the man waved his arm to the right.

'Have to turn right,' said Gaston.

With some difficulty, the heavy lorry started down a minor road. Up came a boy riding a big cart horse with a potato sack in place of a saddle.

'Hey, young feller, Lusigny, Lusigny-lès-Beaune? Do you know it?'

The boy looked at him stupidly.

'Oh come on! Do you or don't you know it? Lusigny?'

There was a silence. Then the horse stretched out its neck, revealed an enormous expanse of yellow teeth, and let out a comic neigh. Immediately the boy, as if by contagion, burst into demented laughter.

'Forget it,' Gaston advised. 'You can see he's an imbecile.'

'But what sort of a lousy hole is this!' Pierre exploded. 'They're doing it on purpose, aren't they?'

They came to a junction with a little cart track. There was a signpost, but its arm had disappeared. Pierre jumped down on to the bank and inspected the grass round the post. He finally found an iron arm covered in green mould bearing the names of several villages, including that of Lusigny.

'Here! You see? Lusigny, three kilometres,' he said triumphantly.

'Yes, but she told you five hundred metres,' Gaston reminded him.

'Which goes to show that we goofed!'

The lorry began to move, and turned into the track.

'You aren't going to take us down there!' exclaimed Gaston.

'Yes I am, why not? Look, there's no problem.'

The lorry advanced, rocking like a ship. Branches scraped its sides, others brushed against the windscreen.

'We aren't out of the wood yet,' Gaston groaned.

'Defeatism brings bad luck.'

'Sometimes, it's simply foresight. Huh! Look what's coming towards us!'

Advancing round a bend, there was a farm tractor towing a cart that blocked the whole width of the road. Both stopped. Pierre got out and exchanged a few words with the man on the tractor. Then he went back to his place beside Gaston.

'He says we can pass a bit farther on. He's going to reverse.'

A delicate manoeuvre began. The lorry crawled on at a walking pace, pursuing the tractor, impeded by its cart. Eventually they arrived at a point where the track was slightly wider. The lorry kept as far to the right as it could without imprudence. The tractor began to pass it. The cart couldn't make it. The lorry reversed a few metres, then went forward again, steering to the right. The way was clear for the cart, but the bulk of the lorry was leaning dangerously over to the right. Pierre stepped on the accelerator. The engine roared to no avail. The right-hand wheels were embedded in grass and soft earth.

'That's it! We're stuck!' Gaston observed with gloomy satisfaction.

'Don't worry, I have it all worked out.'

'You have it all worked out?'

'Yes, look, we've got a tractor, haven't we? It'll tow us out!'

Pierre got out, and Gaston saw him parleying with the tractor driver. The man made a gesture of refusal. Pierre pulled out his wallet. Another refusal. Finally the tractor began to move, and the cart passed the lorry. Gaston jumped down and ran to catch up the tractor.

'Hey, we're going to Lusigny. Lusigny-lès-Beaune. Do you know where it is?'

The driver gestured in the direction he was going himself. Shattered, Gaston went back to Pierre, who was searching the back of the cab, looking for a cable.

'Great news,' he told him. 'We have to turn round.'

But they hadn't reached that point yet. Pierre had unwound the cable and got under the radiator to fix it to the winch. Then he went off more or less at random with the other end of the cable, looking for something to anchor it to. He hesitated in front of one tree, then another, and finally decided on an ancient wayside cross standing at the intersection with a mud path. He wound the cable round the bottom of the plinth and returned to the cab. The engine of the winch began to hum, and they could see the cable slowly moving towards them, twisting and turning on the stones in the path, then becoming taut and vibrating. Pierre switched off, as if he wanted to meditate before the final effort. Then he started the winch up again, bending over the steering wheel as if to participate in the effort that would get the forty-tonne lorry out of the rut. Gaston watched the operation from a short distance behind the cab. He knew that if a man is standing in the wrong place when a steel cable breaks, he can have both his legs severed by one fell whiplash. The vehicle shuddered, then very slowly began to extricate itself from the soft earth. His eyes fixed on the ground, Pierre followed the progress of the lorry, metre by metre. Gaston was the first to see the cross begin to list in an alarming fashion, and then suddenly crash down on to the grass, just when the four wheels of the trailer were finally beginning to get a grip on the road.

'The cross! Look what you've done!'

Relieved at having got out of that particular difficulty, Pierre shrugged his shoulders.

'We'll end up in prison, you'll see,' Gaston insisted.

'If that bastard had only helped us with his tractor, it wouldn't have happened.'

'You can tell that to the gendarmes!'

The lorry resumed its bumpy progress along the uneven road.

'The scenery is certainly very pretty, but don't forget that we have to turn round.'

'We're bound to get somewhere soon.'

And indeed, a kilometre farther on they arrived at a little village square, with a grocery-cum-bar, chemist's shop, and rows of rusty tubes supporting the folded tarpaulins of an absent market. On the far side was a war memorial, with its statue of a private soldier going over the top with fixed bayonet, his boot treading underfoot a German spiked helmet. It wasn't exactly ideal for manoeuvring the lorry, but there was no choice. Gaston got out to direct operations. They had to take advantage of a sloping alleyway and introduce the fore part of the tractor into it, then reverse, turning the wheel hard to the left. The trouble was that the next time they couldn't use the alleyway to give the lorry more room. It had to back as far as possible, right up to the war memorial.

Gaston ran from behind the trailer to the cab window, giving Pierre directions.

'Straight ahead as far as you can go! . . . A bit more . . . Stop . . . Right hand down now . . . Back . . . Stop . . . Left hand down . . . Straight ahead . . .'

It was really like moving around on a pocket handkerchief. The absence of passers-by or inhabitants further accentuated the malaise the two men had felt since the start of their escapade. What sort of country had they ventured into? Would they ever get out of it?

The most difficult operation was still to come, for while the tractor's bumper was practically brushing against the chemist's window, the back of the trailer was now directly threatening the war memorial. But Gaston had a quick eye. He shouted, ran up and down, exerted himself. Good old Gaston, who detested wasted effort and the unforeseen, he'd really come into his own, today!

If the lorry advanced just one more centimetre it would smash into the shop window, with its display of cough drops, tisanes, and rheumatism belts. Pierre turned the wheel as far as it would go and began to reverse. He had a vague feeling that Gaston was being too careful, and making him waste precious centimetres with each manoeuvre. You always had to force him a bit! He reversed. Gaston's voice reached him, from a distance but quite clearly.

'Come on! Gently. More. More. Gently. Stop, that's it.'

But Pierre was convinced that he still had a good metre to play with. That little bit extra would mean avoiding one more turn. So he went on reversing. Gaston's voice rose in panic.

'Stop! Hold it! Stop, for Christ's sake!'

There was a scraping sound, then a muffled impact. Pierre finally stopped, and jumped out.

The private soldier, who had been holding his bayonet in both hands, no longer possessed his bayonet, or his hands, or his arms. He had defended himself valiantly, however, for there was a huge scratch along the metal side of the trailer. Gaston bent down and picked up some fragments of bronze.

'Well, so now he's lost his arms,' Pierre observed. 'But after all, that isn't so bad for a disabled ex-serviceman, is it?'

Gaston shrugged his shoulders.

'This time we really will have to go to the gendarmerie. No getting out of it. You and your lousy Sticks-lès-Beaune, that's it for today!'

The formalities kept them nearly two hours, and night had fallen when they left the gendarmerie. Gaston had noticed that Pierre – sombre, resolute, and as if beside himself with suppressed rage – hadn't even asked the gendarmes the way to Lusigny. What had they been doing in this village with their forty-tonner? Their answer to this question was that they had been in urgent need of a spare part, someone had told them about a garage, a whole series of misunderstandings.

All they had to do now was get back to the motorway. Gaston took the wheel. Pierre was still locked in a stormy silence. They had travelled about two kilometres when they heard a succession of crackling sounds so loud that they drowned the noise of the engine.

'*Now* what is it?' said Gaston anxiously.

'Nothing,' Pierre grunted. 'It isn't coming from the engine.'

They drove on until they came to a pale but blinding light blocking the way. Gaston stopped.

'Hold it,' said Pierre. 'I'll go and see.'

He jumped down from the cab. It was only a Bengal light

burning itself out on the road. Pierre was just about to climb in again when a wild, grotesque fanfare rang out, and he was surrounded by a group of masked dancers brandishing torches. Some had toy whistles, others had trumpets. Pierre struggled, trying to escape from this absurd round dance. He was deluged with confetti, a Pierrot enveloped him in streamers, the mask of a pink pig stuck a paper tongue into his face.

'Stop it, you bastards!'

A firework exploded under his feet. Pierre grabbed the pink pig by the lapels, shook him furiously, and crashed his fist into his snout, which crumpled under the blow. The others came to the rescue. Pierre was tripped up, and fell. Then Gaston leaped down from the cab with a torch. He yelled:

'That's enough, you lot of morons! *We* aren't here for laughs. We've met your gendarmes, you know. We'll go and fetch them!'

The tumult abated. The lads took off their masks and revealed the hilarious faces of young peasants in festive mood. They were all wearing in their lapels the beribboned tricolour of young conscripts.

'Hell! We've just got called up, so we're celebrating! That's all!'

'And anyway, what the fuck're you doing here at this hour with that crate? You moving house?'

They put their fingers to their temples, with howls of laughter.

'Yeah, that's it, they're moving house!'

Pierre rubbed his back. Gaston hurriedly pushed him over to the lorry and shoved him up into the cab before things turned nasty again.

Driving along the motorway, he kept a watch out of the corner of his eye on the embittered face, the obstinate profile of his companion, which was intermittently visible in the harsh streaks of light coming from the sparse traffic.

'You know, your Lusigny,' he finally declared. 'I'm beginning to wonder whether it even exists. Or whether your Marinette wasn't making a monkey of you.'

'It's quite possible that Lusigny doesn't exist,' Pierre replied after a silence. 'But that Marinette was making a monkey of me – no.'

'Then if she wasn't making a monkey of you, tell me why she gave you the name of a village that doesn't exist?'

There was another silence, then Gaston heard this answer, which mesmerized him:

'It could be that Marinette doesn't exist, either. A girl who doesn't exist, it's only natural she should live in a village that doesn't exist, isn't it?'

It was broad daylight the next day when the lorry, on its way back to Paris, approached the Lily of the valley lay-by. Pierre was at the wheel. He was in the same sombre mood as the day before, and only broke his silence by muttered abuse. Hunched up in his corner, Gaston watched him anxiously. A car passed them and swerved back to the right a little too quickly. Pierre exploded:

'Huh! Tourists! They just clutter up the roads! Then there's accidents, and they always blame it on the lorry drivers! Why don't they go by train if they want to have fun on their holidays!'

Gaston looked round. A two-horsepower Citroën was also, with much effort, trying to pass them.

'Even the two-legged beasties are trying to get in on the act! And driven by a woman, what's more. But if she can't go as fast as us, why is she so keen on passing us?'

To Gaston's great surprise Pierre nevertheless slowed down, and the Citroën passed them with no more difficulty. As she went by, the woman thanked them with a little wave.

'You're being very decent,' Gaston observed, 'but after yesterday's goings-on we can't waste any more time.'

Then he noticed that Pierre was continuing to slow down, had switched on his right-hand directional signal, and was pulling over on to the verge of the motorway. He realized why when he saw the Lily of the valley lay-by on the other side of the road.

'Oh no, shit! You aren't going to start all over again!'

Without a word, Pierre jumped down from the cab. It would be very difficult to cross both sides of the motorway, where the traffic was heavy and rapid in both directions. But obviously, this didn't worry Pierre. He seemed to have become blind.

'Pierre – you've gone mad! Watch out, for Christ's sake!'

Pierre just barely missed a Mercedes, which protested with a prolonged screech of its horn. He started off again and reached the central reservation. He jumped over it and started to rush across the Paris-Provence carriageway. A lorry brushed against him and forced him to stop. He started off again with a desperate leap to try to avoid a Citroën DS. One more leap. An impact sent him spinning, another knocked him over towards the ground, but before he reached it he was projected into the air by a staggering blow. 'It was as if the cars were playing football with him,' Gaston was to describe it later. Tyres screeched, horns sounded. There was a general hold-up.

Gaston was the first to reach Pierre. Helped by three motorists, he got him back to their lorry. Pierre's blood-soaked head rolled inertly from side to side. Gaston immobilized it between his hands. He looked him in the eyes with tenderness and grief. Then Pierre's lips began to move. He was trying to say something. He stammered. And slowly, the words began to form.

'The motorway . . .' he murmured. 'The motorway . . . You see, Gaston, when you belong to the motorway . . . you mustn't try to leave it.'

Later, the articulated lorry, driven by Gaston, was back on the road. It was preceded by an ambulance surmounted by its revolving light. Soon the ambulance turned right into the Beaune exit. The lorry passed it, and carried on in the direction of Paris. The ambulance slowed down in the access road and passed a signpost on which Pierre, being unconscious, was unable to read: *Lusigny-lès-Beaune 0.5 km.*

The Fetishist

A one-act one-man play

(*He appears at the back of the centre aisle and makes his way up it towards the stage. He keeps darting anxious glances over his shoulder, then seems reassured and, smiling at the audience, tells them*):
It's all right. They trust me. They're having a drink at the . . . [name of a bar near the theatre.] They've given me an hour. I took advantage of it to do a little shopping. (*Sending a glance around him.*) There's some very smart people here! Beautiful dresses! I like that. It reassures me. It's polite. It's nice. It's gratifying.

(*He hauls himself up on to the stage. Hangs his hat on a peg.*)

And then, it's healthy to be dressed up! Healthy people are well dressed. The doctor says: 'Undress!' – and that's it. You're already different. You're half-way lost. He – naturally, the swine – *he* is still dressed. Overdressed, even, in his white coat buttoned up to his chin. The patient is standing there looking ridiculous, with his braces hanging down, his trousers corkscrewed over his shoes, his shirt tails flapping. 'All right, you can get dressed!' Then it's okay. But there are some cases, some patients, who don't ever get dressed. Never again! The psychiatric hospital is full of men and women who've never got dressed again. They wander around in combat uniform, in jimjams, in strait-jackets, in their nightshirts. But none of those are real clothes. They don't cling to the skin. Real clothes cling, they're solid, they're like armour. My pals in the asylum, though, for the merest nothing, pff!, they get their so-called clothes taken off them, there's nothing left of them, the patients are stark naked when they go for an examination, or for a shower, when they go to bed, or for shock treatment. Ooh, shock treatment! There's a fellow near me, he has false teeth. They make him take them out for his shock treatment! As if they were afraid he'd bite! They might just as well put a muzzle on him, while they're about it!

(*He examines the audience, shading his eyes with his hand, and picks out a young woman.*)

No, it's not true! Can it be you, my darling, my Antoinette? You can't see a thing with these lights.

(*He steps down into the house. Stops in front of a woman. Looks at her for a long time.*)

No no, of course not. That would really have been too extra-ordinary.

(*He goes back on to the stage.*)

It's twenty years, can you imagine? But I'm patient. I'm still waiting for her. Because she's the only one who can get me out of that hole. Every time I go out, it's as if I were going to look for her. The last time she came to see me . . . (*Long silence.*) The day before, the medical director sent for me. I wondered what on earth he wanted with me. He said: 'Martin, we've known each other a long time now, and there's one point we're agreed on, isn't there? You are perfectly healthy.' Me: 'Oh yes, I do feel well, except that I may perhaps be starting a little cold.' 'No, I mean mentally – you aren't ill?' 'Me? Mentally ill? Well really, doctor, if *you* say not!' 'No, well, what I mean is, we understand you, you're delicate, very highly-strung, and you certainly have bizarre tastes, but you aren't what is commonly called mad.'

How about that! But I thought he was going to let me out! It even scared me a little, at first. Because in the long run, obviously, you get out of the habit of the wide open spaces, you can't quite imagine yourself outside again, with responsibilities and all that! But then the director reassured me, he even told me something that gave me such enormous, tremendous, colossal pleasure that I nearly wept. No, I actually did weep. He told me: 'I'm talking to you like this because Madame Martin is coming to visit you tomorrow – yes, your wife.' So then I wasn't scared any more. I said to myself: she's coming to fetch me. They're letting me out, but she's going to look after me, she's going to protect me. And then the director said: 'She will be coming with her lawyer.' At that, obviously, I winced. A lawyer – what for? The director went on: 'Since you are of sound mind, your signature is valid. So this is what your former wife, well, your wife, wants. She wants to marry again. And to do that, obviously she has to get a divorce first. If you were ill, I mean mentally ill, mad, as you might say, well, it would be impossible. The law is against it. When one of the spouses is insane, the other cannot obtain a divorce. But you aren't mad, Martin, we're agreed on that point, aren't we?' Not mad, not when it came to losing Antoinette. But mad enough to stay locked up – I was losing all along the line! The next day I refused to go to the director's office. I told them I'd sign anything they liked with my eyes shut, anything at all, even my death warrant if that was what they wanted. But I didn't want to see anyone. In the end I did see the lawyer in the common room. I signed, and signed, and signed all the papers he'd brought in his brief-case. It was all over. No more Antoinette. Well, the new Antoinette, the one I didn't know, the one who never wanted to see me again, that one had disappeared, yes, for ever. The other one, the previous one, the one who belongs to our good years – she still exists . . . here. (*He taps his heart.*)

Antoinette . . . When I first knew her she was sixteen. I was nineteen. Our families were neighbours. We saw each other almost every day. But I was shy. She scared me. And yet I finally managed to approach her. One Sunday morning, I was just going out and I saw her on the pavement. She was all in white. She must have been going to Mass. She dropped a glove. I ran and picked it up. It was made of very fine, openwork batiste, white lawn to be precise. I hesitated a moment, partly out of shyness, and also partly because I was tempted to keep the glove as a souvenir, that little fabric hand that I could squeeze in *my* hand, put in my pocket, Antoinette's hand . . . In the end, I ran after her and gave her back her glove. It had happened! – we had met. It would have been too stupid of me to miss that chance! If I had only known! Though I *could* have understood, even then. We met again later, and I still didn't understand, even though . . .

I was doing my military service. In the First Cavalry Regiment. I had a mare I was very fond of. Her name was Ayesha. When I harnessed her in the mornings I had the impression that I was dressing her, dressing a woman, yes, with a headstall, a saddle, a girth, the lot! One day we were out on exercises. Field-service uniform, the helmet, the cavalry magazine rifle, the sabre, the greatcoat rolled up behind the saddle, the flask, all the paraphernalia. Suddenly, round a bend in the road, what do I see? Antoinette! In a ray of sunlight she was white, and all alone, like an apparition. She told me later that she was scared, a young girl isolated like that and faced with a whole regiment of men on horseback coming towards her, who were certainly going to smile, and snigger, and crack jokes, when they saw her! But she wanted to be brave. She summoned up all her energy and walked on, looking away from the soldiers. And then, bingo! The dirty tricks fate plays! The troop was just passing her when she heard a faint popping sound coming from her clothes. Next she felt an abnormal freedom round her waist, and then immediately something light falling on to her feet. She had just lost her panties! She stopped, paralysed, her head swimming, and she kept saying to herself, I'm going to faint, I'm going to faint, I'm going to faint, I'm going to fall on to the ground with my skirt hitched up, the soldiers will come flocking round me, how awful, how awful! And then she noticed a certain confusion among the cavalrymen. One of them had somersaulted over his horse's neck and fallen to the ground. The other horses stopped or stepped aside, so as not to trample him. It was me! I was the only one who had seen Antoinette's little panties landing on her shoes and it had taken my breath away, it had made my heart stop, and I had passed out! It was a bit like the day of the glove, but a hundred times, a thousand times more potent. Antoinette took advantage of it to step out of her panties and stuff them in her bag. She was all set to beat it, she wasn't going to hang about, but then she recognized me. It was her little neighbour lying there on the cobblestones! Some of the men had dismounted, they had slid a greatcoat under the back of my neck, and they were trying to get me to drink from a flask. The liquid ran down over my chin. Then Antoinette took pity on me. Instead of making her escape she came up, knelt by my side, and wiped my face with her handkerchief . . . Well, with what she thought was her handkerchief! Because, after they'd taken me to the infirmary in the barracks, what did I find round my neck? Her little panties! Completely soaked in brandy! I was drunk, yes, but it wasn't the smell of the brandy that was intoxicating me! It became my fetish, that little pair of panties. Three weeks later the war came, the phony war at first, and then a war that was a lot less phony and a lot less funny. Especially for the cavalry! The cavalryman is an anachronism when he's faced with German armoured divisions. Panache – oh yes, we had plenty of panache! One day we were at the top of a hill. And down in the valley, what did we see? A column of enemy tanks. The captain didn't hesitate: Draw – swords! Cavalry – charge! For the honour of the Regiment!

We charged. The Krauts picked us off with their machine guns. Ayesha got a bullet in her chest. I went crashing into the clover. Stunned, but unhurt. All my pals were massacred. I was the only one safe and sound. Why? Because I was wearing my little fetish round my neck. It stayed with me even when I got sent to a camp in Silesia with thousands of others. I must tell you that Antoinette and I had come together in a way through our families being neighbours. Antoinette had become what they call a wartime godmother to me. She wrote to me and sent me chocolate, sugar, jam, and underclothing, too. But it was underclothing for me, men's stuff. I didn't ever dare write and tell her the sort of underclothing I would really have liked.

Men's underclothing . . . That was the most sinister thing of all, in the Stalag, all those men with their ragged clothes that they spent their time patching up as best they could. A uniform. That makes a difference! Naked under the shower, an officer, an NCO, a private, they're just three men, no more, no less, whether ill-favoured or well-built. What's more, the Germans and us, the conquerors and the prisoners, without our uniforms we were all alike. They say that the tailor makes the man. How true! A naked man is a worm without dignity, without a function – he has no place in society. I've always had a horror of nudity. Nudity is worse than indecent – it's bestial. Clothes are the human soul. And even more than clothes – shoes.

Shoes . . . I learned a lot about shoes when I was a prisoner. Every evening, in the huts, they used to confiscate our shoes. That was to stop us escaping. Without shoes we were sub-human, human wrecks, the scum of the earth. And in any case, the main difference between our conquerors and ourselves was in our shoes. Or rather – boots . . . Yes, the whole of the Germany of the time, Nazi Germany, was contained in its boots. You know, right after the war they shot a whole lot of SS torturers. That was an extreme solution, and very crude. All they had to do was confiscate their boots. Yes, really – I mean it! No more boots – no more torturers! Take the most sadistic Nazi torturer, deprive him of his boots, give him a pair of slippers instead, great big peasant felt slippers with buckles. You'll turn him into a lamb. It's like a tiger when you extract his teeth and claws: then all he can do with his paws is caress you, and with his jaws, kiss you. And it isn't only the SS and their boots. The whole man is in his shoes. Well – let's take smugglers, for example. People sometimes say the Basques have smuggling in their blood. What *I* say is that it isn't in their blood that the Basques have smuggling, it's in their shoes – in their espadrilles. Take his espadrilles away from a Basque, make him wear a mountaineer's heavy, nailed boots: no more smuggling!

But captivity was tough because of the lack of women. Oh, of course, there were opportunities sometimes, when we went to work for the locals. My pals took advantage of this. I never did. Because for me, women, they aren't . . . how can I put it . . . They're rather to be consumed elsewhere than eaten on the premises, if you see what I mean. Women are the atmosphere they radiate around them. That was why the camp was terrible: it was all men, and more men. I realized later that men could be some use too, that they too could have a meaning. But I hadn't got that far when I was a prisoner. I really couldn't see why men existed. So when the idea of an escape came up, I was one of the first to be interested.

Every month a lorry went from hut to hut picking up the dirty clothes and taking them to a little factory five kilometres away to be decontaminated. We reckoned that a couple of men could get out of the camp by hiding in the lorry. After three kilometres it had to pass through a fairly dense forest on a lonely road. That was where we would jump out. After that, it was merely a question of walking, food, and luck. Fate picked on me and one of my comrades for the first attempt. We hid in the back of the lorry while it was being loaded with the clothes from our hut. We left the camp without any problem. It was as easy as pie. Five minutes later, we entered the forest. My companion jumped out of the lorry, hid under the nearest trees, and waited for me. I didn't jump. I had fainted. I hadn't been able to stand the sickly stench of the dirty laundry. Men's dirt, a virile stench. And a cold smell, too, maybe that was the worst. It's like a pipe: a warm pipe, even if it's old and dirty, is a smell you can put up with. But a cold pipe is a dead pipe, it stinks. If the body needs its clothes to keep it warm, clothes too need a body to keep them warm. Clothes that have been away from a body for too long finally die. The pile of stuff in the lorry had become dead clothes, carrion-clothes.

I hadn't been able to hold out. Antoinette's little panties had made me faint with joy when I fell on to the cobblestones. The lorry full of the prisoner's dirty linen had made me faint with horror and disgust. When they unloaded the lorry at the factory my unconscious body rolled out in the middle of the bundles. Lucky for me I didn't end up in a boiler! They raised the alarm at once. My companion was caught. The dodge of the dirty linen lorry had become unusable. And it was my fault. My companions were furious with me. I was ashamed. But it wasn't actually my fault, it was my nature. Nothing is my fault! I'm at the mercy of my fate. Because I – though you may not think it – *I* have a fate, and it's terrible to have a fate! You think you're like everyone else. There doesn't seem to be anything special about you. But you're not really free. All you can do is obey your fate. And *my* fate is . . . is . . . (*in a barely perceptible voice*:) frills and flounces . . .

And to prove it: Antoinette was waiting for me at the station in Alençon when I came back from captivity in 1945. She was there with our families, my little godmother. The first thing I noticed was her dress. I can still see it, what's more – a white organdie dress with a little apron with lots of flowers and birds all mixed up. And over her shoulders she was wearing a big shawl made of black wool, as delicate as lace. I was sorry she wasn't wearing a hat. In the miserable conditions I'd been in as a prisoner, I had always dreamed of women wearing rather silly hats, either felt or straw, with feathers, flowers, ribbons, and above all, oh, above all! with little veils! A woman's face is so beautiful and exciting seen through the delicate, quivering shadow of a veil! But that was all finished. The war did away with hats, and the veils vanished with the hats. Women go out hatless, their heads naked, their faces naked. Nakedness is so sad! But even so, Antoinette was my fate, with neither veil nor hat. Three months later, I married her.

I sometimes tell myself: you shouldn't have. A man of destiny doesn't marry, he remains celibate, he becomes a recluse – or else a priest, yes, all alone in a presbytery with an old housekeeper. And anyway, we have to face facts: when it comes to frillies, priests certainly get their satisfaction. Priests – they deny themselves nothing! One day – not long after I'd been released – I passed a shop in the Place Saint-Sulpice. *The Elegant Clergyman*, it was called. Well! – in the window there were things like nylon cassocks, silk stockings in white, crimson, purple, violet . . . And lace surplices, and gold-embroidered chasubles, and mauve, red and black capes. What a sight! I simply had to go in and touch all those supernatural garments. Deep down, though, they made me feel uneasy. Because, you see, all that stuff was still men's clothes. Oh, beautiful clothes, princely clothes, episcopal clothes, archiepiscopal clothes! Nothing in common with the prisoners' rags. The precise opposite, but even so men's clothes, clothes that smelled of fathers, hairy chests, stubbly faces. And as I have already said, it was only later that I realized what men were all about. In any case, I don't want any part of the elegant clergyman, thanks all the same. The religious vocation is just a dead end. So let's settle for marriage. With Antoinette . . .

The wedding night. A real shock. Well, obviously, I'd never had anything to do with women. Before the war I was too naïve, too shy. And as for the ones you could sometimes see . . . and have . . . when you were a prisoner . . . My pals, oh yes, they took advantage of them when they went to work in a commando. There was a great shortage of men in the German towns and villages in those days. There *were* chances. But never for me. They were too badly dressed, those chances. The way they got themselves up – you should have seen it! For me it's very simple – a badly dressed woman disgusts me. You should have seen the undies those Pomeranian peasant women exposed when they were picking potatoes and showing their backsides to the skies!

So there we were, married, me and Antoinette. The same day, we left on our honeymoon in my father-in-law's car. Headed south. I was driving. We had decided to look for somewhere to sleep when we'd had enough of driving for that day. So we landed up in the Auvergne, in the mountains, at Besse-en-Chandesse. Hôtel de l'Univers. Shabby but clean, rustic style. A big room with a very high ceiling and a huge brass bed. The moment you touched it the bed jingled like cowbells, or like a troika. In one corner of the room there was a curtain that slid along a rectangular rod, and behind it there was a wash-basin with a metal bidet. Not exactly the place of your dreams for a wedding night. Still, we had rather asked for it, hadn't we? We sat down on the bed, and it made a terrific noise. We laughed, and then we looked at one another. After that Antoinette said: 'You go for a walk, I'll get ready.' I went out. I lit a cigarette and wandered round the village streets. I was ill at ease. I felt something serious was going to happen. Up till then I had had a stay of execution. That was over, now, and I had my back to the wall, or to the bed, rather, and I had to turn round and face it. Really, though, the thing that was worrying me was what must be going on in Antoinette's little head. Antoinette was a well brought up girl, religious, modest, chaste. Oh, you never had to worry with her, never one word louder than another, never a gesture, never a wink. Only the thing was, she was married now. And her husband was – me. Well then, she must have said to herself, prudishness is a thing of the past, we're turning over a new page, I have a husband now . . .

When I went back into the room, after knocking on the door timidly, Antoinette was lying on the troika. Stark naked! And she was looking at me and smiling, a little red in the face even so. But I didn't recognize her. Oh yes, there was her face, with its smile that I loved, but that big white body displayed there in front of my eyes like . . . like . . . Like something in a butcher's window! And I was ashamed for her, for myself, for us both. I blushed. And how I blushed! And she was still smiling, and holding out her arms to me! In the end I looked away, I was so miserable, and finally I saw the chair. The chair, yes, what a relief! What chair, you're going to ask? Why, the chair she had put her clothes on! It was like a little island of solid ground in the middle of a swamp. So I went over to the chair with confident, slow, automatic steps, a sleepwalker's steps, a robot's steps, steps that know where they are going, steps that don't have the slightest hesitation. I stopped in front of the chair and, well, I went down on my knees and buried my face in the pile of clothes. A warm, soft pile, which smelled good, like new-mown hay in the summer sun. I stayed there a long time like that, on my knees, my face hidden. Antoinette was wondering whether I was saying my prayers or whether I had gone to sleep. Next I picked up the clothes and held them in a bundle against my face, and stood up, keeping them there so as not to see anything. I walked over to the bed and scattered them over Antoinette's body. And I said: 'Get dressed!' Then I rushed out like a maniac.

I was feverish, I was miserable. I had to run round the village at least three times. Then I landed up in a bistro. And I who never drink, I drank. Cheap red wine, glass after glass. Antoinette came and found me there. I was drunk. It seems that I was looking at my empty glass with a stupid expression on my face and saying: When my glass is full, I empty it. When my glass is empty, I pity it. I was the one to be pitied. I certainly was in a fine state. But after all, aren't you supposed to get drunk on your wedding night? Antoinette left some money on the table and led me out, yes, led me, took me, dragged me. To the Hôtel de l'Univers, up to our room, our bridal chamber, to the troika. There, she kissed me. Then I pushed her over on to the troika and, to the accompaniment of a terrific jangling of bells, she became my wife. Dressed, fully dressed, that time!

After that, after that . . . Well, we had to get used to each other. There was a certain amount of trial and error, of hesitation, at first, of course. We had to get to know each other, she had to find out what her husband was like. Oh, and I too, I also had things to learn. Because actually, *I* didn't know what was the matter with me, either. Well, what was wrong with me wasn't prudery. Anything but! It went much deeper than that. It's very simple. For me, a body without clothes is . . . it's a tree without leaves, or flowers, or fruit. A tree in winter, as you might say. Just wood! Then you will ask me: And what about clothes without a body? Now *that's* quite a different matter! They haven't come alive yet when they're in a shop window or inside the shop, but they show promise! Well, the thing is, if you had to choose between a body without clothes and clothes without a body, which would you prefer? Er . . . Actually, I'm only hesitating out of politeness, so as not to seem too dogmatic. But to be quite honest – I wouldn't hesitate for a moment! For me a body is only a . . . a thing to display clothes on, a clothes peg, that's all. And long live frillies!

Then what about Antoinette, you will ask. Ah, but my wife wasn't unhappy! Sometimes it's an advantage to have a husband like me. Antoinette was the best got up woman in Alençon. It was a sort of pact between us, a balance, a funny sort of balance to tell the truth. To start with we had agreed that she would never appear naked in front of me. Never! Nakedness is for when you're washing. Not for me. None of my business. Private. A woman's secret. A shameful secret. Every man for himself in that domain. But as she was very sweet she always chose amusing undies, comic things, if you see what I mean. Only the trouble was, Antoinette had been brought up in a convent. So obviously, her daring innovations were always a bit restrained. And then, we lived in Alençon, and although Alençon is a charming town, and they even make beautiful lace there, when it comes to naughty frillies, Alençon huh?

One day I pulled a little parcel out of my pocket. A surprise for Antoinette. She opened it: a bra. In black satin. Unfortunately, I'd had rather big ideas. Naturally, the imagination embellishes everything. And Antoinette's bubs went bouncing up and down in it like those pink tropical birds, waxbills, in their cage. I had to go and change it. But the lesson had borne fruit. I made a note of all Antoinette's measurements, her size in everything. At first I wrote them all down, then I learned them all off by heart. I could recite them for you now, twenty years later. She was a numbered woman, was Antoinette, measured, indexed, quantified . . . And every two months I brought the whole thing up to date. Obviously – because women change. That way, no more mistakes. And it was necessary, because I rarely came home empty-handed. There was no stopping it, and everything became more and more fashionable, more and more sophisticated, less and less decent . . . It had become a real passion. I took trips to Paris, real pleasure trips, all alone with my ideas. But I also knew all the lingerie shops in the region, in Mortagne, in Mamers, in L'Aigle, in Chartres, in Dreux, and even as far as Le Mans! Because you see, clothes in a drawer, or displayed, or on hangers, they're things that have had life promised to them and that are demanding to be given life. Little souls that need a body before they can really exist. When I wander round displays I have the impression that those little souls are calling to me. They're shouting out: I want to live, me too, me too, take *me*! So I look at them all tenderly, I caress them lovingly, it disturbs me, well, it used to disturb me, especially when I could imagine them on Antoinette's body, warmed and brought to life by Antoinette's body, and I was happy, so happy . . . I used to choose the nicest ones, the most appealing ones, the most poignant ones, and I'd rush back home to submit them to Antoinette, to Antoinette's body which would give them life. It was marvellous to see those dainty, delicate little objects, though they were still dry and flat, swell, blossom like flowers, ripen like fruit. . .

But obviously, this made problems. On the financial side, if you see what I mean. I was a banker at the time: third cashier in the Bank of Alençon. I didn't like my job, because I couldn't see any connection between my little metal grille and the only thing in the world that interested me. True, enormous sums of money passed through my hands every day. But in the first place – absolutely impossible to put a single sou in your pocket. Bank cashiers are all scrupulously honest. Not surprising – they have no choice. It's one of the rare jobs in which theft is totally out of the question. Impossible. Everything is too well counted, checked, supervised. So there's no need to be virtuous. In such circumstances the worst rogue becomes irreproachable. No choice. And then, there was something else. Paper money doesn't mean a thing to me. It has always left me cold. They used to bring it to me in sealed packets of a million old francs. You break open the metal strip, and out come the notes. Stiff, ice-cold, varnished, glazed. Not for me, thank you. Human warmth! Without human warmth – nothing doing. But I saw things from a different point of view the day I did the incineration for the first time. The incineration of old notes. Normally it was the chief accountant who did the incinerating. In the presence of a special official. The chief accountant was on holiday. The second cashier ought to have done the incineration in his place. In the presence of an official. He was ill. So I had to do the incinerating. In the presence of an official. I was burning old, torn, dirty, mutilated notes – but the most important thing about them was that they had been softened. Oh, soft, so soft, like tissue paper, like silk. Those silky notes that no one wants any more – every month they get burned. In the presence of an official, who writes down their numbers. You put them in a metal box. You sprinkle petrol over them. Then you throw a match. Oh, it's soon over! I've seen whole fortunes go up in smoke! The first time, a strange impression, yes indeed. Tears in my eyes, I swear. So I asked to be allowed to do all the incinerating. Why not? I was the only person who enjoyed it. And then, on the security side, there was always the official, writing his report. I became the chief incinerator. But when the official had gone, I stayed there. I touched the sides of the box. Still warm, practically boiling hot. I poked around in the ash with a trowel. Sparks flew. Quite soon I was able to plunge my hand into it. It was so soft! The beautiful pearl-grey ash was as warm as a breast, I scooped it up in the trowel and gently, gently poured it into a bag. And it ended up in my house. My cellar was full of it, little bags full of ashes, each one with the date of the incineration on it and the total amount of the burned notes. It wasn't long before I was a billionaire. I wandered around town, casual as you like, with a bag containing a hundred million francs in my hand. I looked in the shop windows, at the jewels, the luxury cars, and especially at the beautiful clothes. Their prices made me laugh in pity. But I didn't dare go into the shops. With my bag full of ashes, they would have taken me for a madman. Me, a madman? I'm as sane as they come!

One day I was hanging around outside an antique shop. Some really fine period furniture, and worn, faded, discoloured tapestries, just like my silky notes. I hung around, and hung around, and the owner was sitting there, outside his shop, on a big settee, looking at me. He was an old Jew with a beard, he had a funny sort of skull cap on his head and shrewd little eyes. He spoke to me. I don't know what he said. I replied. In short, we had a bit of a chat, and finally I sat down beside him on the settee. Out of the blue he asked me what I had in my bag. I couldn't resist it. I spilled the whole story to him, told him what the ash was, and what the figures written on the bag were – the lot. The old man looked at me with his little eyes screwed up, then he began to laugh. He couldn't stop laughing. It was beginning to annoy me. It's true, I don't like people who cackle for no reason.

'There's a discrepancy,' he said at last.

'Discrepancy? What sort of discrepancy? What d'you mean by discrepancy?'

'A discrepancy between your fortune and you.'

'Don't understand.'

'But of course! You possess an extinct fortune, but you are very much alive. There's a discrepancy.'

'What'll I do, then?'

'Nothing. Just wait.'

'Wait for what?'

'Wait until you've caught up with your fortune.'

'How?'

'By dying. Billions in ashes, that implies a billionaire in ashes.'

It wasn't so stupid! I got the point. To recover that fabulous fortune, all I had to do was get myself incinerated too. So I transformed my cellar into a columbarium. Stacked on shelves were bags full of ashes, with their date, and how much they contained. And in the middle, a sort of niche with an urn. And on the urn, my name, and . . . no date. Not yet. And I began to wait. I waited until I discovered another kind of paper money: the nestling note.

The nestling note! A sensational discovery! And I can truly say that the nestling note changed my life. I remember so well. It was a beautiful April morning. A customer came to the bank to withdraw some money. A lot of money. So much that he couldn't cram it into his wallet. He tried, and then gave up. And he put the notes straight into his pocket, where his wallet had been. And departed. Then I noticed the wallet. He had left it behind on the counter by my grille. I picked it up, meaning to give it back to its owner. But I had barely touched it when I began to tremble. I felt the worn morocco leather, it was very flexible, and swollen like a soft belly. I opened it. Some human things spilled out of it: photos, letters, an identity card, and even a lock of hair. And all this was warm. You could feel that it had been lying for hours against the beating heart of a human being made of flesh and blood. The warmth of the breast, as you might say. And of course, there was also some money. Used notes, velvety and warm. Living notes. Not yet destined for incineration, but as good as. Nestling notes. When I touched them I was just as agitated as when I touched a bra or a nightdress, but in a different way. I had just discovered men's raison d'être. I had hated men for so long. It's true – what's the use of them? But this time I had come to understand them. Women are delicate, soft, perfumed lingerie. Men are a wallet swollen with secret things and silky, sweet-smelling notes. For money does have a smell, provided it's living and warm. It smells good, ladies and gentlemen! That was why I had never understood my comrades in captivity. Prisoners don't have any money. They are poor, impoverished, unclean, and unjustifiable. And when I was buried in the prisoners' dirty linen, what I was really doing was approaching men as I approach women – through their underclothes. How queer can you get! Error, aberration, youthful folly! A man is to be approached through his wallet! This first wallet, found, stolen, found-stolen, was like a personal link between an unknown man and me. But when I say unknown! I knew his name, his date of birth, his address, his profession. I possessed his photo, and that of his wife and two children, Raymonde, five years old, and Bertrand, three and a half. There was also an extremely affectionate letter that wasn't signed by his wife . . . So that was it: on the one hand, women's garments, and on the other, men's nestling notes. What's the connection, you ask me? But it's simple: with nestling notes, you buy garments. Because you see, I soon understood that between nestling notes and garments there's a sort of . . . how can I put it . . . a sort of affinity, of complicity! Yes, complicity. Men's natural function is to provide the nestling notes that get transformed into frillies.

So naturally, I didn't stop at this first wallet. I continued the hunt for the nestling note. A strange kind of hunt, upsetting, dangerous, voluptuous. Ah, the nestling note is something quite different from the wood-pigeon or the grouse! It isn't enough to get up early in the morning. Yes, I became a pickpocket. I picked things out of pockets. Jacket pockets and trouser pockets. But not out of jackets left lying over the back of a chair! No, I picked straight from the animal. Because the prey must still be warm. I was hunting warm wallets. It's like someone who goes hunting . . . well, rabbits for example. The rabbit he picks up must still be quivering. If it's a cold, stiff corpse, it disgusts the hunter. Therefore, jackets and trousers still on the animal. Yes, trousers too, because some men keep their wallet in their hip pocket. Obviously, that's much easier to pick than the inside pocket of a jacket. But on the other hand it's money that doesn't have the same quality, if you see what I mean. The money from the inside jacket pocket is money from the heart, the very best kind of money ever made. It's notes that have nestled in the moisture of the armpit, like eggs in their nest in the spring. The money from the hip pocket of a pair of trousers, oh well, it's easier, but it's backside money, it lacks quality. All the same, though, when the opportunity arises . . . a nice fat wallet sticking out of a hip pocket . . .

At first Antoinette was delighted with all these gorgeous undies that came showering into her drawers until she didn't know what to do with them any more. But then, bit by bit, she got worried. It was all very well for me to tell her that I had had a rise at the bank, she wasn't an idiot and she could count. But it was like a vice with me, a drug, I couldn't stop. And then there was the business of Mademoiselle Francine's bra, which wrecked everything.

Mademoiselle Francine was a cashier, a colleague, in other words, except that she exercised her profession at the Majestic cinema. Usually, though, cashiers are perched high up, they dominate. The Majestic is a cinema in a basement – in a cellar, you might say. The cash desk is half-way down the stairs. Which means that when you arrive, you go down a few steps, then you stop at the cash desk which is a bit lower still. You pay, and then you go on even farther down. Only there's no point any more, because you have already seen the show. Well, I'm speaking for myself. Because Mademoiselle Francine always wears breathtakingly low-cut tops. So when you go down towards the cash desk, obviously, you plunge . . . into the cashier's décolleté. You plunge, and what do you see? You'll never guess: a bra, an adorable little bra in mauve satin trimmed with lace. Well, after that, you could have shown me anything you liked, a western, a thriller, a spy story – there was only one thing on the screen for me: a satin bra, and mauve into the bargain, because my imagination has always been in Technicolor. The worst of it was that Antoinette loved the movies. She dragged me off to the Majestic at least twice a week, and it was the torment of Tantalus for me. I was madly in love, you see! I had to put an end to it.

I made a few little inquiries. I discovered that Francine was the girl friend of the manager of the Majestic, and that he had set her up in a studio flat on the floor above the auditorium. Joining the two – the auditorium and the flat – was a little spiral staircase. All this rather favoured my plans. One evening I went out a little before midnight, telling Antoinette that I would sleep better if I stretched my legs a bit. I made straight for the cinema. I knew that a quarter of an hour before the end you could go in without being seen. No more cash desk; no more usherettes. Obviously, no one would want to go in a few minutes before the end of the show. I hid on the spiral staircase, and waited. The house lights went up and everyone left. The projectionist shut the doors. I stayed there in the dark for quite a while. Then I very cautiously went up the stairs, one by one. I listened at the door for a long time. Nothing. No sound. Was Francine there? I tried to open the door. It was locked. I didn't know what to do. I sat down on the top step. I must have made a noise. Suddenly a ray of light filtered through under the door and I heard a voice saying: 'Is that you, Pet?' Sounds came from inside. I squeezed myself into a corner. The door opened. Francine appeared in her dressing gown. She didn't see me. She went down the stairs. I rushed into the room. I saw only one thing, yes, really only one, in the chaos all around: the mauve bra waiting for me on a little table. I grabbed my fetish and went and hid in my dark hole on the landing again. It was high time. There was the sound of water flushing on the floor below, and Francine came back up. She went in and locked the door. I crept down as quietly as I could. I knew that the doors of the emergency exits are never bolted on the inside. There's a gadget which merely stops you opening them from the outside. I darted off with my trophy. I pressed it to my heart. I was so happy I could hardly walk.

Antoinette certainly suspected something. At the time, she didn't say anything. But that bra posed some problems. No question of her wearing it. In the first place, because it obviously wasn't new. Its smell alone! It drove *me* wild, but there was no likelihood of it going to Antoinette's head. And in any case, I wouldn't have wanted that. I've always been against mixing things. Bigamy, orgies, they disgust me. It was Francine's bra, her essence, as you might say, the key to her very being, if you follow me. No other woman could wear it. And even though I hid it on a shelf behind some of my books, Antoinette found it. One day, when we were quarrelling, she flung it in my face. 'And what's more, you're being unfaithful to me!' she shouted. Obviously, you'll think, that was just a manner of speaking. But according to our system it was, after all, logical. Yes, all right, I *was* being unfaithful to her with Francine – with a bra as proxy. Especially as that came on top of her previous anxiety. She was on edge, was my

Antoinette. She certainly suspected that I was stealing. But after all, those thefts were for her. True, they were dangerous and dishonest, but they were for *her*. Whereas in this case . . . In short, things were already going rather badly when the business of the Metro happened. There, well, I really don't know what got into me! That was what wrecked everything. I must have been mad!

That day she had come to Paris with me to buy our Christmas presents. We'd started doing the rounds of the department stores. Naturally, the only thing that interested *me* was fancy lingerie. But what I hadn't foreseen was the effect it would have on me to see Antoinette in the middle of it all. Masses of pretty little frillies on display, with Antoinette in the middle. Like a barn full of nice dry straw and hay, if you see what I mean, and right in the middle a big wood fire sending out flames and sparks all over the barn. You can imagine the result! With Antoinette in the middle of the store the effect of the fripperies was multiplied tenfold, a hundredfold. They burned me, they set me on fire with pleasure and joy – I was intoxicated. Antoinette must have been getting worried when she saw all the money she had brought for quite different things melt away in purchases of women's clothes and underwear. But it was especially my state of excitement that panicked her. Though it was a little her fault, after all. Her presence in flesh and blood illuminated the displays. The slips, the tights, the stockings, the panties, the bras, all those little orphaned objects were crying out to her. I heard them, I could hear nothing else. I had to obey. I obeyed. I bought, and bought, and in less than two hours we hadn't a sou left, we were cleaned out, me and Toinette both. But we were buried in parcels, in pyramids of parcels. My Antoinette was *not* pleased. But I was floating on air, like in a dream. And that was how, her grumbling, me floating, we made our way to the Metro.

We went down the stairs and then, with all our parcels, we found ourselves semi-wedged in the swing gates. We manoeuvred ourselves back and forth, like shunting engines. At this point a little woman slipped between us, saying 'Excuse me! Thank you!' And pff! – she was through. Only, there was a draught. A ferocious draught was rushing through the half-opened gates. It hoisted up the girl's miniskirt and held it there for a moment, even though she quickly clamped both hands down on her thighs. But in that split second I had seen a suspender belt, and what a suspender belt, it burned me, it pierced me, it practically killed me, yes. In black nylon, gathered, wide, the white skin of her thighs contrasting sharply with the long, very long, suspenders which started at the belt and travelled down to collect her stockings in their little chromium-plated clips. It reminded me of a greasy pole, or rather of the sort of hoop round the top of a greasy pole with sausages and hams hanging from it. I had to have that suspender belt to crown this memorable day! I shoved all my parcels into Antoinette's arms. I told her: 'Wait here for me, I won't be long!', and I abandoned her there, in the draughts, too flabbergasted to protest. And I dashed off! I chased after the girl. I caught her up, and wedged her into a corner. Luckily we were alone. I stammered: 'Your suspender belt, your suspender belt, quick, quick!' At first she didn't understand. Then, without hesitating, I pulled up her skirt. She screamed. I repeated: 'Quick, your suspender belt, and I'll go away.' Finally, she obeyed. In the twinkling of an eye, it was done. I had my trophy. I said thank you and ran back to Antoinette, who was still juggling with her pyramid of parcels in the draughts. I was radiant. I brandished my suspender belt like a Red Indian flaunting his Paleface's scalp. I told her: 'Touch it! It's still warm!' And as both her hands were full, I stuck it against her face. But we had to get away from there, in case the victim made a scene. We rushed out and dived into a taxi. Taxi, station, train, Alençon. Antoinette didn't say a word throughout the journey. The next day, she left me. For good. Went back to her mother. A catastrophe. I deserved it, oh yes, I deserved it! But a catastrophe all the same . . .

Everything was over for me. I didn't go back to the bank. I read the Paris papers. They spoke about the sadist in the Metro. They were hunting maniacs in the underground. My victim lodged a complaint against X, then she switched it to the Paris Transport System. Because the System was supposed to be responsible for the safety of its passengers. It says so on the schedule of conditions. The things you learn from the newspapers! Later there was a court case. The plaintiff, my victim, lost. Well yes, a nonsuit, as they call it! The counsel for the Metro victoriously exploited the fact that at the moment of the attack she hadn't had her ticket punched. So the transport contract wasn't yet in force, and the System had no obligation!

No matter; I had death in my heart. Everything had collapsed with Antoinette's departure. Because my life was very fragile, you understand. I had to invent my own kind of happiness, to construct it. I'm not like other people. Other people have their lives all ready and waiting for them down to the last detail when they are born, lying there at the foot of their cot. But there was nothing waiting for me there. I had to invent it all for myself, by trial and error, by making mistakes and starting all over again. Nestling notes didn't interest me any more. Nor did clothes, for that matter. The great light of my life had gone out. From pure habit I went back to a department store, to the hosiery department. I thought it was to start stealing from the displays again. I did steal, yes, but it was quite a different matter. I discovered what I was looking for the day a store detective caught me red-handed pinching a nightdress. I'd had enough. I wanted to make an end of it.

I went to prison. Then they let me out on bail until my case came up. Ah, but that was the last thing I wanted! I had myself caught red-handed again in the same store! Then the judge sent me to a psychiatrist. I could have got a six months' suspended sentence. First offender, so automatic suspension. And don't let us catch you again! They must have been joking! Thanks to my psychiatrist, they classified me as irresponsible. Acquitted by reason of irresponsibility. Acquitted, released . . . and shut up. In an asylum. For the last twenty years! Ah, the asylum isn't always a bed of roses! Ice-cold showers, beds they strap you into, strait-jackets, insulin comas, shock treatment. Not always a bed of roses, no. But you have your little compensations. When you've been good, they sometimes let you go for a stroll. With my two favourite male nurses. You walk around. You look in the shop windows. Sometimes they even go for a drink and let me go shopping, when they are in a good mood. Today I was in luck. There's a sale on in a department store. Great piles of pretty undies.

(As he speaks, he pulls a clothes line out of his pocket and hangs it up from one side of the stage to the other. Then from his other pocket he

extracts an unbelievable quantity of women's underwear, which he fastens on the line with clothes pegs.)

Heaps and heaps of them, at your fingertips. Tight ones and loose ones. (*He brandishes a pair of tights and a nightdress.*) I've always wondered which had the most charm. There are two schools of thought. Tight things, now, they hug the figure and at the same time confine it, keep it firm. But they lack imagination. They don't speak to you. They're laconic, severe – they're disciplinarians. Whereas loose things, floating things – they are the ones that set you dreaming! They're chatty, they're a continual improvisation, they invite you to slip a hand in . . .

(*The clothes line is now completely covered. He steps back and observes his handiwork. In the meantime the two male nurses – white coats under their overcoats, white caps – have entered at the back and are coming up the centre aisle.*)

And when they float in the wind, they're so beautiful!

(*A fan in the wings animates and inflates the clothes hanging from the line.*)

And then – I have to stand to attention! Stiff as a post. With respect. And desire.

(*He stands to attention.*)

Everyone to his own flag. With some people it's the tricolour. With me, it's frillies.

He notices his nurses.

Hm, I've got company. It had to happen.

(*He darts over to the underclothes and starts taking them off the line and stuffing them into his pockets. Meanwhile the nurses are coming up on to the stage. They advance on him slowly, inexorably.*)

Wait, wait! You wouldn't want me to lose my little treasures!

(*They surround him and start leading him off. He doesn't put up much of a struggle.*)

Wait, not so fast. Look – what about that pink slip!

(*He eludes them and goes and grabs the slip. He takes the opportunity of pocketing a nightdress as well. The nurses come back and start leading him off again.*)

Hey, not so fast! Here, look – just that little girdle too. It's only a tiny little girdle!

(*He eludes them and goes and grabs the girdle. Plus two or three more articles. When the nurses surround him again, the only thing left on the clothes line is a pair of black panties.*)

Ah well, all right, let's go. Let's go, since we have to. But no shock treatment tonight, eh! You promise, eh? No shock treatment!

(*He turns round and casts a pathetic glance at the panties. In one bound he escapes the nurses yet again, jumps up on to the stage and returns, brandishing the panties.*)

All right, all right, I'm coming. With my flag. The pirates' black flag. Long live death!

(*The nurses lead him off. For the last time, we hear:*)

But no shock treatment tonight, eh! That's a promise. Tomorrow if you like, all right, but not tonight, no shock treatment . . .

Notes

Amandine or the Two Gardens appeared in a children's edition, illustrated by Joëlle Boucher, in 1977. On this occasion *Le Monde* published the following interview with the author.

LITTLE GIRLS' BLOOD

Your heroine in this story – and even its supposed author, as it is told in the first person – is a little girl of ten. Coming from you, we naturally expect the story to have a hidden meaning. Is there a second level on which we should read Amandine?

Yes and no. In actual fact the second level is so transparent that it merges with the naïve narrative. The theme is initiation. It is an initiatory story. Amandine lives with her parents in a house and garden that are models of order and cleanliness. One day, thanks to her she-cat, she suspects that there must be something else in life. She climbs over the garden wall, and discovers . . .

Let it come as a surprise to the reader.

Let's say that she discovers herself to be in the turmoil of pre-adolescence. The limpid, calm world of childhood is cracking and becoming overcast for the first time. It's the first shadow cast by puberty upon innocence.

So Amandine is initiated into love by her cat.

There would be a great deal to be said about the initiatory role of domestic animals. I don't think it is as immediate as people sometimes make out. The classic formula we read everywhere which maintains that children brought up in the country are 'taught the mysteries of life through observing animals' is extremely debatable. I have noticed that many rural children who may well have witnessed the whole cycle of reproduction in cats, dogs, hens, rabbits, cows, etc., nevertheless remain totally ignorant of human sexuality and reproduction. They simply don't see the connection. For a child of seven or eight, it isn't so easy to imagine papa and mama in the position he sees adopted by the bull and the cow, or the cock and the hen. The perception of man as one animal among the rest is made more difficult by the fact that sexuality is usually presented to the child in its most socially elaborate, conventional and mythological form – via stories, magazines, songs, the cinema, television – and only much later in its physical nudity. This is why the role I assigned to Amandine's cat is that of introducing her to the emotion of love rather than to physical love. At the end, the little girl is emotionally troubled and matured rather than informed about sexuality. This is the important distinction between initiation and information.

And yet, she's bleeding . . .

Yes, that trickle of blood she discovers on her leg after her escapade, and which she can't explain, is going to give the censors something to mutter about. It is justified, though. Every initiation is more or less bloody.

But isn't this idea of the initiation of a little girl refuted by all ethnography?

That is precisely the most debatable, and the most interesting point. It is true that in most societies there is an initiation ceremony for boys. Nothing happens for girls. Why not? No doubt because boys do not from birth form part of the community of men. Brought up by their mothers, they belong to the society of women so long as they are pre-pubertal. Initiation marks the passage of the boy from the society of women to that of men. It is usually accompanied by physical ordeals that prove him worthy of it, and by mutilations that are its price. This may go very far. In *La Mort Sara*, Robert Jaulin reports on the initiation ordeals to which he submitted himself in a Central African tribe. He was enjoined to die, and then to be reborn, with as his 'mother' the sorcerer presiding over the ceremony. This is obviously the most radical way imaginable to break the bond with the original mother, and to replace her by a quasi maternal bond with the group of the men.

What remains of all that in our society?

Much more than people think. The initiation of boys is not lacking in our customs. However, as the beliefs and rites now only subsist in the form of unconscious vestiges, initiation is only experienced on a crude, elementary level. At school, the 'big boys' bully the 'little boys'. 'Rookies' are also bullied. Fathers inflict mutilations on their sons on 'medical' pretexts that do not stand up to examination, such as circumcision or tonsillectomy. And naturally, there are school exams; the baccalaureate is the initiation rite of the middle classes.

These ordeals imposed on boys as the price of their entry into the society of men – are they preceded by a time of exclusion from their community?

Most certainly. The adolescent of today is doubly excluded from the society of men. In the first place, on the sexual level. With all its apparent 'permissiveness', our society is probably one of the most puritan that we have ever known. The adolescent had far more opportunities to make love a hundred years ago. But it is above all on the professional level that the exclusion is the most savage. Seniority reigns supreme. The present-day unemployment is above all the unemployment of the young. Celibacy and unemployment, those are the two evils which a good old traditional initiation would remedy.

And what about girls?

Initiation cannot have the same meaning for them as it does for boys. Brought up by women, like their brothers, they obviously do not have to break with that milieu and become integrated into another group, like boys. Normally, they are destined to remain within the gynaeceum. Just as in our society girls are spared most of the bullying we observe taking place among boys. Not to speak of circumcision; there is no corresponding form of clitoridectomy in our society. But it is remarkable that tonsillectomy should be inflicted much more frequently on boys than on girls. The truth is that women are integrated into society as if from birth to such an extent that they can identify themselves with it. Balzac illustrated this function of women particularly well. His heroes are introduced into society by the women who hold its keys (the famous 'salons'). Conversely, Vautrin is at the same time an enemy of society and an enemy of women. It's the same thing.

No initiation for girls, then.

There is, but in their case it is a sort of reverse initiation, *centrifugal* instead of *centripetal.* I mean: an adolescent boy leaves the feminine group and becomes integrated into the masculine group. For him, initiation allows him to claim a certain status. What can a girl do? As a prisoner of the gynaeceum, she can try to get out of it. To go where? Therein lies the whole problem of women's liberation. Between the gynaeceum and the society of men, there is not yet a unisex society waiting to welcome her. So what remains is an initiation-rebellion. I am thinking particularly of the young Arab girls' fight against the compulsory wearing of the veil. For the adolescent girl, initiation can only be a permanent flight. Amandine jumps over the wall. And goes to see what is happening in the *other* garden.

The Fetishist was first performed in 1974, by Raymon Fuzellier in Berlin and by Olivier Hussenot in Paris, both performances being directed by Étienne Le Meur.

Also by Michel Tournier
and available in Minerva

The Midnight Love Feast

An Arabian Nights from this most distinguished of French writers.

Yves Oudalle, one-time captain of a fishing trawler and still in love with the sea, and Nadège, his wife, no longer get on. There are arguments. Then silence. Finally they decide to separate and invite all their friends to a party – a fish banquet in celebration of love and of the sea – at which to announce the sad news. The guests arrive and each, as in Boccacio's *Decameron*, tells a story.

One by one the stories follow – fairy tales, modern tales, fables, legends, some realistic, all enchanting; and their enchantment gradually reaches Yves and Nadège. As the night draws on the stories grow more powerful and more beautiful until by dawn they are incomparable. When the last guest has left, Yves and Nadège open their curtains to let in the rays of the rising sun, and realise there is no need to part.

The Four Wise Men

The legend of the Magi is one of the most potent episodes in the Christian tradition. This dazzling novel performs the feat of bringing them to life – Gaspard, Melchior and Balthasar, each in quest of what he loved most, and has lost.

But Tournier departs from the Bible story with his unforgettable addition of the fourth King – Taor, the one who came too late for the Nativity.

'Imaginative, macabre and dreamlike'
Graham Lord, *Sunday Express*

'Enthralling . . . a beguiling work of art'
Paul Bailey, *Standard*

'A true masterpiece'
New Statesman

'Dazzling . . . intriguing'
John Weightman, *Observer*

'An astonishing elaboration of the Epiphany legend . . . The most peculiarly inventive novel of the year'
Victoria Glendinning, *Sunday Times*